Where No Lilies Grow

Published by Big Bold Letters Publishing

Cover image by Jamey White

"The best thing to hold onto in life is each other."

- Audrey Hepburn

PROLOGUE

A portly man wearing dark jeans, heavy steel toe boots, and an untucked flannel shirt—all of which are adorned with splotches of dust and clay-colored dirt—sprints, as fast as his pudgy legs can go towards a trailer, stampeding through the other workers and up the stairs. He jerks open the door and immediately reaches for the desk, his other hand flat against his chest, panting as if he'd just finished a 5K.

After finally catching his breath, he takes off his hard hat, sets it on the desk, and reaches for the phone. His hand shakes as his chubby fingers repeatedly press the wrong digits, which flusters him more each time. Finally he takes a deep breath and concentrates on entering the seven numbers in the correct order. Success.

Another man answers, slightly annoyed. His voice course, as if he regularly gargles with gravel.

"Yeah?"

"Sir, we got a big problem over here at the Food Giant site in Merilu."

"Stevens? That you?"

"Oh, yes sir, sorry."

Mr. Bennet has called Shane by his last name since he first came in for an interview. Oddly enough, calling people by their last names has always been one of Shane's biggest pet peeves, and he strongly believes, though he has no proof to support his claim, that somehow Mr. Bennet knows this and does it simply out of spite, to show his power. But owning one of the South's biggest construction companies does entitle you to such perks as calling your employees by their last names—or pretty much any name you want to.

But Mr. Bennet happens to like Shane, which is why he selected him to be the new Safety Supervisor last month. Although well-deserved and way past due, the promotion came as a huge surprise to the 38-year-old unmarried man who's been working for the company for nearly six years.

"Yes sir, I got it."

"Good. So, get on with it; what's the problem?" Mr. Bennet prompts. "I don't have time for chitting *or* chatting; I'm already late for an appointment."

"Well, sir, the crew had just gotten here—to the house," Shane, still trying to catch his breath but knowing that his boss is an incredibly impatient man, struggles to quickly tell the information. "And we were getting ready to tear it down—the house, that is... We were about to knock it down... And then, well, then we saw it...and that's what I'm calling you about—what we saw."

"Well you're lucky I even answered the phone. Damn

contractor's been calling all morning with questions—what a moron. Next time start out the call with, 'This is Stevens.' Got it?"

"Bottom line it, Stevens, I told you I'm in a hurry. You're tripping over your words like you're asking me out on a date. And you know I'm married, Stevens."

"Yes sir, I'm well aware. And Mrs. Bennet is a lucky woman. But what I'm trying to say is, well, you really need to come down here—right away."

"Dammit, Stevens, I told you I can't. Do the words *late for an appointment* not mean anything to you? But, listen, I'll tell you what...I was planning on stopping by there this afternoon, so why don't you just wait and show me whatever it is then. Now, are we all settled?"

Shane is noticeably getting irritated—the way he shifts his weight from one leg to the other and the way he slowly cracks his necks from side to side. Still struggling with the responsibilities of his new position, he doesn't want Mr. Bennet to think he can't handle the situation by himself, but at the same time, he desperately needs his boss' help.

"Sir, listen. We can talk about this now or later—doesn't matter to me. But trust me, if you don't come down here right away, you *will* be hearing about it on the six o'clock news. I told everyone here not to call the police or anything until I talked to you, but the crew was already here working before I got here, so I figure my message was probably too late."

Shane pauses to listen for Mr. Bennet's response.

Nothing.

"Sir," Shane says, louder, his voice carrying the strain from the tenseness of his throat. "We have a Code Black."

∞

As part of company protocol, all employees are required to communicate using the company rhetoric, as designed by Mr. Bennet. Code Black is the most extreme of the "Three Levels of Efficiency and Productivity." Code Green means everything is running smoothly; Code red means there is a problem that needs immediate resolution.

But what distinguishes Code Black from Red is the need for Mr. Bennet's prompt attention (opposed to one of the managers), such as a disaster or anything that would most likely end up on the news. Shane has only had to respond to a Code Red once while in his position. An incident involving a severed thumb.

Having never been involved in a Code Black incident, he really isn't sure how to handle it, past contacting Mr. Bennet.

"Sir?" Shane questions the silence.

"Ok, Stevens, what's the damage? I need to prepare what I'm going to say."

"Well, like I said, we had just gotten to the house and went in to do a routine check. And, well, sir, there were several dead bodies all over the living room. Men, women—even police officers, sir."

Shane is hesitant with each word. Not only is he worried about what his boss is going to say, but he's had a phobia of dead people coming back to life ever since seeing *Night of the Living Dead*. It's so bad that he doesn't attend funerals, no matter how close he was with the departed.

"Yeah, it looks like a real massacre in there, sir. Blood everywhere—the floor, the walls. But what's really strange was when we opened the door, several birds flew out. Doves, I believe. And even stranger, there was confetti all over the floor, like it was sprinkled around over the blood. I don't know—it was really wild."

"Doves? Confetti? Stevens, this has to be a joke. And I swear to God if it is..."

"No, sir, I'm serious. It's a pretty brutal scene. Pools of blood, guts strewn all over the floor."

"Jesus, Stevens, spare me the gory details. I'll be right there," Mr. Bennet replies. "And don't talk to any goddamn news reporters!"

༄

A black Mercedes pulls up to the Food Giant site where Shane paces in front of a trailer before stopping and waving his hardhat in the air. An older, well-dressed man steps out and motions for Shane to follow him inside the trailer.

"You made it here pretty fast, sir," Shane comments with a slight smirk, knowing that no matter how much his boss downplays the severity of the situation, he's also panicking on the inside.

"Fast car," Mr. Bennet answers, looking around, scowling at the lack of commotion. "So where the hell are all the cops, the reporters? Stevens, this doesn't look like the scene of a massacre. I swear to God if you're pulling my chain..."

"No sir, I swear. I asked around, and I know for certain now they're on their way," Shane says, moving in front of his boss, who was walking towards the trailer door. "Should be any moment now."

Mr. Bennet groans, then walks over to a mirror on the bathroom door and begins adjusting his tie. Then he pulls out a small lint brush from inside his coat and gives his suit a few brisk swipes.

Shane speaks up, "Uh, I'm ready to go over to the house whenever you are."

"I'm not *going* in *there*," Mr. Bennet huffs, surprised at the notion. "Not after what you described on the phone. I'll be puking buckets. And this suit's too expensive to get puke on it."

"Well, sir, how're you going to know what to say when the reporters ask you questions about the crime scene?"

Mr. Bennet, who's now moved on to searching the office, clearly looking for something in particular, jerks around towards Shane. His entire face wrinkles up, his agitation written all over it.

"*Crime scene!*" he repeats, appalled at the description. "Listen to me, Stevens, if any reporter asks you a question, you do *not* call this a crime scene. You could call it an 'unfortunate accident' or a 'devastating event.' Hell, you could call it some 'new radical art exhibit' for all I care. But you do *not* call this a crime scene. Are we clear?"

"I understand, sir. The disturbing incident"—he waits a moment to see if this phrase would agree with his boss, but after no immediate objection or even a reaction, he continues—"is pretty gruesome, but it's not like we could get blamed for anything. I mean, those people were just there when we showed up. So why, if you don't mind me asking, does it seem like we're going out of our way to keep our asses covered?"

Mr. Bennet, having found the lighter he'd been searching for, sits on the edge of the desk, then takes out a cigarette and lights it, looking distinctly calmer now that he's taken a drag.

"You don't know how shit like this works, do you, Stevens?" Mr. Bennet began, not waiting for an answer. "The press is going to have a field day with a story like this. And our names are going to be stuck right smack in the middle of it."

&

Now standing right outside the trailer, Shane begins to sweat and Mr. Bennet cusses as they see a police car pull into the driveway, followed by another, and then an ambulance.

Shane turns away from the oncoming vehicles and motions for Mr. Bennet to do the same. Frantically, the newly promoted employee of six years—now wondering in the back of his mind whether or not the increase in pay is worth having to deal with situations like this—reaches into his pocket and removes a thick, folded bundle of paper covered with a dark, dried stain of blood.

"Sir, I know I shouldn't have taken this—"

"Dammit, Stevens," Mr. Bennet interrupts. Is that from the house? What the hell are you doing with it?"

"I know, sir, it was stupid. I should've left it alone, but I didn't know if it had anything to do with this project or the company or what. I mean...I don't know. My first reaction was to take it. I'm sorry, I couldn't help myself."

With cops now out scouting the scene, and a couple of them walking towards Shane and Mr. Bennet, a news van makes a sharp turn down the driveway.

"Ok, ok, just keep that out of sight," Mr. Bennet advises, pushing Shane's hand down towards his side and tucking the letter down into his fist. "Where was it exactly?"

"One of the women was holding it," Shane talks low. "I sort of had to pry it out of her hand."

Mr. Bennet turns back around long enough to wave and flash a fake smile to the nearby officers and to the news reporters getting out of their van, also beginning to walk his way.

"Anybody see you take it?"

"No sir," Shane replies, still trying his best to talk in a low, discreet voice. "I waited until no one was looking. I figured you needed to see it first."

"Stevens, you're an imbecile. But you're loyal, like a dog. Regardless, we have to push forward. What's done is done. So, what's it say?"

"I don't know yet, sir. I haven't read it."

Mr. Bennet lets out a heavy sigh that Shane is all too familiar with. Shane asks him what he should do, and Mr. Bennet advises him, in so many words, to sneak back into the trailer when he gets a chance and read the letter.

Then Mr. Bennet, like a great actor, turns around and greets the officers with a toothy smile and hearty handshakes. Getting right down to business, the officers begin questioning him, and even Shane. Moments later, a team of news reporters swarms over. When the cameras turn on, all eyes are now on Mr. Bennet, leaving Shane a chance to slip away and go into the trailer through the back door.

He carefully draws back the curtains of the small window to make sure no one is watching him or following him. Then he gently unfolds the letter and begins reading.

1

That summer sure was an angry one, but at least it went by quick. Flew by like the pages of a Jane Austen novel on a rainy day. But that was actually a good thing because rainy days back then were few and far between. The air was dry and the sun drained the life out of all of us. But like each year, I considered myself lucky to have survived another southern scorcher.

That same summer I turned twelve, one year away from being a teenager, though I already had the responsibilities of one. I cooked, cleaned, helped Mama out with other chores. I even knew how to drive because Mama made me and my sisters learn, just in case of an emergency.

Since the heat outside was so exhausting, it shut me up inside when the sun was blazing midday. Gave me lots of time to sit in my bedroom and do some reading, a little sewing, and a lot of thinking. But I was still a kid and weather's not something that keeps a kid inside too long. Before you knew it, I'd be back outside running wide open through the yard, loving every second of life. No cares, no worries. Feeling invincible.

Me and my sisters would stay outside for hours, losing

ourselves in a game of tag or hopscotch or swinging on the swing we made with the help of one of the limbs from the big oak behind our house. Or we'd head out for the creek just a little ways from our house. I'm sure we drove Mama crazy, "rompin' and tearin' up the yard," as she would say.

But she knew we were safe and that the three of us would always look out for each other, so she didn't worry too much. What she did worry about, though, was the condition of our yard and the garden. And not from the constant beating it took from our sneakers. But it'd been nearly three long, scorching weeks without a drop of rain, and the grass started to dry up and turn a yellowish-brown puke color. We did what we could to save it, but we also had to watch how much water we used.

I remember feeling sorry for the plants and even more so for the flowers. I was drawn to flowers, like I had some kind of kindred connection with them. And if I could've been anything else in the world, that's exactly what I would've been. Because a flower didn't have to worry, didn't have to feel pain or fear. They were beautiful and didn't even have to try.

But we all knew it was hard times that summer, especially the older folks who tended their fields and gardens. They had a different take on things than us kids, because without the rain their crops wouldn't grow. And without their crops, they wouldn't have any money. Mama talked to us about how everyone was in real bad shape, and she even started making us pray twice a day instead of just the once at bedtime.

"One prayer," she said in her deep but beautiful Southern drawl, "can be fer whatever you want it to be on. Save up that one fer your bedtime prayer. But the other one, say it durin' the day. Make that one fer all us families here in Merilu, 'long with everyone else in Alabama who's sufferin' from this dry spell."

So I did just that. And I expect my sisters did too. I don't know exactly how they worded their prayers, but I reckon we all asked for the same thing in pretty much the same way—for God to take care of his children. That's all anybody can really ask for.

Growing up was hard enough without something like that on your shoulders. Some people thought about moving, heading up to Tennessee or even to Kentucky where they had supposedly seen several rainy days. But I didn't want to move. I liked where I lived, and I couldn't imagine growing up anywhere else.

The small town of Merilu, Alabama, was about an hour or so northwest of Montgomery. My family was born there, and until I was about 18, I'd never been anywhere outside of it. It was all I knew.

Merilu was a quiet factory-run town where no one was home on Sunday mornings. Either you were at church or you were at work at Fleabings, the fifty-plus-year-old textile mill that was king of the city. Pretty much every girl I knew's daddy and brothers and boyfriend all worked there. Some of the mothers in town even worked there too—the ones with big families or children who were already grown. Even Mama worked there, only part-time, after my father left. She stitched up fabric on a production line along with the other women. But she refused to work on Sundays so me, her, and my sisters could regularly attend the Mantioch Methodist Church, right on the corner of First Avenue and Mantioch Street.

I'd been going to that same church ever since I could remember, so it's not like I even had a choice in the matter. I had to be deathly ill before Mama'd let me miss a service. But I didn't mind. I liked going because all my friends went there too.

Mantioch Methodist was a quaint building with several rows of wooden benches lined up on both sides of the pulpit, and it was typically filled with a congregation of about seventy-five or so folks, children included. Down the hall from the sanctuary were a number of classrooms where we had Sunday School, and in the front of the church swung a long rope from the bell tower.

Outside, a crack ran down the sanctuary wall where lightning once struck it long before I was born. I often wondered why someone didn't patch it up, but I'd heard that the preacher wanted to leave it that way because it had to have been some sort of sign from God. I wasn't sure whether or not he meant it was a good sign or a bad one.

Mama said she liked the preacher because he was a

charming, aged fella who let everyone know that if you were going to come to his church, you better be ready to worship. He also led the choir most Sundays and could play the fire out of the piano. I liked him too because he was funny and because his name was Buddy.

And the singing at Mantioch was beautiful. We had one of the best choirs in the state, in my opinion. But I'd never heard another choir, so my opinion wasn't exactly a sound one. Everyone else there thought the same, though, but their opinions might have been a little biased also.

The sermons were a mixture of funny stories and inspirational wisdom. Sometimes Pastor Buddy got passionate about a topic and his voice would get so loud it was almost frightening to a kid's ears. Nonetheless, his words would always set a fire up under us as we looked towards a new week, especially since everyone had been so down and out about the rain, or lack of.

Yeah, it was the kind of church where everyone was in attendance because they wanted to be, no matter what was going on at home or what flu-bug was going around. I was baptized there when I was seven-and-a-half, my sister Carolene when she was eight, and my other sister Jolene when she was almost ten.

❦

It never failed that Mama always cooked me and my sisters a big breakfast every Sunday morning before we left for church—a feast of scrambled eggs with cheese, buttermilk biscuits, French toast, link sausages, and fresh squeezed orange juice. I always cut up my eggs and sprinkled them all over my French toast and then doused the whole thing with Karo syrup. Still do.

But for some reason this upset Carolene and she'd yell at Mama, "Jessabelle's doin' it again!" and I'd be scolded to stop playing with my food. I never figured out what all the fuss was for. It was *my* food and I wanted to eat it the way I wanted to eat it. It's not like I didn't devour the whole pile in a matter of moments anyway. And then I'd hear it from Mama for eating too fast.

Carolene was my loudest sister, and with shiny blond hair that had a touch of curl throughout, she was the most beautiful of us. She was also the tallest, if only by half an inch, and—most importantly, especially to her—first to fill out in the chest. Boys swarmed to her like bees drawn to honey. And Carolene flirted just as much as the boys did, if not more.

She'd parade around in dresses all the time like a model or pageant queen, practicing waving her hand with her arm stiff. Later in school she actually did go on to win a pageant or two, plus be crowned Homecoming Queen her junior year.

What I never could stand was that Mama seemed to always side with Carolene. Just like the time Carolene snuck into my room right after I'd cleaned it and scattered my clothes everywhere, supposedly looking for her hairbrush. Then next thing I knew, Mama was getting on to me for not picking up my room like I was supposed to. I got two weeks' worth of punishment for that little incident. But after I pleaded with Mama that I didn't do it, she told me I really didn't have to do the extra chores, but not to say anything about it in front of Carolene.

Mama admitted that Carolene needed a lot more attention than me or Jolene. We could always talk like that. I could tell Mama secrets and she'd really keep them. She also confided lots of things in me, and I swore I'd never tell a soul. Never did.

My other sister, Jolene, however, was kind of plain like me. Although she was slightly chubby (never outgrew her baby fat), Jolene had a pretty face. She never thought that was enough, though, and she would often skip meals and complain about how me and Carolene could eat whatever we wanted and not gain an ounce. Which might've been true at the time, but that luxury ran out soon enough.

It seemed I was the only one of us girls who really didn't care about being pretty. I knew if a boy was going to like me, he was going to like me for me, no matter if I wore a dress or had curls in my hair or not.

Jolene didn't see it that way. She tried hard to be pretty and was jealous of Carolene for not having to. But Jolene also had big dreams, and this I actually looked up to her for. She inspired me to set my own dreams and goals, giving me something to aim for and even look forward to.

Me and her disagreed on what to become of ourselves, though. Because above anything else, Jolene wanted to be famous, like a movie star or, of course, a model. She had cutout pictures of beautiful actresses like Marilyn Monroe and Betty Grable pinned up on her vanity, and she told me stories of how she was going to be in a picture with Cary Grant and how he was going to fall in love with her in real life.

But even though she had big dreams and longed for fame, Jolene was lazy, so I never took much stock in those kind of stories. Because despite being the first Johansson triplet to be born, Jolene was always last. Always the last out of bed and the last to the table. The last one out of the bathroom, which we all shared, and the last one to finish her chores.

Me and my sisters may have been triplets, but you'd never seen three people so different. And I hated that. I mean, we loved each other and enjoyed spending time with each other, but I wanted us to be closer. I longed for something to one day bring us together.

2

Just like Carolene, Jolene liked to get me in trouble. But she was simpler in her plots and would flat out lie. When we'd be yelling at each other, she'd pretend to cry and point at me saying I hit her. Of course I hadn't.

And one Sunday morning at church when everyone was sitting in the pews waiting for the preacher to welcome everybody for coming and give updates on the folks who were sick and not doing so good, Jolene told Mama I wasn't in there yet because she saw me playing in the Sunday School room.

"Her and this boy was runnin' 'round chasin' after each other, laughin' and gigglin' and carryin' on," she told her.

Of course that was an outright lie. I mean, yes, I had been running around, and there *was* a boy involved, but I was merely trying to retrieve my hair bow from the grubby hands of an older kid whose name I honestly no longer remember. We ran in circles around the desks, and that boy, who was a good foot taller than me, held the hair bow above my head just out of reach. After several minutes of pointless running and many failed attempts at jumping up to snatch it, we stopped and stood there in a face-off, my face beet-red and his fat cheeks flush like two huge ripe apples.

Having a really vivid imagination, I pictured what's-his-name taking a lighter to my hair bow and laughing like a madman as it went up in a terrific orange flame. I countered by taking off my shoe—but it wasn't one of my normal Sunday shoes, this shoe had a long slender heel on it like they wore in big cities—and slinging at him as hard as I could. I watched as the tip of the heel, which was a quarter of an inch thick, caught him right in his eye. Blood gushed everywhere and the eyeball itself even fell to the floor and bounced around like a rubber ball. All I could do was point and laugh.

I shook off the disgusting daydream and even glanced down at my shoes just to make sure there was no blood, no eyeballs. And as I stared at that boy from across the room, sweat beginning to build up on my eyebrows, my mouth opened and out snuck words I'd only heard mill workers use. Words I remember my father using.

"Gimme back my goddamn hair bow, you son of a bitch!"

All murmuring and egging on came to a halt, and I immediately realized what I'd said. And not just that, I'd said the big one, the granddaddy of all cuss words. I felt dirty, ashamed, like I'd just committed the ultimate sin. I just knew the preacher would have to sit down with me and preach to me just the two of us, and probably even baptize me again. But those thoughts came and went quickly, and it wasn't before long that the running had commenced again.

Mrs. Dodson, a close friend of Mama's, came around looking for me and sure enough found me wrestling on the floor with that boy. I'd finally caught him and was holding nothing back. Right as I was trying to pry his fist open, Mrs. Dodson grabbed me by the arm, made him give me my hair bow back, and scolded me like I was one of her own kids.

"What on Earth are you doin', young lady? Your mama's been worryin' herself sick over you. Now come along."

I tried to plead my case as she dragged me down the hall towards the sanctuary. It was a long, tiresome walk down a pale hallway that seemed so unfamiliar, though it was one I'd walked down about a million times before. Mrs. Dodson, her silver hair pulled back into a tight bun that looked like it'd been stuck to the back of her head with glue or maybe Velcro, opened the sanctuary door to reveal a crowd of people huddled together in the middle of one of the pews. It looked like a pack of dogs fighting over a slab of meat.

"Wait here, understand? I'll be right back," Mrs. Dodson instructed as she let go of my hand and ran towards the crowd.

Even Pastor Ellis had come over to join the group. He had his shirt sleeves rolled up, which I knew from past experience meant something serious was going on.

I looked around for Carolene and Jolene but didn't see them. But I did end up making eye contact with a skinny little girl named Beatrice Lynn who I knew from school and was sitting by herself. I motioned to the crowd of people and mouthed the words *what's wrong?* She stuck up her middle finger at me in response. Beatrice Lynn and I'd never gotten along, so her answer didn't surprise me.

I rolled my eyes at her and walked closer. But the closer I got to the mob, the more the insides of my stomach started tightening up, like somebody had stuck their hand in there and started squeezing on my guts.

First, I attempted to look around fat Mr. Hansby, but it was like trying to look around a water buffalo. So then I tried to jump up and catch a glance over Miss Raleigh's broad brimmed felt hat, but that hat was so big it nearly blocked out all the light coming in through the windows. Finally, I ended up standing on a pew on top of a stack of hymnals before I finally saw a woman sprawled out halfway on the floor, her body facing the pew, and her head resting on a pillow someone must have stuck under it.

I screamed, "Mama! Oh God, what's wrong with her?"

Fighting to get inside the circle of onlookers, I lost my balance and nearly fell to the floor, but Pete Bromley, a boy I also knew from school, grabbed me and helped me down. Then he put his arm around me and told me not to worry, that my mama would be okay.

Our family doctor, who happened to be the pastor's son, came over and tended to her—broke out his stethoscope and took her blood pressure and everything.

"Alright, now go on back to your seats," Dr. Ellis instructed, shooing people away like a police officer at a crime scene. "She's gonna be fine, just fine. Don't you worry."

Now that the crowd was clearing out, I was hoping to be able to run to her, be by my mother's side, but Mr. Henson took hold of me and held me in place with his strong arms as I kicked and squirmed for freedom. I thought about biting him but quickly thought better of it. But I'm pretty sure I did elbow him a few times in the stomach.

☙

I sat next to Pete Bromley for the rest of the service while the doctor was tending to Mama in the back. He had a couple of other folks helping him out, but I wanted to be one of the ones helping, and so did Carolene and Jolene, but Dr. Ellis wouldn't let us. Pete tried to cheer me up by singing in a deep voice when it came time for the last song. I smiled just so he would think he was helping.

Even when the preacher was up at the pulpit, my mind really wasn't all there. I kept turning around, staring at the back of Dr. Ellis, waiting for him to stand or move (basically get out of the way). My whole body fidgeting, I was still trying to figure out what had happened to Mama, and still wanted desperately to run over to her. I knew the doctor said she'd be fine, and I believed him, but I'd never seen anyone close to me ill like that. All I knew was there was a pain in my stomach and I just needed to see her—alive and breathing—to get rid of it.

I wanted to believe this would never happen again.

I wanted to really bad.

3

Later at home, no one hardly spoke to each other for the rest of the day. Mama rested on her bed until time to cook supper. Me and my sisters had offered to cook or at least help but she said no, said she wanted us not to make a fuss over her.

So, Mama fried chicken while I sat in my room thinking. I blamed myself for everything. I just knew I had been the reason Mama passed out in church. I figured she probably worried herself sick about where I was and what I was doing, just like Mrs. Dodson had said. More than likely she was boiling mad too.

I could just picture her, pacing the aisle, blood rushing up to her face like mine did in my battle with the hair bow thief. And then Mama probably started to panic, her heartbeat getting faster and nearly out of control. I imagined her grabbing for the back of the pew to catch her breath and her fingernails grinding into that hard wood, whittling away at it like my grandpa used to sit on the porch and whittle blocks of wood into different kinds of toys for us when we were little.

I figured it didn't happen like that—not exactly—but that kind of thinking tore me up. So after an unusually quiet supper I went straight to bed. I laid there sobbing like I'd just skinned my knee up, praying that Mama would get better and never have one of those incidents again. I asked God to keep her healthy, because I wouldn't know how to live without her. If her life ended, mine did too.

Then I curled up under the covers and pressed my face up against my doll, Annie, and clutched her tight. It wasn't soon before I drifted off to sleep.

The next day I overheard Mama on the phone with Dr. Ellis. From what I could understand from only hearing Mama's side of the conversation was that she'd had some sort of seizure. And I think she scheduled a day to come in for a checkup.

When she hung up the phone, I asked her if she was going to be okay.

"I don't want you to be sick," I pouted and hugged her.

"Now, Jess, listen to me," she began. "I don't want you or your sisters to worry 'bout me. I'm tryin' to get the help I need, and when I do, I'll be just fine. Just remember what the Good Book says 'bout there bein' a time for everything. Live by those words, ya hear me? The one I'm keepin' in mind right now says there's a time to scatter stones and a time to gather 'em. Know what that means?"

I shook my head no. I really didn't know, but I would've wanted her to tell me even if I did.

"Well, this ain't exactly the official meanin', so don't hold me to it, and I'm sure it ain't like the preacher'd tell it, but I just like to think it means that there's times when we oughta help out others and then there's times when we need to help ourselves."

I guess the blank look on my face said enough. Mama smiled.

"Baby, I'm tryin' to get better so I can be around to take care a ya'll and see ya'll grow up. And I will, I promise. And a promise is somethin' ya don't ever break."

∽

Throughout the next few years, though, the seizures started happening more frequently, always unpredictable and unannounced. Once it happened in middle of the dairy section in the grocery store. And another time when she came up to the school to see some dumb play me and my sisters were in.

But the seizures never stopped Mama from doing things she enjoyed, like hanging laundry on the clothes line to dry on a pretty spring day, meeting the ladies at church once a month for a Friday night Bible study, and playing with us girls outside—catching lightning bugs, stomping around in the creek behind our house, and starting mud fights, which always ended with somebody getting hurt on accident. Usually it was Carolene who always managed to find a tree stump or root to trip over.

Mama called me and my sisters "a mess of tomboys" on account we liked to roughhouse so much. But she admitted she was a tomboy when she was growing up, too. Simply put, she was a big kid, and despite the closeness of my siblings and me, she was my best friend.

Carolene hated being called a tomboy and it would make her try even harder to be girly. And that meant spending all the money she earned from doing odd jobs and selling the jams she made on trendy clothing and accessories. Her room looked like Vogue magazine's closet—at least that's what I told her, which actually made her smile and she thanked me for the compliment.

Just as foolish, Jolene would dress up in her best clothes and makeup and sashay around the living room quoting Loco Dempsey: "All my life ever since I was a little girl I've always had the same dream. To marry a zillionaire."

I thought they were both pretty loco alright.

But for me, I guess the girliest thing I liked to do was pick the snow-white lilies that grew around that creek behind our house and make beautiful bouquets for Mama to put in the window or on the table.

I also remember lying down among that same patch of lilies is where I had my first kiss. Both of us were fifteen, except Pete was four months older than me. We laid there holding hands and I thought about how my name would sound as "Jessabelle Bromley" while he rambled on about working for his daddy or something. That night was also the first time I saw a shooting star.

As I watched that streak of light dart across the sky on its way to only God knows where, I had one of my girliest moments, picturing my wedding, or what I wished it'd look like. Pete would be standing there by the preacher, dressed in his nicest suit with his hair combed and slicked back. And then I'd enter the room in my white dress, the train so long that both of my sisters would have to walk behind me holding it so I wouldn't trip, so huge it would slap both people on either side of the aisle.

Then after the wedding we'd rush away to a private tropical island where we'd finally make love on the shore, the ocean splashing over our bodies. I knew our love would be endless and would survive all obstacles, just like you might see in one of those mushy movies like *An Affair to Remember*.

But I knew that lying there on the grass by the creek that night would probably be the closest thing I'd get to living out that fantasy. Knowing my luck, I figured mine and Pete's romance would end bittersweet, more like in the movie *Roman Holiday*. Nonetheless, I made a wish on that shooting star and I knew something good would come of it, even if it was nothing like I'd pictured.

☙

But me and Pete stayed together all throughout school, stuck to one another like swallowed chewing gum on a set of ribs. He even stayed with me through my time at college. At my graduation Pete told Mama he was proud of me and that he wanted to marry me. Of course that made Mama cry, and I remember seeing her crying pretty much the rest of the evening. She told me, away from earshot of my sisters, that she'd never been prouder.

College wasn't expected of any of us. Carolene didn't want to go, and Jolene had tried it but quit after the first quarter because she didn't like it.

"I hate goin'!" she declared. "I hate the teachers and I hate havin' to read those stupid textbooks."

As for me, I started at Hopefield College about a year later (I first spent some time working and saving up some money) and ended up receiving a degree in history. I swore I'd never forget the day I graduated, and I don't think I could if I tried. And trust me, I've tried.

My hair, which was normally clown-nose red and straight as an ironing board, was actually curled that day, a major accomplishment on both mine and Mama's behalf. She even let me use some of her makeup. Watching closely in the bathroom mirror, I spread some pink eye shadow over my eyelids and traced black eyeliner across my lashes, then brushed on some light pink blush I borrowed from Carolene, and painted my lips in the hottest pink this side of Tuscaloosa, the lipstick courtesy of Jolene.

I had on so much makeup that I finally thought I looked beautiful, but the rest of the family just laughed at the sight of me. I didn't care though. How many of them had just graduated college? It was my big day and I wasn't going to let my sisters spoil it.

Mama pulled me aside before we left for graduation and gave me some advice, the same advice she'd given me several times before, but this time it seemed to mean a lot more.

"No matter where ya go," she said, dabbing off my lipstick with a damp cloth, "and no matter how ya get there, remember that life's a backdrop. You understand?"

I nodded.

Though Mama's advice made me feel like a real adult, I sure did act like a big kid that day, dancing around the living room in my graduation gown, holding my diploma tight with both hands, and foolishly asking my sisters if they wanted to touch it or if they wanted to read the name printed on it. Mama just laughed and said I made her so proud and that she was going to hang my diploma right over the fireplace.

ೞ

That night Mama'd even prepared a special supper of all my favorites. I dug into the bowl of mashed potatoes and plopped a huge scoop full right next to my turnip greens. My eyes bulged and I couldn't wait to get started.

Carolene and Jolene weren't picking at me anymore since their mouths were full and they kept shoveling more in. That's one thing about my sisters—no matter how much they envied beautiful actresses and wanted to look just like them, when it came mealtime, Carolene and Jolene could pack away some food—and so could I when it came to my mama's cooking. She said cooking for us girls was like cooking for three grown men.

"I'm lookin' forward to tryin' Carolene's newest batch of blackberry jam," I announced, reaching for a buttermilk biscuit.

"Shoot, I forgot to get it out of the pantry," Mama said, darting into the kitchen.

A few seconds later there was a crash. My eyes jumped towards my sisters' and we shot into the kitchen as if the whole room was up in flames.

And then I saw her. Mama was stretched out across the tile floor, shaking like she'd just grabbed hold of an electric fence, and lying in a swelling puddle of blackberry jam. Carolene fell to her knees and started crying and praying aloud.

I tugged on Carolene's arm and told her we didn't have time for all that, that she needed to get up and help me and Jolene with Mama. She wasn't a big woman, but it took all three of us to pick her up.

4

That was one of the rare moments where I wished my father had been there. He'd ditched us when we were six for a younger wife and a better life. He didn't even want children, he said, much less "three fussy girls." I've always wondered why it took him six years to realize that.

Mama still jerking around, we hauled her over to the couch—Jolene had her by the shoulders, Carolene underneath her back, and I had her feet. Once we got her resting comfortably with a pillow behind her head, I placed a damp cloth over Mama's forehead and Carolene put another pillow under her feet, thinking it might help to raise them. Jolene called Dr. Ellis and told him to come as quick as possible. It was all we could think of to do.

Dr. Ellis—who was old enough to be our father, but who Carolene said was beautiful enough to be her husband—finally drove up and rushed inside, carrying his "bag of tricks" with his stethoscope dangling around his neck. He checked her pulse and everything and said we needed to hurry and get her to the hospital. Dr. Ellis helped us carry Mama to his truck and we took off down the road like we'd just robbed the nearby

Picket's Market.

As we traveled down the bumpy back roads towards town, I sat in the back with Mama, laid her head in my lap, and stroked her hair like she often did mine when I was sick. Jolene and Carolene, who I'm sure was deeply worried about their unconscious mother, did find it to be an opportune time, however, to sit up front next to Dr. Ellis and talk to him, though he wasn't paying them much-if-any attention.

It was about ten miles to the hospital, but that trip seemed like it took a hundred. Probably because every minute that passed I knew was one minute closer to losing my mother. She was the strongest woman I knew, having raised three rowdy girls pretty much all by herself, and now she was dying in my arms in the back of an old pickup truck on one of Dr. Ellis' shortcut streets. I began to cry.

By the time we were on the main road and I finally realized where we were and just how close we were to the hospital, my heart began to flutter. I wasn't sure if it was a heart attack or a panic attack or what. I beat on the back window and yelled to the doctor, disregarding the fact that he was older and no matter his high stature, to "quit yappin' an' hurry it up."

When Dr. Ellis turned to look back at me, he paused for a bit, noticing that something was clearly wrong. But it wasn't like there was anything he could do at the time. He couldn't pullover—and I didn't want him to—and he couldn't drive any faster. I guess all those possibilities were running through his head as he looked at me. And it couldn't have been no more than a second, but a second's all it takes for a deer to leap out in front of you. And that's just what happened—Dr. Ellis' truck smashed right into that deer like a bulldozer into the wall of an old house.

Dr. Ellis slammed on his brakes but it was too late. A loud *THUD* came from underneath the truck as it was tossed up into the air like we'd gone over some high train tracks.

I stayed in the back with Mama, my heart still pounding out of my chest, but Dr. Ellis and my sisters got out to evaluate the damage. The poor deer looked to be in about the same condition as the front end of the truck—all banged up with its lights knocked out.

Dr. Ellis drug the deer out from under the car and over to the side of the road into a ditch.

"So we just gonna leave it there?" Carolene asked, somewhat appalled.

"Ladies, listen," Dr. Ellis tried to remain calm, "I feel horrible. I really do. But there was no way to save it, nothing I could do. And I think we have a more pressing case to deal with, don't you agree?"

There was no denying he had a point. So we were back on our way just as quick as if the whole incident never happened, just sitting there in silence. But my mind was racing 90 miles an hour, and I didn't know which was going to blow up first, my heart or my head.

No more than a minute later, whether it was for my sisters' sake or just to settle his own guilty conscience, Dr. Ellis tried to further justify the abandonment by rambling on about how he didn't know how he could've helped that deer anyway, that he wasn't that kind of doctor. Jolene and Carolene could tell it was eating him up inside, so they didn't press the issue.

∞

About two more miles and we were there. The Sara Ann Lewis Memorial Hospital, named after the first female doctor in Lewis County. And the county itself was named after old Doc Lewis' great-grandfather, Col. W. C. Lewis.

Soon as the truck was in park, Dr. Ellis, Jolene, and Carolene jumped out of the front and helped me carry Mama's comatose body inside.

"Help! Help us!" I cried out as we entered the hospital, not knowing what else to do or where to go and forgetting all about my panic attack at this point.

But Dr. Ellis had already gone to sign her in and get a nurse.

"I'll take her, ma'am," a woman with a warm smile who smelled of sweet perfume told me as she pulled Mama's body from my grasp.

Then a couple of fellas helped her place Mama on one of those rolling beds and I stepped aside. They rolled the bed down the long hallway and into a room, and we were told to read the newspaper in the waiting area on the other end of a different hallway.

Dr. Ellis left us to follow the nurses to the room. I sat and cried—now, I thought, was the time to sit and weep—and then I paced the hall some, then cried while pacing. Carolene sat and bit her nails, an old nervous habit, but Jolene couldn't sit still no longer than I could.

"My nerves are jumpin' like a scared cat," she declared, hopping to her feet. "I'm goin' outside for a smoke."

That was obviously a new habit, or at least one she kept hidden from me.

"Eww," my face crinkled up like I was watching some maggots eat. "You're gross," I called out as the glass front doors closed behind her.

I looked across the room and saw a little girl crying—she couldn't have been no more than five or six, pressing her face tightly against her baby doll. That sent me back nearly fifteen years, back when I was a girl her age clutching my own baby doll, the same one I still clutched later as a teen whenever I was sad.

Mama had made me that doll for my third birthday, which I immediately named after my favorite TV star, Annie Oakley. Actually it was the *only* TV star I knew, being that it was the only show I watched that we could pick up. We'd gotten that TV set when me and my sisters were three years old, a Christmas present from my father to all of us.

I was momentarily lost in thought, and I wish I could've stayed there. But I snapped back to reality when Dr. Ellis walked into the waiting room, a solemn look painted on his face, and motioned for us to follow him back to Mama's room. We gathered around her bed, not sure what to do or say. I glanced first at Mama, but quickly cut to Carolene. When I saw her tearing up, my eyes jumped over to the bed, then to the clock on the wall, then back at Mama.

About a minute later, Jolene rushed in, smelling of cigarette smoke and looking puzzled. The silence told her everything she needed to know. Mama had finally had the seizure that would be the end of her struggles, the last battle, the final straw. We all held hands as Dr. Ellis said a prayer.

My feet shuffling across the floor like a zombie, I left the room my mother had just died in and walked outside for some fresh air. In that moment I realized something. Lightning bugs and mud fights, French toast and Karo syrup, the creek behind our house, pink blush and eye shadow, all those years of college and that framed diploma—everything we considered to be so important was now meaningless. The only thing that really mattered was the moment we were in right then.

And in the moment we were presently in, we had a big decision to make: what to do with Mama.

With no money saved for a proper burial and no other plans figured out, our only options were to either leave her at the hospital—which I knew we couldn't do—or take her with us. So, I asked Dr. Ellis if he wouldn't mind driving us all back home, Mama included.

He looked deep into my eyes and knew I was serious. Reluctantly, he agreed.

◈

This time Jolene and Carolene sat in the back of the pickup with me. Once again I safely held on to Mama while the other girls were busy struggling to keep the wind from tossing their hair around.

As we approached the area where we'd hit the deer, I kept a close look out for it. I thought we might even stop to pay our respects, to apologize for not trying to save its life.

When we got to the spot where I was certain we had left it, there was only blood, no deer. Carolene and Jolene looked too, but it wasn't there. It must not have needed our help after all. Or maybe it just wanted to go off to die alone, and not on the side of the road for all to see. Either way, Dr. Ellis kept driving and life continued on.

It seemed like the trip back to the house seemed much quicker than before. But nonetheless, it was plenty of time for us Johansson girls to think of a plan for what to do with our mother's body.

Dr. Ellis stayed with us at the house for a while. I told him there was no need, but he insisted. So I put on a pot of coffee while Carolene inappropriately flirted and Jolene stood outside smoking.

"Take any cream or sugar, doctor?"

He shook his head no and drank two cups within a matter of fifteen minutes. So I started brewing a second pot.

I don't know about my sisters, but I was waiting for him to say the magic question, the question that I'm sure was on every nurse's mind as they courteously turned a blind eye as we carried Mama's body out of the hospital:

What the heck are you gonna do with her body?

But he never did. And I wasn't sure why. He hugged us all goodbye and wished us luck before walking towards the front door.

We all three escorted him to his truck, glancing at each other to see who would be the first to break the awkward silence, the sun beaming down on us and the heat sucking all the life from our bodies. I felt the pain of our flowers, all swiveled up and dying from another dry spell like we had before. And just like last time, the weather was once again on top of everyone's prayer list.

But I knew something miraculous was about to happen, I could feel it—and I could already smell the rain in the air. I followed the doctor's gaze up to the sky and saw the clouds were dark and full, swollen up like my Uncle James' stomach at Thanksgiving. And before I could even make mention of them, they finally just burst. You could hear the crops let out a huge sigh of relief as the first drops of precipitation in two weeks splashed onto their welcoming leaves.

Dr. Ellis stood there a moment laughing and praising the Lord. I didn't know if I should be happy it was raining or sad because of Mama, so I just cried.

With his arms held up to the sky, Dr. Ellis looked at us and declared, "See, girls, God'll always hear you if you talk loud enough."

Then he got into his truck and waved all the way until he pulled off onto the main road. The three of us slowly walked back inside, soaked but unfazed.

We didn't know it at the time but that wouldn't be the last drought we'd have to suffer through. At the time I thought the one we had back when I was twelve was the worst, but throughout the years there would end up being far more severe ones that required a whole lot more praying.

☼

"Ok, ya'll grab her arms and I'll get her feet," I yelled out, takin hold of Mama's icebox ankles.

5

We'd gone back inside and were attempting to find a place to keep Mama for the time being. We assumed there would be visitors coming by all week once the word got out, so we had to act fast. We knew the hospital workers wouldn't say anything about her leaving with us, and neither would Dr. Ellis, but we figured that the fewer people who knew, the better.

With Jolene holding up Mama's shoulders and Carolene's hands under her back, we carefully took Mama's body to the parlor and laid her on the couch. She looked very much at peace, we all agreed, but something about it just didn't feel right, plus it was too much out in the open. The first guest we had over would've wanted to go in there, or maybe their kid would've gone in there to play.

So, we moved her into the back room and placed her in her rocker. Jolene placed a pillow behind her head and I draped her favorite blanket across her lap while Carolene did nothing but complain.

"I don't think this is gonna work either. Settin' up in her rocker like that, she looks like somethin' out of a scary movie. Plus I still don't think she's hidden good enough. I thought we had this all planned out! Why is everything fallin' apart?"

Unfortunately, she was right. The place we all had agreed on in the back of Dr. Ellis' truck fell through, and even our fall back location had done fell through. Everything *did* seem to be falling apart.

And then it hit me—the perfect place.

Carolene and Jolene helped me lift Mama out of the rocker and carry her to her bedroom, carefully laying her on the bed. It just felt like the right place because her bedroom was at the end of the hall, and with the door closed, I knew no one would go in there.

"We could even keep the door locked if we needed to," I said and the others agreed.

I placed a pillow behind Mama's head and Jolene laid her arms by her side. She actually looked really tranquil, like she was simply resting in bed, and we agreed that she would've wanted it like that. We covered her up with a blanket and closed the door on our way out—and locked it.

The three of us walked away and tried not to think about Mama being back there. Throughout the week we entertained guests and told them that Mama was resting peacefully now. We just didn't mention that she was resting peacefully in her own bed.

ஐ

Once the visitors slacked off, we started throwing around ideas of how we were going to bury Mama and where.

Jolene had some good ideas—one being bury her in the yard of the house she grew up in, down in Conecuh County. But I wasn't sure her family still owned that house anymore, plus I wasn't too keen on traveling with a dead body. Once I mentioned that latter part to Jolene, she was absolutely against the notion, making us fully aware that she "ain't travelin' out of the city with no dead body."

But Jolene did end up thinking of a good plan, one that was a lot better than Carolene's idea to sneak into the local cemetery during the night and bury Mama in an open spot nobody had claimed yet.

Entertaining guests and arguing over burial sites had kept us pretty busy since putting Mama's body in her bedroom. But there was one major issue we hadn't taken into account...

Before the week was up, the smell of rotting flesh had crept under the door, down the hall, and began to spread through the rest of the house. Since we were staying in the house, we'd kind of become desensitized to it. But one of our last visitors, who didn't come by until that weekend—Mama's great-uncle Herbert, had caught wind of the stench, and it took some heavy explaining before he accepted that nothing was wrong and left.

"It smells like death in here," he proclaimed, Carolene nearly pushing him out the door.

I could almost see the smoke coming from his heels as his frail body tried to hold its ground.

"Rottin', stinkin' death, I tell ya!"

"Oh Uncle Herbert, ya worry too much. I'm sure it's just some dead rats, or maybe a possum right outside," Carolene assured him. "Nothin' to fret about."

"Heck, I barely even smell anything," Jolene interjected, telling the truth.

"I'll personally call someone to come check out our critter problem right away, I promise," Carolene vowed, giving the poor old man one last nudge out the door.

Then she shut the door fast, commenting that he was a strong man for his age and size. He had only walked from a block away, so I wasn't too worried about him.

"Ok, we gotta move fast," I declared, sending Jolene down to Picket's to get whatever she needed for her plan. I would've loved to have seen old Mr. Picket's face when Jolene came to the counter with her arms full of a dozen or so rolls of toilet paper.

When she got back, Jolene opened up the packs of toilet paper and handed me a couple of rolls, keeping a couple herself. Carolene looked the other way in disgust as she held Mama upright while me and Jolene began wrapping the rolls of tissue around her until no more of her body was visible. And then we wrapped some more.

Once we finished wrapping her up, we all took a step back and anxiously admired our work. Sadly enough, she looked like a mummy from a horror picture.

"Oh I can't stand to see her like this!" Carolene shouted and ran into the other room.

Mama's body nearly fell over, but me and Jolene caught her and stood her back upright. Then I looked over at Jolene and she followed my eyes. She knew what I was thinking and we exchanged nods.

After pleading for Carolene to come back in there, she slowly made her way, like a turtle crossing the road, back to where me and Jolene, and Mama, stood. She hung her head down, arms crossed, as I explained my idea.

"I know it sounds bad," I explained. "But we really have no other option right now. It's just what we have to do."

She didn't like the idea. In fact, she hated it. But she agreed it was the best solution.

&

Over the next couple of years, we somehow managed to make it, taking it one day at a time. At first we didn't do very much, stayed pretty reclusive. I guess you could say we were sulking, wallowing in our sorrows—living out the lyrics of a country song.

But time cures all wounds, and so does love. After taking a long break from it, we all started dating again. At first it was just an excuse to get out of the house, but before we knew it, our relationships started getting serious.

I was actually the first to finally marry and move out of the Old House. I wanted to get away from Merilu, but Pete didn't want to leave, so we didn't. We moved across town into a big house next to his parents. He said he'd been planning that ever since we were kids. True or not, it was romantic, and it won me over.

About a year later Carolene got pregnant by a local man named Scott Hand. Even though Scott was a drunk, and everyone knew it, they got married and had another kid. I guess Carolene was so busy taking care of three kids (Scott included, since he stayed drunk and helpless all the time) that we lost touch.

Jolene was the last to move out. Just like Carolene, she ended up going through a lot of men. But one day she called me up and swore she'd finally met the man of her dreams—a fella named Rodney who was from a town right outside of Merilu.

Though they hadn't dated for very long, she just *had* to move in with him. From what I heard, everything seemed to be going okay for them, even though they were beginning to struggle with paying the bills ever since Rodney was laid off from Fleabings. But it wasn't before long until he got a call about a job from one of his Army buddies.

"You gotta come up to Detroit, Rod," the guy told him. "I got you a good job lined up at GM if you want it."

Jolene said it was the answer to her prayers and, of course, went with him. But with the distance and all, me and Carolene both lost touch with her. But I can't say that was all her fault. Because I actually hadn't talked to her that much since I moved out. Jolene was always so wrapped up in every boy she dated that she basically lost her own identity. It's like we just didn't have anything to say to each other, nothing in common anymore.

Once we were all moved out of the Old House, none of us ever visited it, and we really didn't know quite what to do with it. I knew it wouldn't have been that hard to sell, sure, but we'd have to clean it out first. And, well, heck, it'd probably been a good four years since we'd left Mama's body in a corner of the attic, along with a few boxes full of other things we didn't know what to do with.

6

Months flew by and turned into years. Probably even quicker than you could tear through the pages of a Sherlock Holmes mystery. And when Pete worked nights at Fleabings (his job working for his father ended soon after it began, when Pete found out how hard it was to work with family), that's how I spent those evenings: covered up with a blanket in bed, flipping through pages of Holmes' next adventure.

Some nights I sat in bed thinking about Mama and my life growing up. I loved to fall asleep in the middle of replaying one of those fond childhood memories.

I even had dreams about Mama sometimes, but in them she'd always be turned away from me, or not have a face at all—very strange. I'd call out to her and she'd speak but never look at me. At times the dreams seemed so real I'd wake up screaming, tears and sweat dripping off of me. No matter, I was always glad to dream about her.

Though Jolene was gone to Detroit, I finally got back in touch with Carolene and we'd talk about how things were going, often about her marriage troubles. She'd confide in me every time she'd have a fight with her husband. Scott would come home drunk from the bar some nights and they'd get into a horrible brawl about nothing important. Carolene would always call first, asking to come over. Then I'd hear a mousy knock on the door, and there would stand my beautiful sister, often with a black eye or other bruises or cuts.

Carolene would stay the night, and we'd sit up and drink coffee and talk about our problems. Usually in those situations, though, I stayed quiet and let her spill her guts. She'd tell me how Scott would push her around and tell her she wasn't pretty, which for her may have been just as hurtful as any black eye.

I asked her why she wanted to stay with such a man.

"Just leave him," I told her. "Obviously he don't deserve you."

But her answer was always, "It's not that simple."

"Aw heck, it couldn't be any simpler," I replied. "I mean, just let Pete Bromley lay a hand on me and see if I don't pack my bags and hightail it outta that house so fast his head'll spin."

Carolene smiled and took comfort in my strong words. No matter if they were true or not.

Then the conversation would usually turn to Jolene—*Have ya heard from her?* The answer was always no, not a call or a letter or anything.

∞

It's kind of funny how life goes in a circle sometimes. One minute I'm picking out curtains for me and Pete's bedroom and the next I'm hanging up curtains back at the Old House.

I admit it wasn't exactly my idea to move out, but Pete thought it was best, at least for a while. It was no big deal, though. We just needed some time apart, as Pete said.

When I first got there, I put my stuff in my old room (which I'd shared with Jolene—one bed on each side of the room, separated by a quilt "wall" she insisted on having) then walked around reminiscing about old times. I even strolled through Mama's bedroom, which we'd left looking exactly the way she'd left it. And, yeah, the room, no matter how many candles we'd lit in there afterwards, still had somewhat of a stale, lingering stench to it ever since the incident we later dubbed "The Herbert Fiasco."

But the one room I never went in was the attic.

∽

Come that next week, the very day after I got the phone line hooked back up, I got a call from someone named Mr. Poole who said he worked for the City. He had a husky voice and was quite cut-and-dry, with no time for pleasantries—must've been one of them people who always claimed to be busy, or at least thought what they were doing was so important they didn't have time for small talk. I felt sorry for his wife, if he was married, because that was actually a problem I had with Pete—he was always working.

"Am I speaking with Mrs. Jessabelle Mavery Bromley," he asked, "formerly Jessabelle Mavery Johansson?"

I was a little taken aback and not sure if I should say yes or not. Besides my wedding, of course, I hadn't been called by my whole name since I was a kid and Mama used to yell at me. If she ever said "Mavery" I knew I was in for it. Heck, my name's long enough, so if she was going to put that much effort into the name she called me, I knew she was going to put twice the effort into whipping me.

"Uh, yes?" I asked more so than confirmed.

Mr. Poole went on into his spiel about how the town is expanding and a proposal for a new grocery store had been accepted by the City Council. Next thing I knew he was making me an offer to buy the house (actually the lot—the house was to be bulldozed).

The amount of money Mr. Poole told me was hard to turn down. Of course there were a million ways the money could've been spent, after it was divided up between sisters, of course. Carolene probably would've wanted to go on a clothes shopping spree, get her nails manicured—all the stuff those movie stars do. I wasn't sure about Jolene. If she still acted the same as before, she probably would've just gone on that shopping spree with Carolene. As for me, maybe I would've just put it in the bank, save it for when me and Pete decided to have kids.

I knew it sure would've been nice to have gotten the money several years ago, though. Then we could've actually afforded to bury Mama's body in a nice burial plot. But there was no need in dwelling on what could've been. If I was going to accept Mr. Poole's offer, then I needed to focus on getting Mama's body out of the attic before any City people came around. I hated to think about them slamming the house with one of those huge wrecking balls then, whoops, out falls Mama. That probably would've made the local news, even the national.

"Could I please have some time to think about it?" I tried to sound as gracious as I could. "Maybe I could call you back tomorrow?"

He was reluctant but gave me until the next day to think about it.

&

Sitting in a tub full of hot, soapy water was just what I needed to melt away my anxieties and soothe my throbbing head. And the silence was nice, too—gave me time to consider the deal from earlier. *Could I really give up the Old House just like that? Just to be torn down?*

I lay on the couch, resting my feet and my eyes, comforted by the warmth and softness of my bathrobe, just enjoying the peacefulness. That is until later that afternoon when the phone rang again.

I figured it was Mr. Poole calling back, so I was hesitant to answer. But I've always hated to hear a phone ring constantly, so I picked it up. My jaw dropped to the floor as if it weighed ten pounds. It wasn't the husky voice I was expecting, rather a voice much more surprising.

"Hey, Jess, it's Jolene."

Though I hadn't heard her voice in so long, the sound of it was comforting and any feelings of hostility I had towards her instantly melted away. I mean I still wanted to wring her neck for being so stupid and following that man all the way up north, but I knew there had to have been something big going on for her to suck up her pride and call.

I was so caught off guard, my words mashed together in a sort of garbled nonsense. I tried repeating my response but Jolene cut me off.

"Listen, Jess, I don't have long. Long story short, I'm in trouble and I need your help."

"What do you mean? What kind of trouble?" A chill ran down my spine as I asked, "Are you hurt? Do you need to go to the hospital? Where are you now?"

"Whoa, Jess, calm down. I'm not hurt or anything."

I sighed in relief. Even had to pull up a nearby chair so I could sit down.

"Well, first things first," I said. "Tell me where you are."

"Ok. But don't be upset...'cause I'm callin' from jail."

7

Seems Jolene had tried calling me at my house—Pete's house. And he obviously didn't do like he said he'd do if someone called for me—that is, make up some excuse why I wasn't there then tell me so I could call them back. But I let it slide since it was my long lost sister and he probably thought it was urgent.

"So Pete told me ya'll were separated and you were stayin' at the Old House for a while." (Gee thanks, Pete—you didn't have to offer *that* much information, though.) "Said you had a new number over there but he couldn't remember it. So *then* I had to call information. You know how much pleadin' I had to do to make so many calls? Anyway. So, real quick, tell me..."

And next was the question I feared. The question I hated and dreaded. The question that made me sick to my stomach and beg for a dagger to be driven into my heart.

"What happened?"

My eyes automatically rolled back and I sighed deeply.

"Jolene, it's a long story. Besides, you're the one callin' from jail. I could ask you the same question!"

"Yeah, you're right," she agreed. "And I swear, Jess, I didn't do anything bad—it was all that idiot Rodney's fault. You gotta believe me.

Of course I believed her. I'd always had a feeling that guy was bad news. I figured if Jolene had threatened him or assaulted him or something, it must've been in self-defense.

"Jess, I gotta get outta here. I can't take it much longer. I feel like the walls are closin' in on me, and the people in here..."

Jolene lowered her voice to where I could barely hear her, but I figured since she was doing it on purpose I wouldn't ask her to speak up.

"You should see the people in here. I'm scared, Jess."

Several seconds ticked away in silence and Jolene even questioned if I was still there.

"Yeah, I'm still here. I just...I just don't know."

"Don't know what?"

The innocence and surprise in Jolene's voice made me realize she was depending on me. We were raised to always look out for each other, especially since we didn't have a father around. And we swore to always be there for each other anytime one of us needed something. And no matter how huge of a feat it would be, this time was no exception.

"Ok, Jolene. Me and Carolene'll come bail you out."

"Oh, Jess, sweetie, I know ya mean well, and I really appreciate it, but I just needed to hear your voice is all. I don't want ya to go to all that trouble. Besides, it's a lotta money.

Since this was the third time the cops were called out to the house, bail was set for one thousand dollars. That would be askin' a lot of *anybody*, and honestly, I was debatin' on whether or not I should even call. 'Cause I knew you'd be wantin' to fix everything."

"Jolene, listen. You're my sister, and I'll take care of it," I assured her. "Heck, if you *can't* depend on your own family, who *can* you depend on?"

Jolene said about a million thank-yous, all the while pushing me to say how I was going to get the money. It was a lot and I'd have been curious too—even skeptical, especially since me and Pete were on a hiatus.

"Listen, it's a long story." I told her. "All I'm gonna say right now's that the city's already gave us half the money we agreed on for sellin' the house, so we'll just use that."

Yeah, I lied, but I felt I had to. Plus it wasn't a total lie—Jolene's situation made up my mind for me. Now to just get Carolene on board.

"Woah, wait," Jolene screeched the brakes on my story. "You're sellin' the house? Why? To who? What about Mama?"

Jolene's voice got soft again.

"She's still in there, right?"

"Jolene, just calm down. It's all gonna be okay. I told ya, it's a long story, and I promise I'll tell ya the whole thing on the way back."

"What do you mean *on the way back*?"

"Well, that's my one condition," I tried to sound firm. "If me and Carolene drive all the way up to Detroit and spend that much money to bail you out of jail, then you gotta come back home with us."

I was shocked that there was no sign of hesitation or uncertainty in her voice. Either I had made a pretty strong argument or she secretly wanted to come back home and was just too prideful to say so. Either way, she was quick to answer.

"Deal."

∽

Come sundown I'd thrown in the towel and gotten ready for bed. It'd been a long day and that was all the surprises I could take. Plus I knew the next day was going to be even longer.

I layed there in bed a while, my eyes closed, trying to shut my mind off. When I finally got relaxed enough to doze off, I was out like a bear in winter.

That is until I was forced awake early that morning by someone pounding on the door. I looked out the window and saw it was still dark, so I flipped the light switch on to see the clock striking a quarter after three.

I was generally a light sleeper and, depending on how quiet it was in the house, would usually pop right up at the shuffling of a visitor's feet as they walked towards the door. But this time it took me a little while to get moving.

I lay there a few more moments listening as the

knocking continued. The sheets, smooth like silk, were pulled up to my neck. And the blanket, heavy and warm, was wrapped around me tight, making me feel like a safe, content burrito.

But I pulled myself up anyway and sat on the edge of the bed, sweeping the floor around me with my feet in search of my slippers. The knocking had stopped briefly but started back up again. I wasn't afraid to answer the door, just didn't look forward to what awaited on the other side of it.

Because a knock on the door past midnight and before six a.m. is never a good sign. Either someone was hurt or someone was in distress.

This time it was both.

8

Carolene stood there, suitcase in hand, head hung low, a complete wreck. Black streaks ran from her eyes, and her hair, which she always fixed before leaving the house, even the times she would come over crying and wanting to talk, was an unwashed mess. Even her t-shirt was on backwards.

I rushed her inside and onto the couch, tossed her suitcase aside, and threw a blanket over her shoulders. I expected her to be emotional, but the flood of tears that came pouring out of her could've filled up a bathtub.

I gently rubbed my hand back and forth across her back and told her everything was going to be okay, even though I didn't know what had happened yet. But once she finally calmed down enough to where she wasn't shaking and wiping tears from her face, she opened up and told me her story.

"Nothin' I ever do is good enough for him," Carolene sobbed.

I assumed this had to do with her husband being drunk because she'd told me several times before that Scott was a different person when he was drunk, that he liked to show his dominance and break things—her things. Sentimental things, too, such as, most recently, a set of Mama's glass mixing bowls she'd taken from the Old House when she moved out.

"'Member how we'd use 'em to mix up a batch of cookies when we was growin' up?" she'd asked me a few weeks ago over at Pete's house. "Well, he took 'em one by one and slung 'em 'cross the room all the while yellin' at me, callin' me a lazy, good-for-nothin' this and that."

After that she just sat there on the couch, repeating *Nothin' I ever do is good enough for him* before trailing off into a mixture of sobbing and whimpering.

"Ok, Carolene, listen," I began, holding her hands with mine. "Marriage is hard, but you can pull through this. I don't know what to tell you about Scott's drinkin' problem, though—he just needs to get some help, get into some kinda alcoholics program. Hopefully he'll do that. But as for you, the best advice I can give you is that there's a time to tear and a time to mend. Sometimes we have to tear walls down so they can be rebuilt stronger. And sometimes we just have to thread the needle and sew as much as we can, for as long as it takes us, in order to patch up what's been torn."

Carolene shook her head in understanding, but I knew my words didn't make the pain go away. Words can only go so far and only help so much, but that was all I could provide her right then.

"I don't know how or why men do this," I told her, "but they just have this way over women, a way of controllin' them.

They'll push you into doin' somethin' stupid or regretful, but once it all comes out in the open, you're somehow the bad guy. Or bad woman, I should say."

This seemed to perk her up a bit, and she added:

"Exactly. And they never apologize. You always have to be the one to do all the apologizin'. It's like men can do whatever they want, and women are the ones stuck pickin' up the pieces."

"Yep. Women never let the bad stuff go. We dwell on it forever."

☙

Some time had passed and Carolene had settled down enough to eat. Claiming she was starving and hadn't eaten since breakfast the day before, she raided the fridge and pulled out all the sandwich meat and cheese and pickles. I fixed a sandwich too and joined her at the dining room table.

"I'm sorry to lay all this on ya, Jess," Carolene said with her mouth full.

I shook my head and waved it off as nothing.

"So," she said, still chewing, "tell me what's been goin' on with *you*. I don't mean to pry, but you and Pete musta had a big fight or else you wouldn't be here. Right?"

I was surprised a little by my sister's bluntness. She stared at me and ate a pickle while waiting for a response. But I was silent and just made a confirming facial expression.

"Yeah," she continued, "I embarrassed myself by goin'

over to Pete's and askin' to see ya. It'd been a little while since I'd been over there so I didn't know you'd been stayin' over here. What happened?"

"Oh, well, yeah, it was uh..."

I didn't like it when the tables were turned. I was better at giving advice, not receiving it. Plus I didn't like airing out my dirty laundry. So I finally stumbled out some words and told her that me and Pete had a fight, mostly a misunderstanding really.

"It was nothin'. Just typical marriage stuff. And I've only been here about a week. No big deal. We'll work it out soon enough."

I left it at that. I think Carolene could tell I didn't want to go any deeper into it. I changed the subject to the house offer, since I did have to call Mr. Poole in the morning to tell him our decision.

"So, listen..." I started, hoping to sum up the story as short as possible. Plus I didn't want her asking questions I didn't know the answer to.

"A man from the City called and wants to buy this house so they can put up a grocery store. He's gonna give us half the money now and half later, once the contractors are paid or sign some papers or somethin'."

"Hmm," Carolene grunted as she thought. "I don't know... How much money we talkin' 'bout?"

"Ten thousand dollars. Five thousand now and five

thousand later."

Carolene's eyes bulged in surprise and she even started laughing as if it was a joke. But I guess my face didn't read that I was joking, so she went back to being shocked.

"Ten thousand dollars? Wow... I mean, I know we could all use the money, but, wow, I don't know... What do ya think about it?"

I explained to her everything that I'd been wrestling with and outlined the pros and cons. As far as I was concerned, the pros definitely outweighed the cons, and the whole thing just made sense—we'd get some much needed money and it'd force us to finally put Mama in a proper resting place. Heck, even Merilu would be a winner since the grocery store would make more jobs.

I must've made a pretty good argument because it didn't take Carolene long to respond.

"It's gonna be kinda weird, but okay. Since it's for the best."

I told her I'd call the man back in the morning and tell him our decision. It was a very bittersweet moment, though, because I hated to think of not ever being able to come to this place again, unless it was to buy a sack of potatoes.

But I had to push past that because there was still one more bit of information I needed to spring on Carolene, and I didn't know how to subtly say it.

"So, yeah, I'm headin' to Detroit in the mornin', if ya

wanna go along..."

"WHAT! Detroit? I mean, where'd the heck that come from? It ain't like that's just down the street."

"Your other sister moved there—'member her?"

A look of understanding crept onto Carolene's face, and even a slight look of embarrassment. But I wasn't looking for a response, so I continued.

"Well, long story short... For what reason—and, no, I didn't ask her—she's in jail and I told her I'd come bail her out, as long as she came back to Merilu. So, what do you think? You up for it?"

"Ummm."

But before any real words could come out she'd already picked up another pickle and had begun crunching on it, which I assumed was a way of buying herself some time to think without appearing indifferent.

"No pressure," I added, "but I kinda already told her we'd both come..."

No reaction, just more chomping. She must've really been mulling it over because she grinded each bite of that pickle down finer than relish.

"Ok, let's do it."

"Woah, now are you sure you're really up for it? I mean, it's only been like an hour since you were able to stop cryin'."

And then a smile snuck onto her face, and I could tell it was genuine. I'd seen that look before. She didn't have to say anything else for me to know she was serious.

"Oh but what about your kids?" I asked, feeling like I should bang my head against the table for having forgotten about them.

She told me Scott was planning on bringing them over to his mother's house come morning anyway, to stay for a while. Carolene assured me they'd be fine and that she was up for it—said she was up for anything that would keep her mind occupied.

❦

I knew the rest of the night would be restless, but I didn't expect my body to be *that* achy in the morning. Nonetheless, I fixed myself a cup of coffee and called Mr. Poole back to tell him we'd accept his offer. He didn't sound surprised, or even happy, just briefly ran through their plans. I paid as close attention as possible, but he talked so fast, and his technical jargon was so over my head, that I was still lost when he asked if I had any questions.

I didn't know what to ask him about his plans, but I did ask him for a month to get all our stuff out. I explained that we'd have to go through the whole house and that there was stuff *everywhere*. Then we'd have to divvy out everything and find a place to put the rest.

He gave me one week. And told me to come pick up the money, which I rushed out to do because I knew we'd need it on the road.

When I went down there, I even pleaded with him to give us more time, but he didn't budge. I wasn't worried, though—I had faith we could do it. Then come this time next week, it'd be goodbye Johansson house, hello Food Giant.

※

"Should we go ahead and start loadin' your car?" Carolene asked, a cup of coffee in one hand, reaching for her bag with the other.

I was shocked she was up and ready to go that morning. Perhaps she'd had a couple more cups of coffee than I'd had or something, but whatever the case, she was definitely a lot spryer than me.

When I didn't answer, just fidgeted with my sleeves, she put down the coffee and the bag.

"Jess, you gotta strange look on your face..."

"Well, the thing is," I started. "My car's been makin' this awful racket lately, and shakin' when it's in park."

I didn't figure the news would come as a surprise since I'd somehow ended up with our old family car. It was the car I remember taking our first family vacation in, and the car my father later let my mother have after he bought a new one and took off in it.

"Roy—you know, the mechanic down the street, the oldest of the Jones boys—came by the other day and took a look at it and said it needed a new transmission. Said not to drive it 'les I had to, and no further than just across town. So,

I'm thinkin' we prob'ly won't make it all the way to Detroit if we take it. I was kinda hopin' we could just take your truck..."

"*My* truck! Uh, Jess, *I* don't own a truck. You mean *Scott*'s truck. As in the man who hates me and wants me completely outta his life. As in the man who told me not to drive too fast as I left the house in it yesterday. Not 'cause he was concerned 'bout my safety, but 'cause he didn't want anything to happen to his precious truck. And you wanna drive it all the way to Detroit?"

"Yeah...? So I'm guessin' it'd be a problem?"

"Jess, that man loves that stupid truck! He'd seriously kill both of us if he knew we even left the city in it. Much less if he knew we took it on a road trip. He's expectin' me to bring it back any day now."

"Carolene, I know it's a lot to ask, but we ain't gotta whole lotta options."

"Well, what's he s'pose to drive while we're gone?"

"His work truck," I told her. "He drives it around most of the time anyway, right? And you just said he wasn't expectin' it back right away."

"Ugh!" Carolene groaned and walked away, but at least that was a sign she was considering it.

As I waited for her response, I fixed us another cup of coffee. My stomach was still knotted with anxiety from the long, worrisome night, so I was hoping the coffee would settle it. My cup was nearly half empty when a soft voice finally spoke up.

"This is nuts, Jess. And I know I'm prob'ly gonna end up regrettin' this. But ok, whatever, let's do it."

My face lit up and I reached out and hugged her tight. I hated it had to be that way, and I didn't want Carolene to dig herself a deeper hole, but I knew it had to be done for the greater good. We had an agenda, and we were on a strict deadline. No matter the consequences, we had to see it through to the end. Whatever it took.

"But," she stated while we were still embraced, so I pulled back to look her in the eye. "Ya know all that sewin' and mendin' you were talkin' about?"

I had to think a second but then smiled and said "Yeah?" when I remembered my advice to her about fixing marriage problems. Then Carolene let out a deep sigh.

"Well after this, I'm gonna need a whole lot more thread."

9

Though it was Carolene's husband's truck, I drove. Carolene hated driving but loved to ride, and would hold her arm out the window and let her hand fly in the wind. I worried she'd get her hand hit by a mailbox or another car or something, but I was glad to see her smiling. Plus she seemed happy, carefree even, though I knew that was far from the truth.

But I did need Carolene to hold and help read the map. She tried her best to navigate but often got confused and so we'd have to pull over and figure it out together, if not ask someone for help. I felt like an idiot holding the map and turning it different angles so my sister could follow the path of a road, but if that's what it took to travel in the right direction, then I was okay with it.

"Ya think we oughta take Highway 111 and go up through Sparta?" she asked. "It looks like the best route as much as I can tell."

I told her it sounded fine to me, long as we stayed on the route. The furthest north she'd ever been was Chattanooga, and I hadn't even been that far, so we were seriously cruising on not much more than a tank of gas and a prayer.

The sun beamed down, making my eyelids heavy, and the lack of sleep from the night before was already wearing on me. My eyes crossed a few times so I tried to force them to stay open wide, which didn't last long before they began watering and I had to shake it off.

Carolene had nodded off a couple of times already, but she acted like she hadn't. Maybe she really didn't know she had.

I figured the best thing to keep us awake and alert was to talk, so I told her about how it felt being back at the Old House, and she told me about her kids—Daniel, 5, and Susan, 6, who they called Suzie.

"Jess," she said timidly. "I'm scared I won't see 'em again. I'm scared Scott won't let me, that he'll take 'em away from me."

"Well, don't worry 'bout that," I responded, having given little consideration to that notion. "He can't just not let you see 'em. And if he tries to, that's what the courts are for, right?"

"I guess so. I just miss 'em."

And just like that, she was staring out the window again, lost in thought, and I was back to watching the lines on the road double as my eyes drooped.

It's funny how the things we don't want to talk about are often the topics that come up when we're searching for something to say. Even funnier, silence is generally more comforting than words on topics like that, which kind of defeats the point in bringing it up in the first place.

"Hey, look!" Carolene shouted out, snapping out of her trance, pointing over to the side of the road.

It was a small, handmade sign advertising "fresh, hot coffee and food!" After driving for four or so hours, coffee and food sounded amazing. And judging by the excitement in Carolene's voice when she saw the sign and by the furious growl of her stomach, I knew she agreed too.

&

Unsure of where exactly the place was, we just did like that Toucan Sam character and followed our nose to a red-painted building about a mile off the main road.

"Rosie's Diner," I read aloud, as if I were telling my stomach so it would shut up.

Me and Carolene walked into the diner and sat at the bar, told the waitress we needed a minute. Everything on the menu sounded so good, and my stomach really didn't care what I picked as long as I did it soon.

I tried not to look around, just look at either my menu or at Carolene. I'd seen enough movies to know that two women traveling alone were bound to lure some strange men over, wanting to talk to us and buy our meals. And sure enough, before we could even get our order placed, we were approached by the strangest looking man I'd seen in real life, opposed to on TV or in movies.

Like I said, I figured he was going to hit on us. But

judging by his bizarre appearance, I began thinking maybe he was just going to try to sell us something. But either way, I wasn't in the mood for company.

"Sorry, mister, but if you're lookin' to buy our food, we don't want ya to. And we don't need any life insurance, either, if that's your bag."

As if he didn't hear me, the man continued to take a seat on the barstool next to Carolene, who studied him like a live model in an art class. She watched as he tipped his black top hat to the stone-faced waitress, who flashed him what could possibly be considered a smile, as she took our order.

The man must have been a regular because when she brought us back our drinks, she brought him a cup of coffee, a jar of honey, and a bowl of sugar. I couldn't help but stare too as he doused the coffee with enough honey to cover a pancake, plus seven teaspoons of sugar.

Then he turned towards Carolene, winked at her, and took a sip of the sweet concoction that used to be coffee. His nose wrinkled and his body shook as if he'd just taken a big gulp of Champagne and the bubbles had tickled his nose. Then he chuckled to himself, curiously—the coffee mixture still dripping from his long, curled mustache.

Carolene laughed and stuck out her hand to introduce herself. The stranger delicately took it and kissed it, leaving behind a wet, sticky ring of half coffee mixture, half saliva. My disgust must have been apparent because he quickly pulled out a napkin...from his sleeve.

But instead of simply wiping it off, he first took a salt shaker and gave it a couple of shakes over the wet area, then placed the napkin over Carolene's hand. After rubbing his own hands together, the stranger held them over the napkin while reciting a few muffled words. His movements were precise, and his eyes concentrated on the napkin.

I couldn't help but to smirk when he started muttering and waving his hand around like he was polishing some furniture. But then my jaw dropped when he yanked the napkin away to reveal not only a dry hand, but also his signature.

Carolene held up her hand to examine it, and I leaned over to look as well. The penmanship was beautiful, and I found myself a little jealous, since my teachers always complained about my sloppy writing.

"Frankie..." she read, pausing to study the last name.

The waitress set our plates in front of us. Then in a voice almost as dry as the toast, and without even looking at the signature, she answered Carolene's unspoken question.

"VanTastic."

10

Though I was still uncertain of his intentions, Frankie VanTastic sure was a sight to behold. His hair was gold; his teeth white and sparkling. And he was actually quite charming, with a Burt Lancaster type of appeal. At first I knew there was something magical about him, but not in the since he wanted us to believe. He just had a mystical aura that was intriguing, which worked to his advantage as I later found out.

But what really set him apart and made him appear so strange was his outfit. Actually, *costume* might be a more fitting term. To complement his loud, deep-purple suit was a matching vest and bowtie. And his shirt, or blouse, was ruffled on the front. I was pretty sure I'd seen Jayne Mansfield wear one just like it in one of her pictures, except she filled it out a lot more, to say the least.

I was actually surprised he didn't have on a cape, like one of those magicians on TV. Or maybe he usually did wear one but it happened to be in the dirty laundry on that particular day.

While I continued to try and keep my guard up around the stranger, my easily amused sister had already become mesmerized by him as he ran through a routine of cheap card tricks. Carolene sat there shoveling eggs into her mouth, all the while watching as Frankie VanTastic shuffled cards. She was as wide-eyed as a hoot owl, occasionally covering her mouth as she giggled like a child.

"Hmmm," Frankie now studied the cards, looking deep in thought as he flipped through the deck, the cards all facing downward.

Clutching a single card with both hands, Carolene held it close and grinned like she'd just been asked on a date.

"Hmm. Selecting the correct card from so many would certainly be an art. But did you, my dear, happen to draw the two of hearts?"

His rhetoric was more fanciful than his signature. But the way the lines rolled out of his mouth, it was like he'd said them a hundred times, and I couldn't keep from smiling. I didn't know how he could ramble off such lines like he did. Though his whole persona was entertaining, there was definitely an air of arrogance about him.

Carolene's face lit up and she grabbed my arm to make sure I was looking as she held her two of hearts card up for me to see. We had an uncle who could do all sorts of card tricks and he'd already explained a lot of them to me, so I wasn't too impressed.

"Yeah...wow," I remarked dryly, sounding a bit like the waitress. "That's amazin'. So, Care, ya 'bout ready to get back on the road now?"

"I ain't finished eatin' yet!" Carolene scolded me with her mouth full, then turned to Frankie, her hand covering her mouth.

"You'll hafta excuse my sister," she apologized to the stranger who she was so sure I'd personally offended. "She's always been so guarded and reserved."

I flashed her a cold glare. He responded in laughter, a deep, hearty laugh. I admit I was a little relieved that I hadn't offended him—after all, that wasn't my intention.

"No fear, my dear, there's always one. A skeptic, a cynic, since I first begun. But if you will, follow me to the back. There is something I must show you and you'll see I truly have the knack."

He motioned to a booth in the back of the room and I immediately shook my head 'no' to Carolene and grabbed her arm.

"Are you kiddin' me? We need to go now—things are gettin' creepy. Besides, we're on a deadline, remember?"

I guess her curiosity was aroused because she pleaded with me, trying to convince me to stay for just a few more minutes, and I, of course, gave in. I told her I'd order one more cup of coffee and that we were leaving when I finished it.

After settling up with the waitress, I turned to see a fading cloud of smoke where Frankie had been sitting. Curious, I leaned back to look down the diner to the back booth and there he was, finishing what appeared to be a piece of pie.

Carolene jerked her head to look at me, her face filled with excitement, then rushed over to Frankie's booth and sat across from him. I rolled my eyes as I stood, coffee in hand, and slowly walked over and sat beside her. Frankie started up his flowery speech as soon as my coffee cup touched the table.

"Fancy meeting two ladies of such beauty and grace. What brings the likes of you to such an ordinary place? You must be passing through, stopped to rest, then moving on. 'Cause I've never seen two ladies so lovely dining all alone."

Carolene melted, then giggled. This man was definitely bringing out the kid in her.

"We're from a small town in Alabama," I answered before Carolene could tell the stranger too much information about us. "We're just on a road trip, I guess you'd say."

"Yeah, we're on our way to Detroit to get our sister," Carolene blurted out.

My eyes instinctively cut to hers, and I'm sure she could feel the heat from the hole I was staring into her. But that wasn't enough, so I punched her on the leg, discreetly. Her reaction wasn't so discreet.

"Oww! What in Heaven's name, Jess? I'm just makin' conversation with the nice man. It's not like he's gonna follow us all the way to Detroit to kill us or anything."

"Great!" I exclaimed. "Any other gruesome ideas you wanna give the man we met five minutes ago? A man who"—I turned to look at him—"no offense"—then turned back to Carolene—"looks like somethin' right out of a Dick Tracy comic strip?"

Frankie chimed in, obviously to defend himself, before Carolene could say anything.

"Ladies, a killer I am not; a stalker I find absurd. I only seek good conversation, a friendly word. Let us introduce ourselves, perhaps discover a common bond. Ask me a question, any question, and I'll wave my magic wand."

"Ok, fine..." I proceeded. "So you're a magician?"

"A magician, my sweet, performs at birthday parties and fairs. I do not perform for kids or at such juvenile affairs. I make the impossible possible, and I do it to survive. You could call me an illusionist, like Houdini, except better."

And then he lowered his head towards us and spoke in almost a whisper.

"I'm still alive."

Cue more giggling from Carolene, then cut to me rolling my eyes.

"Wow!" Carolene marveled. "So are you from here? Or do you stay on the road?"

"I do not live here, nor do I live there. You might say I do not live anywhere. I travel around, yes, looking for business and such. But there are a few places I frequent and admire very much."

Then he covered his empty pie plate with a napkin, just

like he did with Carolene's hand, and, I swear to God in Heaven, he pulled the napkin away to reveal no plate—only his fork remained. Me and Carolene watched cautiously as he turned his head to one side and made a discouraging face. Then simply by waving his hand over the fork in one quick motion, the utensil was gone. And in its place was a business card, which Carolene quickly picked up and read aloud:

"Frankie VanTastic. Master Illusionist. Psychic Advisor."

"Psychic advisor? You mean like a fortune teller?" I said sarcastically. "Yeah, now ya just took the little entertainin' act you had goin' and made it weird."

I gulped the rest of my coffee and told Carolene she knew what that meant.

Frankie stuck out his hand, palm up. Carolene wasn't making much effort to get up, so I pulled her by the arm, my teeth gritted, saying, "Come on, let's go."

"Sixty seconds, I promise no more," Frankie begged, reaching out and lightly touching my arm. "I know your time is precious and hard to afford. Don't worry about cost, it's covered, it's free. Just allow me this chance to make you believe."

Without saying a word, the look on my sister's face screamed *pleeeease*, just like a kid. Neither one of us had ever been to a fortune teller, not even at a carnival, so I gave in, figuring there was no harm in it. So I sat back down and told him: "One minute."

He took both of our hands and squeezed them tight, then closed his eyes and began taking deep breaths.

"Don't you have to have a crystal ball?" I asked, halfway serious, since that's the way I'd always seen it done. "Or at least turn the lights out? I think the waitress could prob'ly pull the shade down or somethin'."

"Be quiet, Jess," Carolene shushed me. "He's thinkin'. I mean meditatin'—ain't that the word?"

"No," I told her, in as best a whisper as I could pull off without sounding like I was trying to whisper, "the word is *wastin'*, and that's what he's doin' with our time. Now come on, Care, Jolene's waitin' on us. We gotta go."

And just as I began to work my hand from the sturdy grip of this bizarre magician, he began to speak, his eyes still closed.

"I'm sensing an object, such as a train, a plane, or a ship. No!—it's an automobile, I'm sure of it, that will take you on a great trip."

"Wait," I interrupted. "My sister already told ya that we're on our way to Detroit. And we're obviously drivin' there."

Unphased, he continued.

"This great trip you are on is merely the pair of you. But when you return, you will be joined by an additional two."

"We're goin' to get our other sister," I stressed. "You already knew that too. And that's only one person, not two. So..."

Again, he continued with no delay.

"But on your journey, you must watch out for the blind snake. For he will try to fool you but the bait you must not take. Stand up and be strong, it's his only weakness. For a tongueless snake cannot hiss."

"Right..." I replied, scooting over and pushing myself up from the table. Frankie released my hand and quickly grabbed my arm. Not hard, just enough to stop me. I froze mid-stance.

"Listen!" he snapped. "The dragon lady you must beware of. The one who wants to soar in the sky like a dove. Keep your wits sharp and your mind free. For a lock cannot be opened unless you have the key."

"Sure thing, mister," I said, pulling my arm away and grabbing for Carolene's. "Blind snake, check. Dragon lady, check. I think we got it."

I was a mixture of angry, annoyed, and confused. And I struggled with my goodbye.

"So we're gonna be on our way now. But it was...nice meetin' ya, I guess. And good luck with... Just good luck."

"Fairwell, sweet sisters, and safe travels to both of you. But please heed my warnings, for I promise they are true."

Arm-in-arm me and Carolene walked out of the diner, our faces close, whispering like teenagers.

11

"What a kook!" I shook my head in amazement.

We were back in the truck, about ten miles down the road, and me and Carolene were still talking and laughing about the whole thing. Carolene was a little spooked about the fortune telling part and asked if I thought that was real, but I told her that she knew as well as I did that stuff was baloney—or *hogwash*, as my Mama liked to say. She agreed but said it still bothered her.

Carolene had the map spread across her lap, so I asked her how far it was until the next big city. She estimated that Nashville was about forty miles away. I was glad to hear that, too, because, like I told her, we needed to be thinking about where we were going to stay the night.

"Oh yeah," she realized. "I didn't even think about that before we left. All the money I brought I'd planned on givin' towards bail money." She reached down inside her shirt and pulled out a clip of bills from her bra. "Think we have enough for a hotel?"

"Don't worry," I told her, reaching into my front pocket. "We need to find somewhere cheap, but yeah," finding my pocket empty, then reaching into my other pocket. "I mean, I brought the whole five thousand, 'cause I didn't know how much we'd need for travel expenses, but we still need to use it sparingly—just in case."

"Jess, you're always so responsible and dependable. I really admire that about you," Carolene praised.

Nothing was in that pocket, either. So I checked my back pockets—empty.

"Yeah, well, you may be takin' that back 'cause I can't find it. Carolene, I can't find the money!"

"What do ya mean? Ya took out the money to pay the waitress when you got that second cup of coffee, but you put it right back in your front pocket. I saw ya do it. 'Cause it was—"

"Right before Frankie disappeared for the back booth," I finished. "Ugh! It had to be that stupid magician. That lowdown thief!"

"That can't be right, Jess. Nobody's *that* good. And why would he even wanna steal from us anyway? He was too..."

"Too creepy?" I offered, my blood boiling, my heart still racing from panic.

"Well I was gonna say nice, but yeah, he did give me the creeps. But I still wouldn't have pegged him for a thief. If anything I figured he was just a strange, lonely man, possibly with a few screws loose. But not a thief."

"Care, this isn't a movie, this is the real world. You really need to wake up and smell the pesticide-covered roses, sweety.

Your naïveness is gonna get you in trouble one a these days. Crooks are everywhere, just lookin' to prey on innocent women like you. But I guess I should be talkin' to the mirror since I'm the naïve one that got my pocket picked."

"I just can't believe it," Carolene said, her mouth hung open like she'd just seen a spaceship land. "Well if he did steal the money, can't we just go back and find 'em and make 'em give it back?"

"We've already gone too far," I admitted, feeling defeated and victimized. "I'm sure by now he's long gone. It'd be nearly impossible to find 'em."

"Fine, then let's just go home."

"Carolene!" I snapped at her. "You know that's outta the question. I mean, think of poor Jolene."

"Well what are we gonna do for money then, Jess? I've got maybe ten dollars but that's it. We're gonna hafta, I don't know, *steal* it or somethin'."

"Yeah, right. We'll just have to cut down on our expenses. Like the hotel. I mean, we can always just sleep in the truck or somethin'—no big deal."

"That's fine, Jess, but what about the bail money? That's a lotta money. We can't just make ten dollars magically turn into a thousand."

"I don't know, Care," I confessed, beginning to panic but trying not to show it. "I really don't know."

"Ok, what about a loan from a bank?" Carolene

suggested "I might could get one since Scott's done paid off the loan for his truck."

It was a good suggestion, but like I told her, no bank's going to give a loan to an unemployed woman who has nothing to put up for collateral except her husband's truck.

"Oh. I guess you're right," she admitted, reluctantly. "Well then how 'bout we ask someone for a personal loan."

I cut my eyes at her in disbelief. "From who?"

"Yeah, I don't know—just thinkin' out loud. But if we ever *did* find Frankie VanTastic, I'm pretty sure he has some money he could lend us."

"Not funny."

I appreciated her attempt to lighten the situation a little, but I was too uptight for jokes. I felt like a fool. Even though I had tried so hard to keep my guard up the whole time, trying to protect my sister, I ended up being the sucker.

"Ok, fine," Carolene declared. "Let's just go with my first idea then. Desperate times call for desperate measures. We'll be like Butch Cassidy and the Sundance Kid, except the female versions."

"*Butch Cassidy*?" I repeated. "What's that gotta do with gettin' a loan?"

"No, no," she said, looking down as she picked at her fingernails. "I ain't talkin' 'bout gettin' a loan..."

"Wait a second," I said, sitting up straighter in my seat. "Are you seriously suggestin' we rob a bank? Seriously?"

The words caused me to swerve over the white line a little, so I grabbed the steering wheel with both hands to steady the truck. The last thing I wanted was to get pulled over—worse yet, a ticket.

"Carolene, are you outta your gangster-wantin'-to-be mind? That's crazy talk!"

"I know, I know. But just hear me out."

Carolene sounded so much more focused and sober than she did back at the diner, like she really felt passionate about this plan.

"Ya gotta agree that we're pretty much in a desperate situation. And we really ain't gotta lotta options. Actually none. But think of Jolene. Not only does she not deserve to be in jail, but after what all ya told me about her boyfriend, she'll prob'ly be in danger when she gets out, too. We gotta get her outta there, Jess. We gotta bring her home."

I mulled it over for a good thirty minutes. Doing this would go against everything I stood for—morality and the goodness of human nature. Doing this would make us no better than common criminals, like the ones that made the six o'clock news. But I pictured Jolene's face, and I thought of the pact we made to always be there for each other, no matter what.

I knew the idea was crazy and I just knew there would be negative, devastating repercussions, but Carolene was absolutely right. Desperate times called for desperate measures. And at this point, we were beyond desperate. We were almost hopeless.

"Ok," I agreed.

Carolene's mouth dropped. But it wasn't the face of excitement, even though she'd actually swayed my opinion, but was one of pure shock.

"Against my better judgment, I gotta agree with you. But"—I attempted to say the next lines in my best Edward G. Robinson impersonation—"banks are overrated, see. "Let's knock off a gas station instead."

Carolene laughed.

"Hey, I'm just gettin' into character."

"Ok, a gas station it is," she agreed.

And though Carolene was trying hard to act aloof when it came to the notion of us robbing a store, her hands were noticeably shaking and her foot began to swiftly bounce and tap the floorboard like a dog's leg when it gets scratched in the right spot.

"And speakin' of characters," she added, "who do you wanna be: Butch Cassidy or the Sundance Kid?"

My body began to tingle with fear, excitement, and uncertainty. I was stunned my sister could actually suggest robbery so casually. And I really couldn't believe I was also entertaining the idea. Were we even capable of pulling it off? Were we bold enough? Clever enough? And even if we did succeed, what was the likelihood we wouldn't get caught?

Maybe I was overanalyzing things. Maybe we were just

too desperate to even consider rationality. Or maybe we should've just turned around, waited for Jolene to call, and broke the bad news to her. I kept swaying back and forth with my opinions, but it was a big decision. We hadn't even really considered the danger involved. It's not like we knew what we were doing. I mean, forget getting arrested, there was a very good chance we could wind up getting ourselves killed.

I pictured Carolene getting shot in the back, blood gushing from her mouth as she fell to her knees and collapsed onto the tile floor. Me, I'd grab her gun and start firing back at the cashier. One shot to the arm, another to the chest, and ending with a shot to the head, splattering blood and brains all over the back wall and the rack behind the register that held the dirty magazines. I hadn't had such violent thoughts since I was a kid. Back then I just chalked it up to an overactive imagination. But now I was afraid these gruesome thoughts might actually become reality.

But I guess it's true—there's a time to search and a time to give up. And this was not the time to give up. We may not have exactly been searching for something, but we were on a mission, and we had to keep pushing forward. Whatever it took.

So I drew in a deep breath and told myself I would not be scared. Whenever the time came, I would be ready. So I grabbed Carolene's hand and smiled.

"I'm whichever one Robert Redford was."

12

As we drove, letting our minds wander, the miles raced by like pigs escaping from a slaughterhouse. And by the time I checked the time, a good thirty minutes had passed, maybe an hour—heck, maybe more. We ended up passing on through Nashville and decided to stop at a rest area somewhere right over the Kentucky line.

We'd made pretty good time so far—wasn't even sundown yet, but we still had a long way ahead of us. I had to use the bathroom and Carolene wanted to go in and freshen up a little—splash some water on her face, run a brush through her hair. I figured it was killing her to feel so dirty.

Though she claimed to want adventure, road trips were not Carolene's glass of milk. I knew it'd be hard on her since she always liked to spruce herself up and never went a day without fixing her hair. But before we left I told her we couldn't pack much, just a few necessities. She hadn't really complained about it yet, but like a storm on a gray, cloudy day, I knew it was coming.

I don't exactly know what Carolene had been thinking, but ever since the notion of robbery was brought up, I tried to remember that movie. It started coming back to me—how Butch and Sundance started out as bumbling bank robbers at first and then they started getting the hang of it. Since the robbery we were planning was going to be our first (and last, for that matter), I knew we were bound to run into a heap of trouble. I just hoped it didn't end the way the movie did.

Not just *Butch Cassidy* but any movie I'd ever seen about robbers or thieves never turned out well, no matter why they were doing the robbing or thieving. And if it did turn sour, we'd be sitting ducks because it's not like we had a—

"Gun!" Carolene suddenly exclaimed as if she'd been in deep thought and the idea jumped out of her mouth without her even knowing it. "That's what we need—a gun."

"What?!" I shrieked, looking around the bathroom, praying no one else was in there.

We must've been thinking along the same lines, but I was floored by Carolene's sudden change of character. I mean, I was still struggling to get in the mindset of a robber. I just couldn't shake the fact that this was actually happening. But Carolene...she seemed determined, fearless. Excited even.

"So," I began. "What's got you so fired up about doin' this? 'Cause I'll admit, it's kinda scarin' me a little."

"I'm sorry, Jess. It's just...I've been waitin' for the chance to break out of my mundane life. I want excitement. Danger. Adventure."

I nodded as I processed her testimony. Something had

been boiling inside Carolene for a long time. And I had the feeling I was about to find out what.

"I haven't told you everything that happened with me and Scott," she began, her face long, her eyes avoiding mine. "I was cheatin' on him."

The news took my breath away. Knowing all I knew about Scott and their relationship, I guess it shouldn't have come as much of a surprise as it did. I didn't need to know the details, and I could've saved her the heartache of proclaiming her sins aloud, but instead, I listened as she poured out intimate details of her new relationship—how she felt like she was finally swept off her feet for the first time by this guy, and how she wished she would've met this guy before Scott. And how the only reason that her and Scott stuck together this long was for the kids.

"I know there's no good excuse for it, Jess, but you have to understand. Me and Scott's relationship had gotten so horrible. He was always drunk and callin' me names and sayin' I was worthless."

"So last night when you came over...?" I nudged her for more, now intrigued.

"Yeah, Scott found out about the affair and he sorta lost control. He pushed me against the stove and lifted a skillet and made me tell 'em who the other guy was."

Carolene started to say his name, but I told her I didn't want to know. So she just told me it was someone Scott worked with, which had made him even angrier.

"So when I left to come see you," she continued, "he told me next time I came back better be to get my stuff. And he said his truck, of course, better look just how he left it. Said if anything of mine was still there next week, he was gonna burn it."

And that's when the flood gates opened. I tried to comfort her and give her all my attention, but I couldn't help worrying about someone walking in on us.

"I'm so sorry, Care," I responded, waiting for the right words to come to mind.

"Jess, he made me feel like everything was my fault," she fought back the tears. "He called me a whore. I was beggin', screamin', and cryin' out for him to just listen to me, to my side of things. I know I messed up bad. I know I did. But everything we once had together was gone. No more love, no more affection, no more excitement."

Mama once told me that tears, like yawns, were contagious. And just like every time Carolene had come over to the house, upset and crying, though I'd be trying to stay strong, searching for the right words to say, I'd see her crying and the tears would just start pouring from my eyes too. This time was no different.

"But that," she pointed back in the direction of the diner. "That was excitement. That mysterious man with his fancy language and his magic tricks. It was like we was in a movie."

"Care, listen," I said while taking her hand, "that man back there wasn't excitement—he was a thief. He took all our money. Money that we're talkin' about breakin' the law to get back, not to mention riskin' our lives in the process. I know you don't wanna face facts, but you're blurrin' the line between fiction and reality. And this ain't fiction, Carolene. I have no idea why, but here in reality there are bad, bad people all around us, just lookin' for any way to make a buck. Even if it means takin' advantage of some innocent women on a road trip."

Carolene was quiet now. Not sure if she was sulking or just processing everything. I let her hand go and dried my eyes, then reached over and tried my best to dry hers.

"Don't worry," I said. "We'll figure it out. Remember, there's a time to embrace and a time to refrain."

"What's that one mean?" Carolene spoke up, admitting that she couldn't remember the definition of the word *refrain*.

"I think it means there's a time to seize the day and a time to just...leave it be."

"Oh. So what's today then?" Carolene asked, biting her thumb nail, awaiting my response.

I figured our luck of no one entering the bathroom while we were in there being all emotional was running out, so I motioned to the door. As we walked back to the truck, the words of the passage echoed in my head as Jolene's face came to mind.

Jolene had always talked about feeling trapped and wanting more out of life. Now she was trapped again. Trapped behind the iron bars of a horrible relationship that was killing her.

I wondered what Jolene was doing that very second. All I could imagine was that she was alone, crying, and scared.

As we climbed back into the truck, I started it up but sat there for a moment, letting the cool air from the air conditioner blow against my face and dry my eyes. Now I knew what had to be done. We had to shake off the fear and go get our sister and bring her home. At home, of course, we still had to deal with the house and burying Mama, which made me sick to my stomach worryin' about. But it all had to be done.

"Today..." I replied.

I was only halfway thinking aloud, but I needed to hear myself say it. Probably even more than Carolene needed to hear me say it.

"Today we seize."

13

I thought it'd be best to take another peek at the map before we got back on the road. I added it up to be about 500 someodd miles left to Detroit. Figuring up miles and deciding between different routes on the map had taken my mind off of things, but I was quickly brought back to reality, before I could even get the map folded back up, when Carolene blurted out:

"I think I know where we could get a gun."

She seemed so excited, so eager. Oh God, what had we become?

"And where's that?" I asked, pulling back onto the highway, wishing I had a cup of coffee in my hand.

"A pawnshop."

She had a point. That was a good place to look and probably one where we wouldn't look quite as suspicious.

"Ok, we'll ask around for one when we get to the next big city."

We could've stopped at Bowling Green but decided to push forward until we got to Elizabethtown. I actually had a second cousin that moved there a few years before Mama died. I knew there would be no chance we'd run into them, but I'd heard from them that it was a nice place and I just wanted to see it for myself.

And just from driving around downtown, it really did look like a nice place. And the couple we asked for directions to the nearest pawnshop were real courteous and helpful.

"Fred's Pawn and More," Carolene read aloud the front of the building as we parked, just a few blocks down from where we'd gotten the directions.

According to the local couple, this place had everything you could want—and plenty of things you didn't want—and was the cheapest in town. Plus it didn't close for another hour.

The first thing I noticed when we walked in was the eight foot tall Indian man holding a homemade welcome sign. Shotguns and rifles covered the wall behind the counter. And as I scanned the rest of the room, I saw a drumset, a bookcase full of record albums, TVs, lamps, and even a few old signs. One was a tin Coke sign that said "Enjoy Ice Cold Coca-Cola" and I wished I could've bought it. Heck, I could've spent the rest of the evening in there just looking around.

"Judgin' by the looks of this place," I whispered, "I don't think Fred needs *more* of anything."

Carolene snickered as a bright yellow tank-top walked our way. Thick black hair grew wild under the tank-top, spreading like vines up a trellis. The man this hairy forest belonged to was, in fact, Fred himself. And Fred was a talker, telling us how long he'd lived in Kentucky (14 years, though not always in Elizabethtown), all about his family back in Brooklyn (his parents moved to Kentucky when he was in diapers), and strangely enough, how he recently passed three gallstones. That made me feel a little queasy, but I did learn that apples were the miracle food when it comes to gallstones.

"What can I do for you ladies? The name's Fred Berman. If I don't have it then it ain't worth havin'."

"Well," I started, my voice trembling a bit. "My sister and I are lookin' to buy a gun. And"—I casually looked around the room—"it looks like you gotta lotta different kinds here."

Fred smiled and clapped his hands together, then walked over to the glass counter where he raised his arms and happily showed off his furry armpits.

"So, you wanna gun. Well that just happens to be what I specialize in."

"Oh really..." I began as me and Carolene timidly approached the man who'd already taken down a double barrel shotgun and was looking down the sites with the barrel aimed towards the ceiling. "Yeah, that's a real beauty alright, but we're lookin' for...somethin' smaller—ya know, a smaller kinda gun."

"A handgun," Carolene added. "A pistol."

I was at a loss, my mind blank. I felt like I did the first time I ordered in a Chinese restaurant as a teenager, which ended with me folding back up the menu and just ordering "noodles and rice."

Gently placing the shotgun back, Fred asked us for our price range. Carolene told him just as cheap a deal as he would give us. I nervously shifted my weight from one side to the other and Carolene now scanned the room, pretending to browse.

"Yeah, ok, I got some real cheap pistols. Like..."

Fred browsed his display case, then smiled at the sight of one and gently held it up for me to see.

"Ahh, this is one of my favorites—take a gander?" he offered it to me but I declined—a shiny, black hand cannon that looked too heavy for either me or Carolene to handle, which he described as a ".38 with a little wear 'n tear."

I asked him how much it was and his answer floored me. I waited for him to start laughing but he didn't.

"Wow, I'm sorry but two hundred dollars is *way* outta our price range."

That was a major blow to my confidence. Doubt began creeping back into my gut and I fought to keep it from taking over. Maybe Carolene sensed this, but she joined the conversation again, trying to bargain with him. He said we were pretty so he'd cut us a deal: $175 for the gun plus one box of bullets.

"Well what about just the gun without the bullets?" I asked.

I thought it was a reasonable question, but this threw Fred for a loop. He started laughing and shaking his head as he put the .38 back in the case.

"So you wanna buy a gun but you don't want no bullets for it... Just what're you all up to?" he interrogated.

I was a deer in headlights, not sure how to respond. I couldn't tell him the truth, and I wasn't clever enough to make up some elaborate story right there on the spot. This idea seemed to be falling apart, and I just hoped we could get out of there without stirring up too much suspicion.

Fred seemed to be studying us hard as he stepped back over in front of the register, his arms folded. And that threw up a red flag for me, letting me know it was time to leave.

"I make you a good deal and now you wanna gimme a runaround. It ain't none of my business what you all are up to, but I ain't got time to fool with no persnickety women. Patience ain't one of my virtues."

"Ya hear that, Care?" I tugged on Carolene's arm. "The man's busy and we can't afford anything anyway. Let's leave him be."

But Carolene stood her ground. I was glad she was with me. She was always strong when I faltered, and vice versa. We balanced each other.

"No," she told me, loud enough so Fred could hear. "We came here to buy a gun and Mr. Fred here's gonna sell us one."

"Well tell me then why the hell you wanna gun but don't want no bullets for it?" he fired back.

"To scare people!" Carolene shouted, aggravated.

The words shot out of her mouth like a bullet from that .38 we could never afford. It was easy to see that weariness and frustration were starting to overcome us.

"Ahh," Fred smirked.

I added: "Well, there's a time for war and a time for peace," hoping to smooth over Carolene's outburst. "We just wanna keep the peace, make no war, and all that stuff, ya know?"

I wasn't quite sure what I was saying, but it seemed to appease Fred, who nodded and smiled.

"Well why didn't ya say so? If that's all you want, I got plenty of replica guns."

He reached in his pocket and took out a piece of gum. Smacking as he chewed, we were guided over to another section to see a couple of rows of guns that looked just like the ones Fred was just showing us. As he walked I could hear him mumbling, and I was sure I could make out something about persnickety women...

"They look just like the real thing, don't they?" he asked, proudly, as if he made them himself. And he might have for all we knew.

"So what are they then, like toy guns?" I asked.

Me and Carolene both leaned close to study them like we were picking out a diamond ring. Fred smirked again. I could tell our ignorance about guns was actually amusing him more than irritating him.

"Something like that. But if you just want somethin' for looks, for intimidation, then this is your best bet. Much, much cheaper than a real gun too. Plus I'll even make you a deal."

I felt myself gaining my confidence back. Maybe this was going to work out, I thought. Maybe we were actually going to somehow keep our agenda after all. I felt the presence of someone above looking out for us, getting us back on track after we hit a bump in the road.

I backed away from the counter and pulled Carolene with me for a private talk.

"I'll be honest, I kinda wish we could afford a real gun," I admitted. "I mean, it's kinda scary, ya know, just the two of us women out on the road. And we ain't ever even left Alabama, so we really have no idea what all's out there. Heck, we've already been scammed once. No tellin' what's around the corner."

"I know, Jess, but we gotta face the truth. We can only get what we can afford. We just gotta get it and go."

I nodded and stepped back up to the counter to tell Fred we were interested. Now he was eating sunflower seeds, spitting the shells into a Styrofoam cup.

"So what kinda deal are we talkin' 'bout?" I asked him.

Fred took out one of the replica guns, a real beauty, placed it on the glass counter, and slid it towards us. Then he looked at me and smiled.

"I like you all. So I'll tell ya what. It's yours—free of charge."

He spit out another sunflower seed shell and my face lit up with amazement. I wondered if he'd had a change of heart and now he felt sorry for us. I didn't like accepting charity, not when I couldn't pay him back in some way, but I was desperate. Nonetheless, Fred seemed to be a nice guy and his generosity was truly a blessing.

"On one condition," he told me, gawking at Carolene as she bent over to pick up some old coins that had fallen from a wooden coin case she was tinkering with. "Your pretty little sister there comes in the back with me to, uh, you know…settle the bill."

14

"Ugh! What a scumbag," I groaned on the way out of the pawnshop. I slammed the door behind me and let out a loud sigh, almost a growl. I marched to the truck and sat there with the window down and my arms crossed.

Carolene was still in the store doing God knows what. After Fred made his proposition, me and Carolene had a very intense meeting and she ended up agreeing to the creep's deal.

"Care, there's absolutely no way I'm gonna let you go near that creep," I warned her, not so naïve that I couldn't figure out what Fred was implying. "A kiss would even be too much to ask, but sex?"

"Well the fact is, we ain't got near enough money to buy anything in here. And I'm sure other places aren't gonna be much cheaper."

"Yeah, but—"

"Plus," Carolene continued, "I thought we were gonna keep our eyes on our goal—seize the day. Jess, this is just an obstacle in our path, a means to an end. We can move past this."

"Oh c'mon, Care, ya can't seriously be considerin' this."

My voice had a touch of anger to it now. Of course I was mad at Fred for proposing such a thing, but I was starting to get mad at my sister who I thought was smarter than that, had more pride than that.

But the more we talked and the more she reasoned, I knew Carolene's mind was made up, and I'd slowly began to come to terms with it. I knew she didn't want to do it, I knew she was disgusted by the idea, but I also knew she would do anything for her family.

"Jess," she told me, her hands on my shoulders, looking me straight in the eyes. "It's gonna be okay. Trust me."

Then she dug into her bra and pulled out the clip of dollar bills and gave it to me.

"Hold onto this, so he don't try to take it too."

And that's when I stormed out of there, back to the truck. I didn't want to see anything or hear anything. I felt queasy just thinking about it. Those greasy hands with the hairy knuckles all over my innocent sister. I had a mind to take one of those guns and put it to Fred Berman's head. I had a hunch no one would miss him.

I sat in the truck with my eyes closed while I cooled off and tried hard to keep from doing anything drastic. And just when my heart slowed back down to a normal beat, I nearly jumped out of my skin from the sound of someone clearing their throat right beside me. I jerked my head towards the window expecting to find Carolene.

"I see ya finally come to your sen—"

But I put the brakes on before finishing the word when I saw it wasn't Carolene. Instead, there stood an elderly black man dressed in ragged, oversized clothing with a straw hat pulled down over his ears. Large bottle cap glasses made his eyes appear huge.

"Oh now you'll hafta excuse me, ma'am, I didn't mean to put a scare in ya. Sometimes I let my curiosity get the besta me."

"No, no, it's okay," I assured him, pulling my hair back into a ponytail—sweat had made loose strands stick to my face. "I'm a little jumpy anyway. But what do ya mean your curiosity got the best of ya?"

"Oh I was walkin' by and seen you settin' here all by your lonesome with your eyes all shut. I didn't know if you was sleepin', prayin', or, God forbid, dead."

"Well to be honest, I *feel* like I'm dead, *wish* I was sleepin', and *need* to be prayin'," I replied, sending us both into a fit of laughter.

I needed a good laugh. Works just like medicine.

"Oh I see," the stranger said with a smile full of yellow corn-colored teeth, very much opposite of Frankie's sparkling white ones. "But why you out here just settin' in your truck? You ain't got no place to be?"

One thing I noticed pretty quickly about the stranger was the way he talked. I noticed it when he first spoke but didn't pay it any mind until he started saying more and more *S* words. This fella had a lisp, and I guess that's why he sounded like he was hissing every time he said a word like *seen* or *settin'*. Pete told me his Aunt Rancy had a lisp but I couldn't quite grasp the sound until I actually heard her talk when she came over to the house for supper.

"I gotta place to be alright," I answered him. "But my sister's in the pawnshop there and I'm just waitin' on her to, uh...finish payin'."

"Oh ok. Well that clears that right up."

There was a brief pause before the man took off his hat and apologized for not introducing himself.

"Oh I don't know where my manners are today. Musta left 'em back in my other trousers. The name's Abraham."

He didn't offer a last name, so I didn't ask. And I didn't tell him mine either, just offered my hand to him through the window.

"I'm Jessabelle. It's a pleasure."

"Oh no, the pleasure's all mine," Abraham said, flashing those corn kernel teeth again. "Now I'm not lookin' to waste nobody's time here today, so let me just say my peace and go on 'bout my way."

I listened as Abraham told me his story, how he served in the Army during World War II and how he'd outlived nearly all of his family and now he didn't have anybody to turn to. Now he just got by "off the kindness of his neighbors"—doing odd jobs for money and sleeping wherever he can rest his head.

And then with sorrowful, puppy dog eyes, he asked if I could spare a few dollars or even some change.

"Oh I ain't lookin' for no handout neither. I'll work it off. Yard work, wash your truck, fetch groceries for ya, whatever you need done."

We were tight on cash, but I figured helping out a nice guy like Abraham was the right thing to do. So I gave him a couple of dollars from Carolene's money clip and told him he didn't have to do anything for me and that we didn't live around here anyway, we were just passing through.

"Oh now that's very kind of ya, ma'am," Abraham praised, stuffing the bills into his shirt pocket and buttoning it. "God's gonna bless ya. He surely will."

"Well I sure hope so."

And then the passenger door jerked opened and Carolene climbed in. She placed the gun in between us and let out a deep breath as she leaned her head back against the headrest.

"Finally," I snapped at her, not meaning to be so harsh, but the word just snuck out of my mouth.

She forced a smile, but I could see the regret and shame behind it.

"Sorry, he had trouble gettin' it up."

"Ugh, so ya really did it, huh?" I was somewhat shocked but definitely disappointed. "Well I guess ya did since ya got the gun with ya."

Abraham just smiled and nodded and pretended like he was part of the conversation, just waiting for me to introduce him. So before Carolene could respond, I went ahead and introduced the stranger to her. It was quick and blunt.

"Abraham, this here's my shameless sister Carolene. Carolene this is Abraham, a homeless vet."

"Oh I'm pleased to—"

"So what all'd he make ya do?" I interrupted Abraham to quiz Carolene on her reckless act. "Was he gross? Did he hurt you? I swear if he hurt you..."

"Calm down, Jess. It didn't happen like ya think."

"Oh, well I guess I'll be on my way then," Abraham tried to interject but went unnoticed.

"What do ya mean it didn't happen like I think? What happened then?"

"I didn't have sex with 'em."

"Yep, I best be goin' now," Abraham spoke up again.

I finally acknowledged the man who was being so gracious to put up with two hysterical women. He thanked me again and we said our goodbyes. Then I turned back to my sister, eager for details.

"Ya have to know I'm embarrassed and ashamed, right?" Carolene said.

Her eyes started to swell up and I sat in silence, just listening.

"So I'm not gonna go into too much detail. But we did *not* have sex. I only...did the oral."

"A blowjob?" I shouted in relief more than asked. I felt so big-city using the slang term. But I was far from small-town rural Alabama, and the subject at hand had no call for civility.

I hated to think about my sister putting her mouth on that filthy man's privates, but I was thankful that was as far as it went.

"But how'd you get out of it?" I asked her. "I figured he was dead-set on havin' sex."

Carolene sniffed and wiped her nose. But when I saw her smirk through the tears, I knew I was about to be proud of my sister.

"I told him what I thought would gross him out. Gross him out enough not to wanna have sex. And then I countered with the oral suggestion."

I began to chuckle because I figured I knew what she was about to say. Carolene may have often gotten herself into a pickle, but she was clever and always came out of it alright.

"It was easy," she bragged. "I just told him I was on my period."

15

After the laughter died down and the tears dried up, I looked down at the gun and was reminded what this whole pawnshop ordeal was about, the next part of our journey: the robbery. And an uneasy feeling settled into my stomach once again.

"Ya know, Jess," Carolene shared, "just because we got this gun don't mean we know what we're doin'. I mean, I've seen enough cop movies to know a *little*, but I'm not sure we could even pass for amateurs. I'm afraid we'll get laughed at."

We may have been from the South and lived on a farm, but Mama never allowed guns in the house. And not having a father around, we never learned how to shoot one. I figured it wouldn't be too hard, just aim it with your finger on the trigger. Right?

But I knew what Carolene was getting at. We needed some pointers so we didn't make complete fools of ourselves. And we only had one shot, because real gun or not, I'm sure we'd still get arrested for attempted robbery if we got caught.

"So you just wanna ask around?" Carolene suggested. "See if somebody would show us how to handle a gun?"

"I don't think that'd go over too well, don't ya think?"

"I guess you're right," she agreed. "We might be asked too many questions. Then people'd get suspicious and think we were up to somethin'."

Which we were, of course. But we didn't want anybody else knowing that. We needed to find someone that wouldn't ask a lot of questions. Someone that I could trust to be discreet about the whole thing. Someone that, in his mind, owed us a favor...

"What about Abraham?" I offered.

"Who?" Carolene asked, her eyebrows wrinkled as she tried to remember why that name sounded familiar.

"The old man I was talkin' to when you came out. He was in the Army. He'd definitely know about guns."

"Ohh," she remembered. "You mean the homeless vet, as you so nicely described him."

"Yeah, I need to apologize to 'em 'bout that."

"Hey now..." she raised her voice. "Don't ya thank ya should apologize to your *shameless* sister first?"

True. So I apologized, told her that I'd just been upset. Then I admitted to her that I was still shook up, though, because now I wasn't sure if we'd find the old man again since he roamed the streets looking for food and work. For all we knew, he may not have even been in town anymore.

Carolene agreed that there was a slim chance we'd run into Abraham in a town unfamiliar to us. Plus we'd planned on leaving the next morning after we got some sleep.

And then, don't ask me why, but for some reason we started talking about Dick Tracy. I guess it was because we were on the subject of guns and crime. We recalled how we loved the comic books and how we'd been so excited to watch the short-lived TV series in the 50's. We also tried to remember the names of the villains—Flattop, Pruneface, Mumbles, etc., and laughed, trying to remember which one we thought Frankie VanTastic looked most like.

I was midway into what I thought was a great Mumbles impression when Carolene began shaking my arm, pointing down the street towards an elderly black man walking out of a bakery eating a roll.

"Oh wow, Jess, look! Straw hat, big coat—that's him, ain't it?"

"Oh sweet Jesus, it is. Let's go."

Carolene followed my lead as we got out of the truck and hurried over to Abraham, who was just moseying down the street, eating his roll one torn off piece at a time. I called out to him as we got near.

"Um, excuse me, Abraham? It's me, Jess. From the truck."

The old man stopped and turned his head curiously over his shoulder while sucking on the tips of his fingers. Judging by the blank expression on his face, I wasn't sure if he was happy about seeing us or not. Using his free hand, he took off his glasses, wiped them with the bottom of his shirt, and placed them back on his face.

Then, as if it merely took him a minute to recognize us, he held up his hand and smiled. Honestly, I was relieved by his friendly gesture. We finally caught up to him, slightly out of breath.

"Well it seems our paths have done crossed again," he said rather warily, which sounded more like: "...theme sour pass thav done croths again."

"I'm sorry to bother you," I started. "And I'm sorry about the 'homeless vet' comment earlier"—to which the old man graciously waved off. "I was just mad at our situation. I really do appreciate all you've done for our country. But I gotta really big favor to ask of ya. And I would even give ya a few dollars for your time. We just really need your help. I promise it won't take long."

"Well I don't see how I could pass up a few dollars," he said, stuffing the rest of his roll into his coat pocket. "'Specially to help out a couple a sweet gals like yourself."

"Thank ya, Abraham, that means a lot to me. And to Carolene, too."

"Oh yes ma'am, I meant it. Ya'll are real fine folks."

I glanced over at Carolene and nudged her to speak up. I knew it was my idea, but now that we were face to face, I felt too strange about asking him for such a favor. I mean, I'd heard his life story, I knew what he'd been through and it felt wrong to be asking him to ultimately be an accessory to robbery. Plus

Carolene was better at talking people into doing things.

"Um, Mr. Abraham?" Carolene sounded nervous. "This may be a strange question, so feel free to say no."

Even though I could see the confusion in Abraham's eyes, he continued to wear a smile. And as Carolene spoke, I couldn't help but wonder if what we were doing was really a good idea or not. But I let her go through with the question anyway.

"But we was wonderin' if...maybe sometime in the mornin' if you'd, well, teach us a little 'bout guns. Like how to hold 'em and whatnot..."

16

Since sleeping in the truck was our only option, neither one of us griped about it. I let the seat back as far as it would go, which wasn't much, and struggled to get comfortable. It took a while to find a position where the window crank wasn't stabbing into my side.

We'd cracked the windows a bit to let the cool night air in and then covered up with an old blanket Carolene had insisted on bringing from the Old House. It was actually quite comfortable, but Carolene almost didn't let me share it, not until I apologized.

It was all because I'd ragged her about bringing it, having deemed it "not a necessity." But that was back when I assumed we'd be spending the night *in* a motel, not in the parking lot of one. Needless to say I ended up eating my words and apologizing for the ridicule.

Come morning we happened to see an elderly couple bringing out luggage from their room and packing their car up, so we went out to help them. They thanked us and wanted to pay us but said they didn't have a lot to offer.

"Nah, there ain't no need to pay us. But if we could use

your room's bathroom to freshen up a bit, we'd be much obliged."

The woman chuckled and the man said to go right ahead. Said he was going to turn in the key, but that it was all ours.

☙

The church clock in the distance rang ten and me and Carolene were now standing across from Abraham on a narrow back road. Actually, it was more like an alley. I held the gun out daintily, as if it were loaded, awaiting instructions.

"Alright now, whatcha gonna wanna do is hold the gun with both hands. Uh, which hand do ya write with?"

"I write with my right," I answered, to which Carolene snickered and I elbowed her in the arm to hush.

"Ok, good," Abraham said. "Now..."

He took off his glasses and gave the lenses a good rubbing just like before, muttering to himself—or to us, I wasn't sure—the whole time.

"Hate these damn things. But ain't got no say-so in the matter. Can't tell a heifer from a polecat without 'em."

Once he had the glasses back on, he took the gun from me, demonstrating as he instructed.

"So ya see, ya gonna wanna grip the handle with ya right hand and put ya first finger on the trigger. Now ya gonna wanna put your left hand 'round the right one. That'll keep it more steady for ya."

I felt a little silly and a little criminal at the same time. Here we were behind the dumpster of a local pharmacy practicing aiming a gun. Luckily they were closed today, so there shouldn't have been anybody around.

But not only did Abraham show me and Carolene how to properly hold the gun, but he showed us how to look tough doing it. And that was the silly part—watching Carolene follow Abraham's lead, reciting lines like *Gimme all your money!* and *Reach for the sky!*

It made us both giggle because those were some of the same lines we said when we did our Dick Tracy impressions. I would be Mumbles and Carolene would be Flattop and we'd point our guns (our fingers) and say:

"Keep ya mouth shut and nobody gets hurt!"

Carolene recited that same line as she looked to Abraham to see if she'd done a good job. I wasn't sure what our new friend thought we were up to, but he didn't mind helping us out. And he sure was a calm, patient teacher. He even gave us some unsolicited tips on when to make our move and how to get away quickly. He was actually quite knowledgeable about the whole matter.

But as we got to know Abraham better, I grew curious about what happened to his family. I knew better than to pry into anyone's personal affairs, but I thought maybe I could help him since I'd had my fair share of loss and heartache. I just wanted to return the favor for all his help.

But before I could ask the first question, Carolene suggested we go down to the diner at the end of the block and buy Abraham some lunch. I could just make out the time on the church clock down the road and it was already way passed my normal lunchtime. Heck, it was nearly approaching my suppertime.

Being out there with Abraham, laughing and telling stories, the time seemed to have flown by. But I really had learned a lot. And now that food was mentioned, my stomach began to growl, so I told her that was a fine idea.

ଏ

We hoisted ourselves up onto our barstools and waited for the waitress to turn around. Finally, a Dawn Wells look-alike acknowledged us, giving Abraham a strange, confused look.

"Now don't gimme no lip today, ya hear me?" Abraham told her. "I'm havin' lunch with my new friends here."

Me and Carolene smiled and picked up a menu.

"Friends, huh?" the waitress gave a quick snorting laugh. "Whatever. Ain't none of *my* business. What can I get you and your *friends* here to drink?"

I wasn't sure what to make of her. Was she just rude or did she know something we didn't? Carolene must've thought the same thing according to her curiously shaped eyebrows and wrinkled nose. I figured I'd just better stay quiet, not ask any personal questions, and not cause a scene.

We all ordered—nothing big, just a sandwich, chips, and a soda. After all, we were tight on funds, especially with another plate on the tab.

And for a few minutes it was peaceful. Everyone just ate, didn't even look at each other. But Abraham was the first to gobble down his food, so he started asking questions.

"So what's two pretty little girls like you doin' out on the road anyways? Ya goin' visitin'?"

"Yes, sir," I answered, trying to chew up and swallow my food quickly. "We're goin' to see our other sister up in Detroit."

It wasn't a lie. It was just enough truth to be social, but I didn't want to air out all our business. Carolene, on the other hand, liked to chat. Just like with Frankie, when you get her going, she didn't know when to be quiet.

"Actually, our sister's in some trouble up there and we're gonna get her and bring her home."

Abraham looked from side to side before whispering, "Oh, some trouble, huh? So's that what the gun lesson was for?"

But before either one of us could respond, the manager had come out from the back, yelling at the waitress.

"I don't care *who* he's with. I told you not to let that bum in here again," he warned her before turning his attention to Abraham. "Don't you remember what I told you?"

The manager threw the hand towel he had draped over his shoulder right into Abraham's face. As the towel fell onto the old man's egg salad sandwich, I thought I could make out steam blowing from his ears. And then the man who was just trying to enjoy a nice meal with a couple of new friends slammed his hands on the bar and started cursing, showing a side of himself that neither me or Carolene were expecting.

Anytime I ever heard someone shout out a string of curse words like that, I was reminded of my father. Because that was the last memory I have of him—telling my mama just what he thought of his life and how he wanted a new one.

I didn't know if a brawl was about to break out or if we were simply going to be kicked to the curb like vagrants. Of course one of us was in fact a vagrant. But not today, I thought. Today he was a paying customer and I made sure the manager knew it, too. I tore into him like I'd just caught him sneaking out of the house past curfew.

He made no response, just threw his hands up and stormed back to where he came from. Just like a dog that'd been scolded by his master. Carolene laughed wildly, even mockingly pointing at the waitress. It wasn't nice, but I don't think anyone in that diner that day would have considered us to be nice people anyway, given our recent scene.

We grabbed our plates and drinks and went to a booth near the back. Carolene slurped down the last of her Pepsi, but I told her I didn't think we'd be getting any refills, so I gave her some of mine.

Even though I thought the manager's actions were a bit uncalled for, there must've been a reason for them. And I wasn't sure if I really wanted to know that reason either. In this case, the less I knew the better. After how nice Abraham had been to us—taking time out of his busy day...well, taking time out of his day nonetheless, to come to me and Carolene's aid, I didn't want my impression of him to be soured.

All I knew was that I really needed to start chewing faster.

17

"Eh, shit like that always be happenin' to me," Abraham grumbled, his voice rising on certain words he obviously wanted others to hear. "Ain't nobody in this town gotta damn bit a decency no mo'."

"What was that all about?" Carolene asked him in a calm voice, just trying to find out the facts but not provoke him any further.

"Foolishness. Damn foolishness is all."

That clearly didn't answer the question, but we didn't press it. That might have been a can of worms we didn't want to open.

"I gotta good mind just to take myself on somewheres else," Abraham muttered mostly to himself, his tone beginning to soften as he calmed down. "If'n I knew some friends that stayed in another place."

I stuffed the last bite of sandwich in my mouth, washed it down with my drink, and signaled the waitress for the check. The pit of my stomach was hurting and I knew it wasn't from the tuna.

"Say," Abraham began, "ya'll seem like ya must travel a

good bit."

I began repeating in my head: "Please don't ask to go with us, please don't ask to go with us..."

"So tell me what's a nice, sunny city I might like to settle down in?"

Whew! Ok, advice I can give, I thought. Even though I didn't have much to offer on the subject.

"Well, we honestly don't travel that much," I admitted. "This is more like a special occasion. But you could always do like they do in the movies—hop on a train and get off wherever it stops."

"Now that ain't a bad idea, you hear me."

"And if you're wantin' to head out somewhere sunny," Carolene chimed in, "you should go down to Florida. Or maybe even travel west, to the coast. I saw this movie a while back that took place in Santa Monica, California. It was beautiful!"

"Well there ya go," Abraham said with a great big smile, showing off that set of corn kernels once again. "Santa Monica sounds like a nice place to go for a place I don't know nuttin' 'bout."

"That does sound nice," I agreed. "I don't know much about it either, but you can't go wrong livin' at the beach."

Abraham chuckled a bit. He seemed to be much more jovial now that he had some food in him and we were away from the rude employees. But to be honest, I was still confused and didn't know where any of this was going. But the waitress had already come by and took my money—which only left us two dollars and some change—so it was time to start saying our goodbyes and get out of there.

"No, ma'am, ya can't beat it. Plus I really do need a beach in my life. Do these old bones some good."

Me and Carolene fully agreed. I thought a beach sure would've been nice right about then. No cares, no worries. A beach is one of the few places an adult can go to feel like a kid again.

"Oh I know these big toes a mine would love to be buried down in some sand," Abraham continued. "And for myself, I'd love to walk out by the ocean. It's a shame I've gone this long without never even seein' it."

Both Carolene and mine's ears perked up like a dog's.

"Wait," Carolene pounced. "You never seen the ocean?"

"But you were in the war," I followed right behind. "How could you've not seen the ocean?"

Abraham seem to be taken aback, somewhat offended. And that was when his demeanor started to change again.

"Oh, uh, well I meant I never enjoyed the ocean," he backpedaled. "Never been there for enjoyment. Seein' it from a boat on ya way to combat ain't no pleasure trip, I assure ya. But what's it to ya, anyways? Maybe I seen it, maybe not. Ain't none a yo damn business, now is it?"

Yep, now it was time to go.

"We're very sorry," I said, scooting out of the booth to

stand up, "but we need to be gettin' back on the road while we still have some daylight. It really was a pleasure meetin' you, and thanks again for everything."

"Yes, sir," Carolene agreed, extending her hand, waiting for Abraham to shake it. "Thanks for all your help."

I stuck out my hand too, but Abraham just sat there with a strange, scorned look on his face. His eyes narrowed, his nostrils flared. My stomach tightened and my fingers began to get cold.

"I'll be frank wit' ya'll," he stated, using the table to help lift himself up. "What I need from ya is a ride."

"Oh..." I said, glancing over at Carolene.

I put down my hand and Carolene followed suit. Abraham was really starting to alarm me now, and I assumed we weren't going to part ways on a friendly handshake.

"I'm sorry, sir, but we can't help ya out there," I replied, taking a step back. "I'm sorry."

"No, ma'am," Abraham said firmly, taking a step closer. "Now ya'll the ones that done brought up all that talk 'bout goin' somewheres new. Out West. California. The beach."

With every step that Abraham took towards us, me and Carolene took two backwards towards the door, hoping that someone would finally intervene and come to our rescue.

"Now I need ya'll to help me out here. Just like I helped ya'll out. Ya remember, don't ya?"

Me and Carolene looked around to see the other patrons

in the diner staring at us, but none looked as if they were about to make a move. Abraham was yelling at this point, and I was scared he was going to say too much.

I began thinking—maybe someone had already gone to call the cops and they were on their way. And when they got there Abraham would still be rambling off everything that happened that day—our gun practice, all the talk about robbery. And then they'd search me, find the gun, and haul me and Carolene off to jail on attempted robbery, even though we hadn't even attempted it yet.

"Don't act like ya'll are better'n me," Abraham pointed, still coming towards us. "Carryin' around your little fake gun. What ya gonna do, try'n rob a bank? Jewelry store? Don't make no difference to me, but I know. Just remember I know what ya'll are up to."

I could hear the low rumble of chattering all around us. Everyone just watching and making comments to each other. One young guy even took a picture of the scene. Maybe they had seen Abraham act out like this before and knew he was harmless, so they didn't offer to help. But I didn't know if he was or not and I was scared.

The door was not even ten feet away now. I knew me and Carolene could out run him. Heck, in his shape he probably wouldn't even try to run. But for all we knew he was carrying some sort of weapon. So we stayed where we were, waiting for the right opportunity to make a dash for the truck.

"Now listen," I tried to reason with him. "We appreciate your help and I hope ya enjoyed your meal. But that's as much as we can do for ya. And we're in a big hurry, so if ya don't mind..."

And as I turned towards the door, the man I not long ago called a friend grabbed my arm and yanked me back around.

"Now, ma'am, I believe you musta stuck yo head in the icebox 'cause it's done got too damn hard to understand what I'm tryin' to tell ya."

I fumbled around for a response but came up blank. Carolene was frozen beside me. But while I was dealing with Abraham, she was looking around the diner trying once again to make eye contact with someone, but everyone just turned their heads away. Either they were all just heartless people who enjoyed seeing us scared or they were scared themselves. And where did the waitress go? I'd thought about calling out for help, but I assumed it wouldn't matter.

"Now listen, ma'am, I ain't gonna take *no* for an answer."

With a wild look in his eyes, Abraham reached into his pants pocket and I felt my heart skip a beat. Carolene now stared at me, probably trying to read my mind, which I'm sure she noticed was blank at the moment. So I was glad she tried her hand at reasoning with him.

"Sir, the fact is, we ain't got no money," she admitted. "And we ain't got no room for another passenger either or we'd love to take you with us. But if you knew what all we'd done got ourselves into, and what we got left to do, you'd understand that time ain't on our side. So if you could just go about your business and we'll go about ours..."

"Well now," Abraham spoke, and I crossed my fingers that Carolene had gotten through to him. "Ya keep tryin' to feed me lines like Corn Flakes, while I'm still over here chokin' on horse shit. Now ya gonna keep shovelin' it in, or ya gonna 'least gimme a chance to swalla'?"

Clearly she hadn't gotten through to him.

Me and Carolene were panicking at this point. The tone in Abraham's voice was enough to send us on edge. But I happened to glance down to see the motion of his hand in his pocket, clenching and wrapping around an object. And that was when I lost it.

"Oh, God," I called out and continued to talk to Him. "Though I often falter, I've tried to act justly, love mercifully, and walk humbly."

I grabbed Carolene by the hand and closed my prayer:

"And I know you got our backs."

We both turned in a mad dash. I jerked the door open and we took off, no looking back. Straight to the truck and jumped in. Doors shut and locked, windows up. Breath in, breath out. Breathe in, breathe out.

There was no Abraham in sight. I figured he waved his hand at the idea of running after us. Me and Carolene were still pretty spry. I even leaped over a storm grate on the way to the truck.

"Pull forward, up closer to the door," Carolene said. "I just wanna see if he's still standin' there."

But he wasn't.

He was lying there. His glasses beside him, his straw hat being carried away by the wind.

"What happened?" I asked.

"I don't know!" Carolene answered. "I was too busy runnin'. You think he had a heart attack or somethin'?"

I hadn't even considered that. I knew he was old and he seemed kind of feeble, but that didn't mean his heart was bad, right? Still, a sudden gust of panic hit me.

"Oh, Carolene, ya don't think he really *did* have a heart attack and *we* caused it, do ya?"

"No way, Jess. I mean, there ain't no way. I mean...let's just go, ok?"

But just before I pulled away, the manager—the man I was way too harsh to earlier, who was probably just protecting his customers from someone he must've had a previous run-in with—came outside, grabbed the old man by his coat, and dragged him out from in front of the diner's door.

As the manager moved him, Carolene gasped and covered her mouth, startled by the sight of blood dripping from Abraham's forehead. But I assured her he must have just been knocked out, a blow to the head, nothing serious. I mean, the manager wouldn't just leave a dead body on the sidewalk, would he?

Though Carolene couldn't watch anymore, I continued to stare, curious. Because it was the strangest color of blood I'd ever seen...

And that's when I realized it wasn't blood that was dripping from Abraham's head—it was pancake batter.

My sigh of relief made Carolene turn around, just in time to see the manager look our way. In his hand was a large, metal mixing bowl, pancake batter running down the side of it onto the sidewalk.

"You're welcome!" he called out. "Now get the hell out of town and don't ever come back here again!"

18

About thirty miles down the road, I looked down and noticed I was doing a good twenty miles over the speed limit, so I let off the gas to slow back down. I guess I was still in panic mode, still running from an elderly man with a weapon. Or what I thought was a weapon.

Whatever the case, he did a good job of making us think he was going to hurt us. And that's the part that haunted me the most—the "what if" factor. It took me a while to shake off that feeling.

ಬ

We drove for at least four more hours, and the road was wearing on me—plus I hadn't driven by moonlight in ages. Carolene had a glazed look on her face, too, just staring out the window, making no comments. Really we hadn't passed anything exciting enough to make comments about.

We'd filled up the truck that morning before meeting Abraham, but the needle on the gas gauge had gone down with the sun. But I welcomed the chance to stretch my legs and use the bathroom.

"Keep your eyes open for a gas station," I instructed

Carolene.

"Already?"

I told her the time and, much to her surprise, how long it'd been since we'd gotten gas. But luckily it wasn't long before we caught sight of a chipped-paint sign ahead on the right. I got out to pump the gas and Carolene rolled down her window to talk.

"Jess, how we s'pose to rob a store if we ain't got the guts to stand up to one old man?"

I looked down and smiled a half-smile.

"Yeah, I know. But it caught us off guard. And we trusted 'em. I mean, I know *I* did. And even though we'd just met 'em, I considered 'em a friend."

"Yeah, I know what ya mean. So, then are ya sure we can do this? I'm just scared somethin's gonna go wrong."

"Care, you ain't backin' out on me are you?" I asked, a hint of anxiety to my voice.

"No, no, not sayin' that. Just...sayin'."

"Oh. Well, don't be thinkin' that way. Or as Mama'd say, that's just stinkin' thinkin'."

That pulled a slight curve from Carolene's lips, but still, she was staring off into the distance now. I wished I could read her mind, just to see how she really felt about everything. But it was probably about the same way as I felt about it—terrified.

I got my two dollars and change's worth of gas and reached into my pocket for the money. It was sad to see our little wad of cash had now dwindled down to nothing. We not only needed money to get Jolene out, but we needed it for ourselves too—for food, gas to get home. Heck, I wasn't sure if we even had enough gas to make it *to* Detroit.

Looking around, I felt a pain in the pit of my stomach thinking about the little bit of time we had left to do all the things we had to do. But if we were going to make it back home and bury Mama in time, I knew we needed to quit thinking and start doing.

Fear was not an option, I repeated to myself, filling my lungs with the cool night air. Fear was not an option—it was a choice. And family trumps fear every time. Right?

After all, there's a time to be born and a time to die. But I just hoped we wouldn't be dying any time soon. Not just yet. Not that night.

"Hey, Care."

She didn't answer but I kept right on talking anyway.

"It's dark," I said, looking around. "Ain't nobody else around."

I took some deep breaths and tried to pump myself up like an athlete, saying motivational phrases aloud but softly to myself. I continued to look around, ever so conspicuously.

"Let's do this. Right here, right now. We can do it. Let's just get it over with and we'll be on our way. Remember, this is for Jolene. No one gets hurt. In and out. It'll be over before we know it."

I was rambling at this point, trying to ease my nerves. I figured Carolene was nervous too, so I told her not to panic, not to cry, and to just not say anything at all. The less we spoke the better. In and out.

"So, ya ready?" I said, turning to face her.

"Huh? Ready for what?"

The question seemed to pull Carolene, who'd been staring intently at the lit-up Holiday Inn sign down the street, from her daze, oblivious to what was happening and what I'd been saying.

"Oh ya gotta be kiddin' me," I threw my hands up and sighed, as if it pained me to know I had to repeat everything.

"I'm sorry! Ya got my attention now. What all'd ya say? I promise I'm listenin'."

"Ugh..." I groaned. "Ok, long story short: we're gonna rob this store."

"Uh..." Carolene searched for a reply.

But seeing that I was serious, she unbuckled her seatbelt and hopped out. I went ahead and finished filling the truck up with gas, trying to think ahead. I mean, what getaway car only has two dollars and some change worth of gas in it?

As we crept towards the door, I overheard Carolene softly repeating to herself like an actor before taking the stage: *Reach for the sky... Gimme all your money... Reach for the sky...*

"Remember," I whispered, looking straight ahead, trying to put my tough-gal face on.

Though my heart was pumping like a steam engine, it felt like my blood had dried up and stopped flowing, leaving my body ice cold. And as I reached to open the door, the gun behind my back and Carolene behind me, I drew in a deep breath that bulked up my chest and held it in for a few moments before releasing it.

"Just like we practiced."

19

There's something almost spiritual about holding the barrel of a gun to a man's head. The omnipotence you possess and the rush of adrenaline thrusting through your veins make you feel like a god.

That was a line I'd heard in a movie once. It was some big-city gangster flick that I only saw one scene of, and it happened to be the scene where the main character lay on the street curb dying, having been shot in a robbery. And those were his last words.

The scene came to mind as I stood there in front of a kid who looked nearly half my age dressed in a bright yellow bowling shirt that read "Cheap Al's Quick Stop" on the pocket. With both hands, I aimed the gun directly at his face, squeezing the grip so tight I felt I could have crushed it.

Our eyes locked onto each other and hung there a bit. From behind me, Carolene told him to reach for the sky, exactly as we were coached. And it even sounded rehearsed, too.

Clearly we were amateurs.

Amateurs or not, the terror of a gun sent the kid's arms into the air, revealing a swamp of armpit sweat. My face cringed and my body instinctively drew back at the sight, just as I did every time Mama would have to gut fish she bought from one of the local fishermen. I felt bad for having made such a reaction, but at least I wasn't smiling from ear to ear like my easily amused sister.

My hands shook and I too began sweating as if I was back in the Alabama summer sun. Being modest, I kept my arms close to my body for fear of being in the exact same sticky situation as the kid.

This was the moment when I was supposed to yell out: *Gimme all your money!* But I couldn't speak. I knew my lines from rehearsal but I also knew I'd get them all jumbled up. My eyes cut to the cash register, and the boy obviously knew what we were after because he immediately opened the register and started stuffing the money into a brown paper bag.

I knew mama was looking down on me with a long face, ashamed of my actions and what I'd let myself become. She raised us the best she could by herself, teaching us right from wrong, always using the Bible as her textbook. And once she passed, I think I could speak for my other sisters when I say we never forgot a word she told us. But I bet it sure didn't seem that way now.

"So what's your name?" Carolene asked him, shifting her body and looking around.

My eyes bulged out like a blowfish and I flashed her a look of astonishment. *What was she thinking?* This wasn't the time for idle chitchat. No one needed to know anyone else's name, that was for sure.

"Shut. Up. Carolene," I emphasized each word, my teeth gritted, hoping she would pick up on the seriousness in my voice, not realizing until after the fact that I'd just said her name.

With his arms back in the air and the bag of money lying on the counter between us, the kid broke what Abraham said was the first rule of robbery: never exchange personal information. And from the crime movies I'd seen, I was aware that small talk was not typically part of the transaction.

"Ted," he blurted out. "My family calls me Teddy, and my real name is Theodore. But most people just call me Ted. I know, it gets confusing."

Ted. Great, now we were on our way to becoming friends. So I had to say something to make him realize we weren't bad people and that we definitely weren't going to hurt him. So I looked him straight in the eyes and asked him a deep, personal question. I know it was breaking rule number one, but I figured since the rule had already been broken, it was alright.

"Ted, would you do anything for your family?"

I'm sure to him the question was way out of left field, but it was a sincere question. His eyes darted back and forth between me and Carolene, and after a few moments he must've realized I was actually waiting for an answer.

"Oh, uh, yeah of course," he more asked than said.

"Well," I tried to explain, "then believe me when I say that we wouldn't be doin' this for any other reason. If ya really love your family, Ted, you'll do anything for 'em. Do you understand? Anything."

I waited a few moments again for Ted to respond. But to my surprise, his eyes teared up, and instead of saying how he understood and that he would have done the same thing if he was in our shoes, he put his hands together and started to beg.

"Please, lady, just don't hurt them. I gave you the money. I swear there ain't no more. Tell me what else you want me to do. Just please don't hurt my family. They may be strict on me, but they don't deserve to be hurt."

I was taken aback, struggling to make sense of things, and the only word I was comfortable saying was, "Huh?"

"Please... What are you going to do to them?"

I looked over at Carolene, uncertain of what was going on. She looked just as confused.

"What *about* your family?" she asked the boy who had tears running down his cheeks. "Ain't nobody gonna hurt 'em. Heck, we don't even know 'em."

"Really?" Ted sniffed and wiped away his tears, unsure of what our angle was.

"Really. Ain't nobody gonna hurt your family," I verified.

"Well I just thought..." Ted continued, running his hands over his head. "I don't know what's happening. I'm so confused. But you're not going to shoot me either, right? I'm only 18."

Oh to be 18 again. Even though that's the age I was when Mama died—and I would never want to relive that again, if there was nothing I could go back and do to change things. But that was before all the relationship trouble began, back when me and my sisters were as tight as the Three Musketeers.

But we weren't teenagers anymore, though we acted like it, now a trio of misfits—two sisters committing robbery on the way to get the other sister out of jail. But Ted seemed to have his own issues, and the hopelessness in the next words he spoke made me feel guilty for making him have to go through this whole ordeal.

"But who am I kidding, you might as well just pull the trigger."

Then he lowered his arms and shoved some loose money that had fallen onto the counter into the bag. It was apparent that he was becoming more agitated and less afraid, slamming the register drawer shut and banging his fist on it as he thought aloud about the consequences from tonight's mishap.

"My boss is gonna kill me anyway. Then after he kills me he's gonna fire me. And after he fires me, my parents are gonna kick me out. They've been looking for a reason to anyway, and this'll just send my dad over the edge."

We watched as Ted sobbed and took out his hostility on the poor cash register. This wasn't covered in our training session. There was no mention of emotions. We were supposed to be in and out, no small talk, no crying.

I wasn't sure what to do, but I still tried to keep the gun pointed at Ted. We still needed to get what we came for. Carolene, however, was a sucker when it came to tears, so she spoke up to try to comfort the troubled youth.

"Ted?" Carolene said in a low, calm voice. "It's all gonna be okay. I know it seems like life can be hard on ya at times, but"—she put her arm around my shoulders—"we all struggle. Heck, we done been through a whole heap a trouble just to get here 'n we still gotta ways to go."

I nodded in agreement, hoping the rest of our trip would go a lot smoother.

"Now just take a deep breath," Carolene continued. "And calm down."

It seemed to be working because the redness in Ted's pimply face started to fade. Plus he'd stopped hitting innocent machinery.

"Listen, Ted, we ain't gonna shoot ya," she assured him. "In fact—"

And that's when Carolene opened her big mouth and stuck her whole foot in it. I knew what words were about to come out, I just didn't expect what followed.

"—this ain't even a real gun. It's just for looks. Ain't even got no bullets in it."

Finding out this bit of information was the opening Ted had obviously been waiting for. He ran straight to a drawer and started shoving different keys into the lock, trying to find the right one. All me and Carolene could do was watch, our legs frozen.

He finally got the drawer lock open and from it he pulled out an old looking revolver. And judging by the way he delicately handled it, I was pretty sure Ted's gun *was* real.

20

"Easy now, Ted."

I spoke calmly, easing one hand out into a stopping motion while the other mirrored Ted in what had turned out to be a gun-wielding standoff—also something that wasn't covered during training. I'd seen this particular scene play out in many movies, and it never turned out good for the ones in my shoes.

"Nah," the kid began his rant. "You gonna come in here and try to pull the wool over my eyes, try to get my ass in trouble, make me piss my pants?"

I hadn't noticed the growing urine stain until he mentioned it. I wanted to say that I'd gone a little bit on myself too, but I didn't feel it was the right time.

"Nah," Ted continued, "ain't no way I'm gonna let you all leave with this money now."

He pulled the bag of bills closer to him. His face was still stained with tears and you could tell his nose was snotty.

"You tried to make me out to be a fool," he snarled. "And that ain't even a real gun? You both must be crazy."

I hated that word—crazy. It was the same word Pete

threw around, calling me that nearly every day over this or that.

"Ted," Carolene grabbed his attention. "Listen to me good. This ain't nothin' personal. It's just about the money. It's a pretty serious situation we done got ourselves into. Ya know, a life or death kinda deal? So just don't do anything stupid. Think about your family, your parents."

Contrary to what she'd set out to do, her words must have made something snap inside Ted because he got a wild look in his eyes, like he was about to do something drastic. And we were no stranger to that look. Just earlier I'd seen it in the eyes of a man I thought was a kind, old gentleman.

"Fuck you!" he threw back. "You don't know me or nothing about me. And I told you what was gonna happen to me if you took this money."

He must've been thinking again over the consequences he'd suffer, or at least what he figured would be the consequences, because he seemed to grow more infuriated.

"And that shit ain't gonna happen," he announced, as if the sound of the words helped to solidify his decision. "Nah, I ain't gonna let that happen."

Even though I was the one with the gun pointed at him, Ted turned his gun towards Carolene, the one who had struck a nerve or triggered a memory in him to send him over the edge.

But it was like Carolene's feet were glued to the floor because she didn't even try to jump out of the way or anything.

Just stood there and watched as Ted, his eyes squinted like Rory Calhoun, his front teeth biting down on his lower lip, slowly squeezed the trigger.

The shot was deafening and must have been powerful because it flung Ted back against the wall of cigarettes and chewing tobacco. Cartons of Marlboros and Newports rained down on top of him.

Carolene slowly lowered her eyes to examine her chest and started sobbing like she did after falling off her bike and skinning up her knee twenty years ago.

My heart fell to my stomach as I gasped.

"Carolene!"

The word seemed to bounce around the room. And I wouldn't have been surprised if they didn't slip out the door and end up waking up a few angry guests in that Holiday Inn down the street.

I dropped my gun and ran to her. Clutched her. I was bawling as bad as when I first saw Mama passed out across that church pew many moons ago. Now we were *both* little girls with skinned up knees.

We grasped each other tight for support. Not just for mental support but physical too. I felt my knees buckling and my legs going numb.

Then I eased my head back towards Ted, trying to see as best I could through hazy eyes. And I watched as that young boy, a mere teenager who had his whole life ahead of him, slid down the wall to the floor, his hands pressed to his stomach. But no matter how tight he pressed, the blood kept gushing out, seeping through his fingers.

I let loose of Carolene and rubbed my eyes for clarity. I was pretty sure my mouth dangled open like a fish but I was confused about the whole situation, and I was trying hard to make sense of it.

"What just happened? I mean, how?"

I looked back at Carolene. Studied her body to make sure I wasn't seeing things. But no wounds, no blood.

"You're not... And he *is*... But that's impossible. Bullets don't come outta toy guns."

Carolene still wept silent tears. But they were now tears of joy. Because she wasn't the one bleeding. She wasn't the one holding her insides in. But she was, however, the one still standing.

Carolene took her sleeve and rubbed her face dry, then looked me in the eyes.

"Jess? I think there's somethin' I need to tell ya..."

21

We stood there a moment trying to put ourselves back together now that the shock was wearing off. But I can honestly say I'd have rather stayed in shock because reality, as I looked at the kid bent over on the floor coughing up blood, wasn't very pretty.

"Ya 'member back at the pawnshop," Carolene began her confession, "how you said you wished we could get a real gun, for protection?"

"Uh huh..." I replied hesitantly. "But we couldn't afford one. So, how...or do I even wanna know how?"

"Oh I promise what I told you was all that happened. The guy was just...very appreciative is all."

Carolene's tears started to dry up and she even smiled when she joked, "What can I say? I guess I'm just that good."

I almost smiled but I held it in. I was still pretty upset that she didn't tell me the gun was real. And by the looks of Ted, that would have been some really good information to know. But Carolene kept on joking about the pawn shop owner.

"Yeah, he was a very horny man," she laughed. "Even

offered me a sword, but I turned it down, of course. Told 'em it wouldn't fit in my purse."

Maybe joking was how she chose to deal with the situation. Maybe she felt responsible. Which she pretty much was, but I wouldn't have dared ever tell her so. But I couldn't help but give a soft chuckle at the sword comment.

"But, Care, why didn't ya tell me it was real? Why on God's green earth would ya keep that a secret?"

"Well," she started, coyly. "I mean, I know ya said you wished we had one, but I know how ya are. I know ya don't really like guns, and I figured you'd be all nervous and scared about havin' a real one with us."

"Ok," I began my argument. "So why'd ya go and tell poor Ted there it wasn't real if ya knew it was?"

I hated to put Carolene on the spot, but she really had a lot of explaining to do. She bit her nails and picked at the ends of her hair, the usual things she did when she was nervous or worried. Her heart may have been in the right place at the time, but her head sure wasn't.

"I just felt so bad for 'em. He was so upset and worried about gettin' fired and kicked out of his house. And to top it off, he was so worried he was gonna be shot."

I grabbed Carolene and forced her to turn and face the kid slumped down on the floor behind the counter, blood dripping from his mouth.

"Carolene, that ain't pancake batter—that there's blood.

Clearly he had a right to be worried, don't ya think?"

"I'm sorry!" she cried out in near hysterics, covering her face and squatting down. "I didn't think you'd pull the trigger! If ya thought the gun wasn't real, Jess, then why'd ya go 'n pull the trigger?"

"Hey, now don't turn this around on me," I argued. "That's just what ya do with a gun. I don't know—instinct, I guess."

That was the truth. I guess if you already have your finger on the trigger, it's just instinct to pull it when you think someone's about to shoot first.

"Plus," I added, and this was my key point. "It ain't s'posed to be a real gun!"

&

After that, we were both quiet, sitting on the floor, mulling over where to go from there. But we were so worried about ourselves, we'd totally forgotten about the other person in the room.

"So what about Ted?" I began. "I mean, we have to call an ambulance or somethin'. We can't just leave 'em here to die on the floor of a gas station. Plus somebody could walk in any second now. I mean, who knows how far the sound of that shot rang out. There could be a swat team on its way right now!"

So Carolene went over to the phone and dialed 911. And then it was like the stage lights cut on and the curtain was drawn.

"Help! Oh God, ya have to hurry. We're at Cheap Al's Quick Stop near the Holiday Inn. There's a man in here with a gun just shootin' everybody in his way. [pause] [cue scream] I hear 'em coming! Please hurry!"

Carolene even did a little curtsy after that performance. But that just meant the cops were definitely own their way now. And fast. But that also meant we could just leave Ted where he was and not worry as much, hoping that the paramedics and the doctors at the hospital could save him.

And that's just what we did.

I threw Carolene the keys to the truck and she flew out the door. I grabbed the bag of money, plus a few packs of beef jerky and peanuts from next to the register—heck, even a thief's gotta eat, right?—and was right behind her.

We tore out of there like we'd just shot the cashier and robbed the place.

ஐ

My sister was obviously a lot better getaway driver than I was because before I knew it we were crossing the city line. And my heart finally stopped racing.

Me and Carolene talked about it and we figured the cops and the ambulance would show up at the gas station and see that there was nobody around except Ted. Then once they saw him they'd rush him to the hospital. And there the doctors would work their miracles and Ted would pull through with no permanent injuries. Just a scar that would remind him of the day he was shot by a toy gun.

And after living through such an ordeal, his parents were bound to let him stay put, and the gas station owner had to let him stay on at his job, after he recovered, if he wanted to return. Because after all, he tried to save the store from being robbed. He was a hero.

We made that scenario our reality, whether it really happened that way or not.

Things got quiet again and me and Carolene just swapped the beef jerky and the peanuts back and forth. Carolene felt comfortable enough to slow down now, though I was just going to let her keep going at that speed since we needed to gain some time back.

Being dark and having pushed thoughts of Ted, who I was sure was getting medical attention at that very moment, out of my mind, I closed my eyes. They were begging for just a minute's rest. I felt my body relax and in an instant I was out.

It was the best three minute's sleep I'd ever had. And it would've been longer if I wasn't forced awake by the sound of Carolene's voice.

"Jess...Jess...wake up. We gotta problem."

I looked up just as Carolene was pulling the truck off onto the side of the road. I could see Carolene's face from the streetlight shining down. It was blank and emotionless, but there was anger and disgust in her voice.

"Why can't we catch a damn break!"

"Huh?" I was still groggy. "Where are we? What's wrong?"

Carolene let out a deep breath as she put the truck in park. Staring straight ahead into the pitch black, she asked me a question that felt like a boxer delivering a knockout blow to my face.

"Know where we can find a spare tire at 10 p.m., give or take a time zone?"

22

We both stood there in the cool night air, staring at the flat tire, the same look on both of our faces. You wouldn't have found a better example of the word *disbelief* in the dictionary. I poked at the tire with my foot and gave the truck's backend a comforting pat.

Broke down, beaten, and deflated.

And the truck was in bad shape, too.

I knew we were in the biggest bind we'd been in yet, but I sure didn't know how we were going to get out of it. I could've changed the tire if we had one, but Carolene said the spare was already put on the truck and Scott never got around to getting a new one.

The only idea I could come up with was to ditch the truck and try to hitchhike the rest of the way. Once we got to Detroit, maybe Jolene would know somebody there that could get us a car, cheap. But I knew Carolene would hate to leave the truck. After all, it wasn't ours and we'd taken it without permission. Plus if we abandoned Scott's truck on the side of the road, Carolene knew she could kiss any thoughts of getting back together with him goodbye. Because nobody's going to try to reconcile a relationship after you've gone and stole their truck and abandoned it in Nowhere, Ohio.

And I hated to leave it, too. The loss of the truck would set us back at least a day or two or three. Also—I knew it was stupid, and I didn't want to mention such a petty thing to Carolene, but I couldn't get over the fact that I'd just filled the truck up with a whole tank of gas. Granted we didn't pay for it.

Yeah, the likelihood of us actually making it to Detroit, getting Jolene, making it back to Alabama, and doing what we needed to do in time was starting to look very slim.

"We could walk," Carolene suggested. "I don't know how far off town is but it can't be that far. Maybe we could stay the night, get a new tire in the mornin'."

It sounded reasonable. Plus we didn't have many options. And I was sure the truck would be fine—I didn't figure anybody would try to steal a three-legged Datsun.

"Hey, Jess?" Carolene asked, her legs together tight and an alarmed look on her face. "I'm sorry 'bout this, but I really need to pee before we start walkin'."

I laughed and agreed. I couldn't even remember the last time I'd gone to the bathroom. I guess it had to be that morning.

And then I remember I did go a little in the gas station...

We both went down towards the trees but stayed in sight of each other and squatted.

"Hey," she called over at me, nostalgia in her voice. "You know what this kinda reminds me of?"

I told her I had no idea. I racked my brain but no thoughts came to mind where we were ever stranded on the side of the road, peeing together in the dark.

"That time we all piled in Dr. Ellis' truck to take Mama to the hospital."

"Oh yeah?" I replied curiously.

"Yeah, you 'member we hit that deer?"

How could I have forgotten that day? I thought about it often. Even still dreamed about it. But I wasn't sure how that night related to our current situation. Maybe it was because we were on the side of the road like the deer? Or maybe it was simply because we had car trouble? But really I didn't know where she was going with it.

"I remember...but what about it?"

Carolene started laughing so much she snorted. Finished, we both stood up and walked back towards the truck.

"Tell me!" I pressed, anxious to know what was so funny. But Carolene's laugh was so contagious, I felt myself already starting to smile, even chuckle.

"Ok, ok," she began, trying to compose herself. "I never told nobody this, but that night, with all that was going on— Mama being sick, the deer getting hit, and I even had some butterflies bein' right up next to Dr. Ellis—I was a nervous wreck and, well...ok, I'll just admit it. I peed on myself."

"What? Really? When?"

"Yeah, tryin' not to pee all over myself while squattin'

over there's what made me think about it. But I mean it was like ALL over me that day," she laughed, waving her hand all around the front of her pants. "We'd just got to the hospital and Dr. Ellis was rushin' us but I couldn't move—I knew my bladder was about to explode. And the entrance looked so far away. But I knew I had to go help with Mama, so I tried my best to hold it in. But after runnin' a few steps, the dam broke and WOOSH."

On my lead, we both busted out in laughter. It was the gut burning, make-you-cough kind of laughter. Something I hadn't done in a long time, and something I really needed after what we'd been through so far.

The laughter faded and now I was left with thoughts of that night stuck in my head. Just what I needed—to be more upset. I tried to think about other things to get my mind off of it, like Jolene, the mission.

And then my ears perked up like a coonhound's.

I cocked my head back at the sound of a low rumble in the distance, accompanied by two steady circles of yellow light. The sound got louder and the lights brighter and I felt a gust of life being breathed back into me. My eyebrows raised as I turned to Carolene to exchange smiles.

That rumble was the sound of our prayers being answered.

We both jumped and waved fiercely, almost like we were stranded on a deserted island and we were trying to flag down a boat. Actually, that was exactly what it was like. We were stranded, and since we had no clue where we were, we might as well have been on a deserted island. And our boat, our saving grace, was speeding right towards us.

"Don't stand too close to the road, Care," I instructed. "Just in case they don't see us."

"Yeah, yeah," she grumbled back, getting further into the lane, waving her arms like she was guiding a plane.

"Carolene, seriously, back up. They don't seem to be slowin' down."

I was two seconds away from leaping towards her and dragging her out of the road when I noticed a red glare shining off the road. The truck was braking.

"Now if it's some guys," I coached, "you do the talkin'. Flirt with 'em. 'Cause this may be the last car we see for a while."

"I gotcha," she replied, trying her best to fix her hair. "I know what to do."

At that moment, above all other moments, I was glad I had Carolene with me. Heck, that truck probably would've passed right on by if it was just me out there. But I felt better now, calmer. It seemed that we may get back on the road again sooner than I thought.

The truck came to a halt beside us and with the window rolled down, two guys who both looked to be in their 30's smiled and greeted us with an "evenin' ladies." The driver said it looked like we must've had a flat tire. He seemed like a nice enough fella, and his awkward way of pointing out the obvious actually made me feel at ease.

"Yeah," I said. "We musta run over a nail or some glass or somethin', don't know. But we ain't gotta spare tire, of course, or we wouldn't be standin' out here all helpless-like."

"Well it's your lucky day," the driver spoke, leaning over his friend to get a better look at us. "I gotta truck just like that back at the house. Gotta spare tire for it too that'd prob'ly fix you right up."

Me and Carolene started talking at the same time, thanking him and saying how we'd pay him for it and how it was a miracle from God that they happen to be passing by.

"Lemme just use my flashlight here to take a closer look at the tire first."

When the driver got out he was much taller than I'd thought. Had to have been well over six foot.

"Wow," I whispered to Carolene. "What're the odds?"

"Tell me 'bout it," she replied. "But I sure am glad of it, though."

As the man approached the truck, Carolene asked him for their names.

"Uh, I'm Dale," he sort of stammered. "And him over there, that's Dave."

Dave, still seated in the passenger seat, didn't smile, but he did raise his hand in somewhat of a wave. Me and Carolene exchanged curious glances then waved back.

Always eager to make new acquaintances, Carolene introduced herself in return, then introduced me.

"Really nice to meet you ladies," Dale sounded sincere. "Where you all headed?"

"Well, if we can ever get there, we're headed to Detroit," I said, a little disgust in my voice. "But it's always one thing after another, ya know?"

I had to crack a little smile at that. Our family has had so much bad luck it was almost comical. It was either laugh or cry.

"Yeah, that's a bummer," Dale remarked. "Well, now that the small talk's over, let's get down to business."

The words made me feel uneasy and my smile vanished. Taking a step back, I cut my eyes back over to Carolene who had already crossed her arms and taken a few steps back herself.

"Um, what kinda business?" I asked.

"Compensation business..."

23

I was scared that my worst fear had come true. And not only did I have myself to worry about, but poor Carolene had already had her run-in with sex-crazed creeps and I felt horrible that she might be put in that position once again, no pun intended. But I wasn't going to give anything up without a fight.

Unknowingly, I found myself backing up further. But Dale moved along with me. Taking two steps forward to each of my steps back. It felt like we were right back at the diner trying to get away from Abraham. Dave continued to sit in the truck, watching us do the predator-prey dance.

"Don't you worry," Dale assured us, but keeping his eyes locked on mine. "We ain't gonna hurt you. We ain't even gonna touch you if you cooperate."

Now I was confused. Relieved, yes. But terribly confused. I wasn't in the best mental state, but I couldn't think of anything else we had that they'd be interested in.

"Come on, you dumb bitch. The cash. Hand it over."

"Yeah, I mean, of course I'll pay ya for the tire. And even give ya money for your time. Let's just calm down and get back in the truck. Ya know, and go get that tire."

A clicking sound I was all too familiar with now pulled my attention towards Dave in the passenger seat. Sitting there, same blank stare on his face, but with a gun pointed at me now. Dale motioned towards our truck with his head.

"Put your hands on it. Both of you."

"I have some money in my front pocket," I admitted. "It's not much, but it's all we have. I promise."

"Shut up," Dale fired back. "Gimme the bag."

"My purse?" I tried to play dumb but was a horrible actor.

"Cut the shit, woman."

Then he looked over to Carolene and told her, "Reach in the truck, grab the bag, and throw it to me."

Carolene's eyes began dripping as she asked him how he knew. So Dale—and at this point I was starting to doubt that was his real name—told us that him and "Dave" had been following us ever since we left the diner in Elizabethtown. Parked a block away at the Holiday Inn, they saw us running out of the gas station with the bag and take off. Having robbed a liquor store a few months back, they knew exactly what was in the bag.

As Carolene reached through the window of the truck, I grabbed her arm to stop her, took a deep breath, and declared:

"I can't let ya take this money."

I immediately thought of Ted's bold act, telling me and

Carolene he wasn't going to let us leave with the money. Dale got a kick out of it, though, looking back at his accomplice who actually broke his stone-faced persona to flash a quick smirk.

"Well, miss, it don't look like you gotta whole helluva lotta choice in the matter, now does it?"

My heart was beating so fast I figured it was about to explode. If it did, I thought, then I wouldn't have to worry about being shot or raped or whatever was going to happen to me. Then I repeated:

"I can't let ya take it."

"Suit yourself," Dale replied. "But we *are* gonna leave here with that money."

And as he spoke, he marched towards me, grabbed me, and put his arm around my neck from behind. In his other hand was a knife.

"You,"—he ordered Carolene—"open the door," and she did as he instructed. "Now grab the bag, nice and slow, and set it down beside me."

With the knife he motioned towards their truck, letting her know Dave still had a gun pointed at her. Sobbing, Carolene moved delicately, carrying the bag towards Dale.

"Hurry it up," he barked at her. "We ain't got all night."

When she got close enough that Dale could reach her, he snatched the bag from her and placed it down next to him. As he did so, he released me, giving me a push for my troubles, and I stumbled to the ground.

Looking up at him, seeing him laughing, just about to take off with the money that we'd gone through a lot to get, including going against all that we were taught and the morals that we were raised on, I was overcome with anger. Actually more so than just anger—it was more like fury, because it burned my stomach all the way up to my throat. At that moment I realized why mama had always said the phrase *I'm so mad I could spit fire* after we'd done something really bad.

There was no way I could let this happen. I had to do something bold. I had to take a chance, make a move.

As Dale picked up the bag and turned to walk towards the truck, I'd gotten back to my feet and brushed myself off, acting nonchalant so I could take them by surprise. I figured I would go for Dave first, since he had the gun. Maybe try to grab his arm and get the gun away from him. I was hoping Carolene would instinctively join in once she saw me running.

I took a few deep breaths to ease my nerves. Carolene must've sensed I was about to make a move because she turned and stared over at me, as if she was trying to read my mind. At least she was aware and wasn't off on another planet like she often was.

Just about to dart towards the truck, I froze at the sound of Dale's voice. He had stopped just shy of the truck and set the bag on the ground, then turned his back to us and began urinating on the back tire like a dog. But the nonchalant command he'd given his partner almost made *me* urinate. And if I hadn't just gone, I'm sure I would have.

"Shoot the pretty one first."

At this point I wasn't even thinking, just reacting. I sprinted to Carolene and stretched my arms out in front of her as if I was blocking her from passing a basketball.

"No, wait!" I pleaded. "Don't shoot her. Please."

Then Dale followed with, "How you know I wasn't talking about *you*?"

I would've blushed under different circumstances, but the comment had no meaning coming from him. No matter who he was referring to, all that mattered was the sound of that gun. So with my head cocked and a sarcastic smile smeared across my face, I channeled my inner Beatrice Lynn and shot him a bird.

"Fine then," Dale said nonchalantly. "I don't give a damn *who* gets it first. Stay like you are and Dave here'll shoot both of you at once."

Dave held up the gun for a better shot, thinking to himself, I'm sure, how awesome it *would* be if he actually shot us both at once. I clutched Carolene tighter than I ever had and braced for the impact of the bullet, if the roar of the gun didn't give me a heart attack first.

Silently, I spoke to Mama, telling her we would be united again very soon, which actually calmed me some. I knew the pain wouldn't last long, and then it'd be all over. I was ready.

Oh God, but what about Jolene? Just as I was ready to

give up, her face appeared, and I realized we'd be leaving her all alone. And I told her we'd come get her—I promised. Was I going to actually break that promise?

I couldn't. I pushed aside the emptiness that had come over me and searched my mind for a solution, praying for strength and focus. But it was hard to think once I heard the cock of the gun, hard not to give into fear.

And then through the corner of my eye I saw it. It was the same miraculous vision we'd seen not long ago, what I'd thought was the answer to my prayers when our tire blew out but had turned out to be a nightmare instead.

Headlights.

As I turned my head, my eyes squinted and my mouth dropped when I once again saw those two steady circles of yellow light heading our way. My fingers were crossed that this time they were, indeed, the answer to my prayers.

But I really didn't know what to expect. It could've been friends of Dale's coming to help him out—he could've been expecting them. Heck, maybe they'd come to dispose of our bodies after Dale shot us.

But I couldn't afford stinkin' thinkin' right then. I crossed my fingers and held onto the glimmer of hope that this was our rescue boat.

I could barely breath at this point, and the lights almost blinded me they were so bright, so close now.

24

The guys must not have been expecting anyone, though, because Dave withdrew his arm to hide the gun, and Dale, after zipping his pants, stuffed his hands in his jeans pockets to look casual, having kicked the bag of money out of sight, into a shadow cast by the truck. Me and Carolene, however, were frozen, frightened. Far from casual.

The car was one of those older Eldorados, red, with a hardtop, and it came to a halt right beside Dale's truck. Inside were two women, both beautiful. Both with the biggest smiles I'd ever seen.

I was actually a little jealous of the long red hair of the woman in the passenger seat. It wasn't the natural, orangey kind of red hair, but cherry red. She must've died it—one thing I'd never done. And behind the steering wheel was what looked to be a natural blond with pink streaks. But I was pretty sure the pink wasn't natural.

"So, what the hell are you dumbasses doing out here in the middle of nowheresville?" the driver yelled out, but I wasn't sure who she was specifically referring to, if not all of us.

"Yeah," the other woman echoed, laughing, "haven't you

seen *Psycho*?"

"Oooh, or what about *Village of the Damned*," the driver added, excitedly. "That was a freaky one. Made me piss myself. You remember that?" she asked her friend, gently slapping her on the arm for validation.

They both got a good chuckle from that memory. And I wasn't sure if Dale looked more confused or agitated, but what I *could* tell was that he looked like he was about to snap.

"Excuse me, whoever you are," he spoke to both women in the Eldorado with teeth-gritting firmness. "We're kinda in the middle of something. So maybe you outta get lost."

Call it a gut feeling, women's intuition, or whatever you want, but when *Pscyho*'s eyes and mine met, she seemed to understand our situation. She leaned over to whisper into the driver's ear, and a few seconds later they were both opening their car door and walking over to us.

Dale went on the defense—standing straighter with his legs spread a little to widen his stance and his hands on his hips. Then he cut Dave a glance that I took to mean "be ready."

"What, you didn't hear me, bitch?" Dale called out, his eyes focused on *Psycho*'s face. "I said get lost."

"Bitch?!" she yelled back, obviously offended. "I don't see no goddamn dogs around here. Do you?" she asked her friend.

"Uh oh," Blondie warned Dale as she held her back. "Now you done gone and pissed her off. And you don't wanna piss her off. So maybe *you're* the ones that outta get lost."

Dale spit to the side, though he barely had enough saliva to even form a spot on the ground. *Psycho* spit in return, outdoing his by three times the size.

"Dave," Dale roared. "You wanna come out here and show these ladies we ain't playing around?"

On command, Dave stepped out of the truck, pistol aimed at the redheaded driver, who must've seemed to be the bigger threat to them at the moment. Dale walked slowly towards the women, warning them to leave.

"I'm starting to see it now. You chicks are just some peace sign wearing, men-hating hippie bitches, out here trying to prove a point or something. But this ain't no peace rally bullshit. Ain't nobody got time for your..."

Dale continued his rant, but I stopped listening when I caught sight of Blondie. All the while Dale was ranting, his attention focused on *Psycho*, Blondie had been staring at Dave, trying to look sexy or enticing, rubbing and caressing her breasts, and even sliding her hand down to her private place. She threw her head back and appeared to be moaning silently. Dave's eyes were glued to her as if he was hypnotized.

"So listen," I heard Dale say. "Why don't you just get back in your little red car and go find some other little hippies to play with."

"First of all," *Psycho* fired back, "we don't like being labeled. So fuck you for calling us hippies."

"Dave, just shoot 'em already," Dale told his friend who wasn't paying any attention to him.

So Dale called his name again. After no response, he turned to see Dave's bottom jaw heavy, his gun lowered and aimed towards the ground. Blondie now had her hand down the front of her dress, rubbing her nipples between her fingertips.

"And second," *Psycho* continued, pulling from behind her the gun that was tucked into her panties. "We don't *hate* men..."

While talking, she quickly fired off a shot straight into Dale's leg and then whipped the gun towards Dave, who snapped back to reality once Blondie stopped and held up the middle finger on both hands.

"We just think they're pretty stupid," *Pscyho* finished. "Now drop the gun, loverboy, and both of you put your hands in the air."

Dave obeyed, chucking the gun off to the side and raising his arms. But Dale just clutched his leg, moaning in pain, trying to stop the bleeding. The shooter *nicely* suggested he go to the hospital.

"Oh, bitch, you're gonna pay for this," Dale threatened. "Just you wait 'n see."

"Damn you really love that B word, don't you?" *Psycho* objected, then told them to "get the hell outta here" while waiving the gun towards their truck.

I watched as Dale struggled to ease his wounded leg into the truck and Dave got behind the wheel, and listened as both of our fearless heroines looked at each other and laughed. Then they simultaneous muttered one word, the same word.

"Dumbasses."

25

Watching those men speed away almost made me cry with relief. I was certain we were either going to get shot or, mugged, or worse. I just knew those close calls were going to be the death of me.

Carolene had her eyes closed and her head back. She looked like she was lying in a tub of hot water. A bubble bath. Relaxing and letting all her cares float away with the steam. I just figured as much because she'd once told me that was her happy place.

After gaining my composure enough now, I looked up at the two women before me and smiled.

"So what'd those punks want?" the *Psycho* woman asked us, holding out her hand palm-up towards her friend.

"What for?" Blondie asked her, dropping the keys into the open hand.

"To lock the gun back up, duh," *Psycho* tried to whisper but I heard her anyway.

Blondie said "oh yeah" and turned back to me and re-asked what the guys wanted.

"My bag," I responded. "They were tryin' to take my

handbag. We'd pulled off the road and they just came up and stuck a gun on us."

The bag! They left it! I nudged Carolene to run over and retrieve it and return it to the truck. Knowing we had the money back, I felt like I'd just crawled out from a pile of bricks and could breathe again.

"Ahh," *Psycho* said, walking back from the car, packing some cigarettes, nodding as if she completely understood the scenario. And I was glad she did because I didn't want to go into any more detail. I wasn't sure yet if I could fully trust them. And I definitely didn't want to make mention of the stolen money.

"Well it's really awesome to meet you," she greeted. "I'm Ana."

Ana offered her hand to me, so I cautiously shook it. After all that had happened, this time I was prepared to keep my guard up longer, just so I didn't get the wool pulled over me again.

"And I'm Gretchen," added Blondie, smiling, her lips full, her mouth wide. "And I'm gonna take a wild guess and say you two are having some car trouble. Or truck trouble..."

She zipped her head around to Ana and asked, "Is it always *car* trouble, or is *truck* trouble if it's a truck? It really don't make sense if it's still called *car* trouble when it's a truck."

"Yeah, but I think it's still called car trouble, Lucy. I never heard of nobody having truck trouble. But, hell, there's always a first time for everything, so I don't see why it can't be truck trouble."

"Well good," Gretchen gladly accepted Ana's response. "Truck trouble it is, then."

"Wait," I stopped their banter, staring at Gretchen. "I thought your name was Gretchen."

"Yep, it sure is."

"But she called you Lucy," I inquired.

"Oh that's just my stage name—Lucy Hotpants."

When Ana finished packing the cigarettes, Gretchen grabbed at them and they pushed and shoved like two kids fighting over candy.

I nodded as if it all made sense. Carolene smiled a fake, understanding smile. She was staying awfully quiet. I think she was really shook up by those men. I mean, despite the dangerous look in old Abraham's eyes and the courageousness of Ted the cashier, that was by far the most scared I'd been on our trip so far. And I figured Carolene felt the same.

"What stage?" I asked, fearful of offending her or, worse yet, showing my ignorance. "You mean like Broadway?"

Gretchen and Ana busted out in laughter, choking on cigarette smoke in the process. Ana had to reach out and grab her friend just to hold herself up.

"You're too funny," Ana responded, now bent over holding her stomach from the pains of laughter. "Broadway!"

I smiled, still unsure of what to do or say next. But I was

glad they showed up, and of course I was thankful to them for saving our lives. I owed them an ocean full of gratitude. But I just had no idea how to talk to them yet. I must've seemed like such an idiot.

"We're musicians," Gretchen said. "We travel and play bars and coffee houses and pretty much anywhere that'll book us."

"Oh wow!" I replied, impressed since I had no talent whatsoever. "So your fans don't know you by your real names—like Marilyn Monroe. I mean, everyone knows her real name was Norma Jeane Mortenson."

"Or like Cary Grant," Carolene finally jumped in the conversation. "His real name's Archibald Leach. I read that in a magazine one time."

"You got it," Gretchen answered.

"So why Lucy Hotpants?" I inquired, not sure if I should ask personal questions.

"Well, because her middle name's Lucille," Ana added, not thinking anything of the question. "So that's why she's Lucy. And Hotpants because of that slammin' ass of hers," she laughed, slapping Gretchen on the butt. "Go ahead, girl," she told Gretchen, "show 'em that ass."

Laughing and dancing around like she was at a bar, Gretchen obeyed and shook her butt awfully close to me and Carolene.

"So what's *your* stage name?" I asked Ana, hoping the

new question would stop Gretchen from shaking her butt before I got hit by it.

"Mine's Annie Oakley."

"Oh, you an Annie Oakley fan?" Carolene perked up.

My sister loved Annie Oakley as much as I did. We used to read about her and *Buffalo Bill's Wild West* show all the time as kids.

One side of Ana's mouth curled up into a smile, like it brought on a good memory. She lit up another cigarette, leaned her head back, and blew the smoke straight up.

"Annie was a tough old broad. Men would say she was as mean as a badger, but that's because she didn't take shit from 'em. Never took shit from *no* man. They'd try to screw her over and she'd turn 'em around and screw 'em right back."

Carolene wore a look of confusion and responded just as innocently as a toddler:

"I ain't so sure we're talkin' 'bout the same Annie Oakley..."

26

Ana suggested leaving the cars and going into the woods a little ways to make a fire to relax and warm up. A fire sounded so nice at the time that all my (and obviously Carolene's) reservations floated away and we jumped on the idea.

Our two new friends claimed to have been Girl Scouts, but they must've left all their scouting skills back wherever they were from because neither one of them could even get a spark going. I kind of felt bad for not helping but I was still pretty shaken up. The last few hours had been both bizarre and terrifying.

Gretchen tried rubbing some sticks together for a bit, then Ana, until it just turned into one big comedic scene. After the laughter died down, Gretchen's cigarette lighter came out to help.

It didn't seem like no time at all before the fire crackled and hissed and lit up the black woods. We all sat around it in a circle (actually it was more of a square)—me and Carolene across from Ana and Gretchen, who I was beginning to let my guard down around.

"You two sure are pretty," Ana said. "And you don't strike me as being from around here neither. So where are you ladies from?"

I smiled at her nice comment and told her. That led me into telling them the story about where we were headed and why, all the way up to Dale and Dave. But I did leave out the part about them following us from the gas station that we'd just robbed and (accidentally) shot an employee. A kid. A kid named Ted.

"That's a man for you," Ana said, referring to the Dale and Dave incident. "They see a damsel in distress and instead of saving her like in the fairytales, they take advantage of her. It's pathetic."

"Yeah," Carolene spoke up. "Like in the movies when the hero comes and rescues the princess and they live happily ever after. That stuff don't happen in real life."

Sensing some sadness from Carolene, Ana came over and put her arm around her neck and pulled her head next to hers, just like they'd been best friends for years.

"You got that right, sweetie," Ana told her. "There's no such thing as happily ever after. 'Least that's how *my* life's always been. But it sure makes for good song writing, though."

∞

After a while of sitting around the fire, I was getting antsy. I glanced over at my sister, whose eyes were glued to the spontaneous concert in front of us: Gretchen picking at an acoustic guitar while Ana hummed along.

"So..." I started, not really sure what we were doing or how long we were going to do it. I was glad for a chance to rest and calm down, but I wasn't exactly in the mood to "chill" or "shoot the breeze" like Ana had said we were doing. I was beginning to wonder what our next move was going to be.

"Hey, don't worry, pretty lady," Ana stopped humming long enough to say. "Relax—get some rest. Don't think we've forgot about you and your truck trouble."

And then she found the melody again, but this time carried it with some *ooh*'s and *la*'s. But Gretchen added, talking over her:

"Besides. Can't really do nothing 'til daylight, right?"

She had a point. I guess if they were nice enough to stick around until morning so they could take us to town, or whatever the plan was, then I figured I could be courteous enough not to push the issue and just be patient.

And then Ana pulled out a Ziploc bag with some cigarettes in it. But I could tell by the way she and Gretchen acted differently than they did about their previous cigarettes that it must've been the special, non-tobacco kind. I'd never actually seen those in person until that moment.

Ana must've seen both me and Carolene watching them intently as they giddily lit one of them up, so she asked us if we wanted a hit. Being naïve about the whole process—what would happen to us, how we'd feel, etc—our first experience wasn't going to be then and there.

"No thanks," we answered simultaneously.

"Whatever. You're loss," Ana shrugged off our refusal.

I was glad she was so nonchalant about the whole thing. It made me relax more. I leaned back, my arms stretched out behind me, my hands flat against the ground, holding myself up.

At that angle, the moon hit Gretchen's guitar just right and I could make out an image. And as soon as I saw it, a chill ran through my body. So I had to ask about it.

"Hey, is that a picture of a dragon on your guitar?"

"Yep," she answered almost proudly, still lightly strumming. "You may not can tell out here but she's emerald green and has flames shooting from her mouth."

"Wow. That's pretty, uh—"

"Oh," she inserted, "and the best part is, she's wearing a pink tutu. Pretty wild, huh?"

While I was stumbling around for an answer and maybe even a compliment, Ana chuckled and added:

"See, sometimes me and Gretchen wish we were doves so we could fly away, go wherever we wanted. Those are actually lyrics to one of our songs."

"Oh, so why a dove?" Carolene asked. "And what's that gotta do with a dragon?"

"A dove because their beautiful," Gretchen answered.

"And because their white color represents purity and

goodness," Ana tagged on.

"But actually," Gretchen continued. "I'm just like the dragon in the tutu, trying so hard to be something I'm not."

"Yep," Ana followed up with a smile and a wink. "I tell her all the time that's exactly what she is—a fire-breathing monster made up like a girl."

Me and Carolene chuckled. And I guess Carolene felt at ease enough to share a similar desire with them.

"Me, I wish I was a flower, so I could feel no pain or fear and just be naturally beautiful."

"But you *are* beautiful," Ana told her. "And besides," she added with a smirk, "if you were a flower you'd have to worry all the time about getting stepped on or getting your head chopped off by a lawn mower."

☙

"Whew wee!" Ana yelped like when I was a youngster taking my first bite of homemade ice cream. "This fire's making me hot! Who's up for a skinny dip?"

Gretchen jumped on the idea as if it were the best idea she'd ever heard, reaching behind her trying to grab a latch or zipper on her dress. Just out of curiosity I had to ask where there was any water around.

"There's a creek somewhere off over there," Gretchen pointed with her head, having finally found the zipper and quickly unzipping. "Don't you hear it?"

I was silent for a moment and then, yep, there it was.

Plain as day. But I actually hadn't heard it until she'd made mention of it...

The idea of sleeping outside around strangers was bad enough, but the idea of being naked in front of those strangers made me feel as awkward as I did the first time me and Pete had sex. I shuttered at that thought, remembering how bad I was. I'd ended up crying in the bathroom for an hour, then came out, all ready to try it again, and found Pete already asleep, snoring, buck naked.

I shook the thought from my mind and tried to decide what our next move was going to be. But it all happened so fast. One minute we were sitting there in front of the fire, listening to Gretchen play guitar and Ana humming along, and the next minute Ana and Gretchen were standing before me, their dresses on the ground as they pulled their long hair back into a ponytail.

Carolene, her eyes glued to the nude bodies before us, leaned over and whispered in my ear.

"They're wearin' earrings on their nipples."

27

I'm not too sure why, but I found myself following Carolene who was following Gretchen and Ana as they led us down to the creek. The moon was bright and lit up the trail, but I still stumbled over branches and rocks. The whole idea of skinny dipping with a bunch of women was unsettling to me, but even more unsettling was another feeling I had—one I couldn't exactly explain. A feeling that involved something I had passed off as nonsense, what I thought was ridiculous.

"Psst, hey, Care," I quietly called out.

But she didn't hear me so I caught up to her and pulled her back to slow her down.

"What?" she sounded defensive. "I know what you're gonna say and, no, I ain't gonna take my clothes off *or* get in the water."

"No, Care, listen," I told her as we both walked, my arm around her shoulders so I could pull her close and talk softly. "Remember what Frankie VanTastic said, "beware of the dragon lady" and somethin' about wantin' to be a dove?"

"Yeah, so?"

"Gretchen's guitar...it had a dragon on it, in a tutu. That

could be the dragon lady. And she said she wanted to be a dove, too. I don't know if I'm just bein' silly and that's all just a coincidence or what."

"But Ana said that about the dove."

"Yeah, but still."

It seemed there'd been a major role reversal when it came to Frankie's fortune telling and I wasn't sure why. Carolene was the sceptic now and I was being the trusting one. But I just had a gut feeling we weren't free from danger yet and wanted to keep my eyes open for any signs.

"I know what ya mean, Jess, but Frankie was pretty out-there, like ya said. The more I think about it, the more I realize just how mad he was. So I'm just sayin'...we should just take his advice or warnings, or whatever ya wanna call it, with a large grain a salt."

"I know, I know, I know. But what about Abraham? I mean, what'd he sound like to you, like when he said his *s*'s?"

I could see the gears turning in Carolene's head, thinking back over Frankie's "premonitions".

"Yeah, but Frankie said *blind* snake, and I'm pretty sure I remember Abraham bein' able to see just fine."

She had a point. Maybe I was *trying* to make things line up to fit Frankie's cautions. I really wasn't sure.

"Well, regardless, somethin' told me I better hold onto these."

Then from my pocket I flashed the car keys that Ana

dropped when she disrobed and took off towards the creek.

Carolene's eyes bulged but she didn't say anything. She couldn't even if she wanted to because, now at the creek, Ana had already started in on us, doing her best to coax us into joining them. I stuffed the keys back into my pocket and told her, once again, thanks but no thanks.

Gretchen eased into the water, but Ana dove right in. Carolene was too curious not to at least stick her foot in the water but yanked it out as if she'd just touched a hot stove.

"Wheeew!" Carolene cried out. "Wow, that's cold. How're ya'll even standin' that?" she asked the girls who, judging from their screaming and shivering, were struggling themselves.

"Yeah it's a little chilly," Gretchen played it off, her teeth chattering. "But it's so damn exhilarating! C'mon, you gotta experience it."

Carolene and I both shook our heads and politely declined, continuously, due to their insistence. But I wasn't going to give in, and neither was Carolene. Ana and Gretchen must've finally realized this after a bit because they finally stopped nagging us.

And then there was a splash.

"Hey! Cut it out!" I yelled at Ana, who was giggling uncontrollably. Gretchen joined in the laughter.

And then she did it again, except this time she splashed me even harder. Of course now Gretchen had to start in. She aimed at Carolene and before I knew it Carolene was soaked. We both yelled even louder for them to stop. But Carolene, who'd had kind of a quiet curiosity around our new naked friends, exploded.

"Stop it, you...you bitch!" she ordered Gretchen.

Ana and Gretchen both stopped with the splashing and cheered as if they were delighted in their defeat.

"That a girl!" Ana praised. "That's how you get your point across. That's how you gotta be with men, too. Both of you. You gotta have a "take no shit" attitude. Don't let them break you down. 'Cause they will if you let them."

I wasn't sure why all of their advice came back around to men and how horrible they were, but I just continued to smile and be thankful that the advice was free. Whether or not I actually wanted it, I could afford advice at prices like that.

After they got their fill, the two skinny dippers walked out of the creek while wringing out their hair and sat down on a piece of flat ground. As they sat, Ana apologized for the harassment, and Gretchen for getting us wet. Said they just wanted us to lighten up and have some fun. As I looked over at Carolene, who was wringing out the ends of her shirt, I told them it was okay, no hard feelings.

Of course Ana and Gretchen had no towels, and I could tell they were shivering. They sat in front of me and Carolene just like before except without the warmth of a fire. Oh, and they were still naked, too.

"How about this," Gretchen said as Ana continued to twist on her wet hair. "We play Truth or Dare!"

I'm sure the lack of excitement was evident in the disgusted look on my face. Every time those girls came up with an idea and I thought *that's the last thing on Earth I'd wanna do*, they'd surprise me by topping it.

"Oh come on," Gretchen begged. "Jess, you go first. I'll start it out easy on you—truth—ask me a question."

"I really don't wanna play. I'm sorry. Ya'll just play and I'll listen."

And then she begged. And pleaded. It was as if she was a kid begging her mom for a toy. And, of course, I finally gave in.

"Fine! Ok, how about... How did you become a musician?

Gretchen admitted she dropped out of high school and left home when she was sixteen. She'd had a slew of odd jobs—waitress, dog walker, housekeeper, even cherry picker—but none for too long.

"Then I learned to play guitar and started singing at some coffee shops, getting paid in tips. It wasn't much, but it sure beat the hell outta cleaning up dog shit."

Feeling somewhat of a connection to her, I told Gretchen how bad I felt about her not being able to find herself, and that I could relate.

"It's okay. I'm happy now. I just didn't have anybody in my life that cared about me. But now I do," she said, smiling and putting her arm around Ana. "And I wouldn't wanna be anywhere else except with her."

Ana kissed her on the cheek and it warmed me inside. Not as much as a fire would have, but I'd given up hope now of one getting made.

"Ok, Ana," Carolene spoke up, "now *you* tell us a truth."

"I don't think it works that way, sweetie" she replied, "But whatever, sure. Whatcha wanna know?"

"Tell us about the last serious relationship you were in."

Ana complied, telling us about her last lover, as she referred to him, who was actually, much to our surprise, not a *him* but a woman named Vicky. She said everything started out amazing, especially the sex, as she so generously highlighted. But having to sneak around and keep their relationship a secret from Vicky's family was exhausting.

"But anyway, that's when I met Gretchen at the coffee shop. We jammed together and really hit it off, so we decided to take our little act on the road. Figured there was more to life than what we knew. We just had to go out and find it."

"Well," I told her, "there's always a time to plant and a time to uproot."

"Right on, kid," Gretchen praised. "Uproot is just what we did. It's what you *have* to do sometimes. If you wanna make it big."

"Exactly," I agreed, straying from our game, hoping we could just continue talking like this. "I often feel stuck in Alabama. I mean, I wanna get away so bad sometimes, but I just can't do it. It's like a magnet that just won't lemme go. And then I get all depressed about it."

Everyone shook their heads as if they agreed and knew exactly what I meant and felt. Then it was quiet for a minute as if my words were being reflected on, or if they'd spawned personal memories. The silence was really peaceful.

But it was soon broken.

"Booo, you all are no fun," Gretchen complained, "Let's get back to the game."

I looked over at Carolene and rolled my eyes. She smiled but looked just as uneasy as I did.

"Ok," Gretchen continued. "How about this... I dare Ana to make out with me."

28

"Whatever, you crazy bitch" Ana rejected and pushed her away, smiling. "I'm filthy and too damn cold."

"Whatever, skank," Gretchen replied. "I bet it'd warm both of us up."

Ana just laughed it off.

"How about I give you a rain check?" Ana replied, which Gretchen gladly accepted.

But looking at Ana I noticed she was shivering harder now, and her face was slowly losing its color. Not being too familiar with any type of drugs, I wasn't sure if what she'd smoked earlier was supposed to have that kind of effect or not. But in my gut I felt it wasn't the drugs.

As for the game of Truth or Dare, Ana's refusal to make out with Gretchen seemed to be the buzzer that ended it.

"See," Ana declared, making reference to our earlier conversation, "no more tears for us now. We just laugh and live one day at a time, having fun and enjoying life."

Judging by the way she continued to shiver and shake, and how she put way too many teeth-chattering *e*'s in the word *see*, I knew something was very wrong. But I wasn't going to be the one to bring notice to it.

"Well," I responded, "there's a time to weep and a time to laugh. So when the cryin's over, it's time to smile and move on. That's all ya can do."

"You know, you got a real way with words," Gretchen said. "You write much poetry or do any songwriting? 'Cause I bet if your sister here'd learn to strum a guitar, then you might make a pretty damn good act. Hell, we might even could tour together. Of course you'd have to open up for *us*."

I just smiled and shook my head. If she thought those words came from my mind, so be it. As long as she took something from them. But I knew who the real author was and I was okay with being his penname.

"Jess's always sayin' thoughtful stuff like that," Carolene praised. "She knows just what to say in the right situation. Me, I don't ever say the right thing, 'specially when it comes to relationships."

"See, that's just like Vicky," Ana started back up on her ex, even more flustered than before, now looking so weak and pale that Carolene cut me a worried look.

Then I glanced at Gretchen who looked awfully irritated. I wasn't sure if she was more irritated at Carolene for getting Ana upset, or the fact that Ana was talking about Vicky again.

"She just left one day without even really explaining why. I figured it was the secrecy, but I was willing to work through that. I came home one day, like normal, to the apartment we shared, and there was a letter on the dining room table. A letter. How fucked up is that?"

"Wow, that's pretty messed up alright," Carolene agreed. "So what'd the letter say?"

I shot her a glance to let her know she was starting to pry to deep. But Ana answered anyway.

"Oh just a bunch of gibberish about not wanting to hurt me and how it was for the best. You know, the usual blah blah blah. I mean, how could it be for the best when I thought *I* was her best?"

Her eyes were hazy and her face tight. I told her how sorry I was to hear that and she forced a slight smile. But the shaking was getting worse and I knew something bad was about to happen.

"Sometimes men—and women too," I said, "can do some really stupid, really hurtful things."

"Absolutely," Carolene added, probably thinking about her own personal issues back home. "And now I'm sure he prob'ly—she prob'ly—regrets it."

Gretchen consoled her friend and I wasn't really sure if either one was listening to us. But that was probably for the best anyway since we were butchering our advice and might've even offended Ana with it.

And then the moonlight hit Ana's face, which not only had lost most of its color now but was working on turning a shade of blue. I immediately felt a knot form in my stomach, and I watched as Ana suddenly fell flat on the ground, Gretchen shrieking and panicking as if she'd just seen a huge snake crawl across her leg.

And as the red-haired girl we'd met only a few hours ago lay there and shook like a thousand volts of electricity was passing through her body, I thought of Mama.

I had tried to block the image of Mama's seizure from my memory, so it was actually kind of hard to remember how the situation went exactly. But I do remember seeing Mama shaking and me, Carolene, and Jolene yelling at each other about whether or not to touch her. By far it was the scariest moment of my life.

Gretchen grabbed Ana and held her tight, pressing Ana's head into her chest and stroking her hair with her hand, speaking softly, telling her everything was going to be alright. Ana continued to shake uncontrollably and even wet herself.

"Maybe ya shouldn't touch her," I suggested. "We've seen this kinda thing before and the doctor later told us it was best not to touch 'em, just let the seizure finish."

"Maybe you should shut up," she fired back at me. "It's all your fault, anyway. We were doing just fine until we met you."

I was stunned. I knew Gretchen was just upset and looking for someone to blame, but hearing her words as she pointed her finger directly at my face actually made me feel guilty.

I liked Ana and Gretchen, and I felt so horrible about what was happening that for a moment I found myself actually starting to believe her. With all the trouble we'd been getting into lately, she might've been right. It might *have* been our fault...

29

"Please, baby, wake up," Gretchen repeated, sobbing hysterically, clutching Ana even tighter than before. "Please, Annie, please."

Gretchen nuzzled up to Ana, face to face, and spoke softly. All me and Carolene could do was watch, like the dramatic ending scene of a movie.

"I love you, Ana. I always have. You're my sun, my moon—"

Ana's body stopped convulsing and went limp, unconscious.

"My shining star."

And for a moment I knew exactly how Gretchen felt. We may have been from opposite backgrounds and were on very different life journeys, but for those few seconds as I watched Gretchen cry out for help, feeling scared, confused, and helpless—I felt as if we were one, and I wanted to help her.

"Maybe we should—"

"Shut up!" Gretchen snapped at me. "Just shut—up. You don't know anything. You sit there and act all innocent like this shit ain't your fault. But if she dies, you get to just move on, go back to your shithole little town and be merry. You have no idea what it's like to lose someone like this, someone you love dearly."

"Actually—" Carolene began.

"Shut up!" she snapped again. "Ana is an angel and she deserves way more than this."

Gretchen moaned, her eyes closed, her head back as far as it could go.

"God I'm so stupid. I mean, who was I to think she'd ever love me?"

As she said this, Gretchen caressed Ana's face softly with her thumb, tracing the outline of her lips. And that's when I realized that the love she was speaking of wasn't a friend-love, or even a family-love.

That's also when I realized I actually *didn't* know what she was going through, and maybe I really *couldn't* understand. Because I'd never lost someone I was *in* love with.

⌘

"Ok, grab her feet," Gretchen ordered Carolene, then told me to grab ahold of Ana's other arm.

"Gretchen, this is crazy," I said, though I followed her instructions and helped lift Ana from the ground. "Even if we get her to the car, we have to find a hospital. And even if we find a hospital...well, I mean, we may be too late by then..."

I didn't want to be pessimistic, just realistic. I knew Mama had been pretty much in the same state as Ana, but we had a doctor with us then, and he knew a shortcut, too. And even then she didn't make it.

"Just get to movin'! She'll be fine. She'll be just fine."

So we did. I understood she was in denial, and I could tell her that repeating *she's gonna be fine* wasn't going to make Ana fine, but I kept my mouth shut. That was just part of the process of losing someone and I didn't want to take that away from her.

The three of us moved as quick as we could, but carrying someone through the woods proved to be no easy task. I stumbled twice and Carolene full blown tripped once, sending Ana crashing down to the ground. It's strange, but I felt like we were a comedy group. Like the Marx Brothers or the Three Stooges. But nobody was enjoying our performance.

Needless to say Gretchen wasn't happy about it either. With every single step she cursed, as precise as the second hand ticking on a clock.

It had taken us about two or three minutes to follow Gretchen and Ana from the campfire to the creek, but it was taking us much longer to return. And when we finally made it back to the campfire site, Gretchen threw on her dress and grabbed Ana's. Then started searching the ground.

"Ok, now where the hell are the keys?" she cried, sounding panicked, frustrated. "Ugh! I can't believe this. Help me look," she ordered.

Me and Carolene were down on our hands and knees,

pretending to inspect the ground for the missing set of keys, moving rocks and sticks and sifting through patches of grass.

"Nope. Ya sure ya brought 'em with ya? Maybe they're in the car."

"They better be."

The way she said that sounded like more of a threat. What would she do when she couldn't find them? I already felt guilty and selfish, but now I started to feel afraid.

We all assumed our positions and picked up Ana. At least it wasn't as far to the cars as it was to the lake. And as we slowly shuffled our feet in dysfunctional unison, my mind raced with ideas.

I figured Carolene had to be wondering the same as me—what we were going to do if Gretchen did leave us there, stranded. Who knows, Gretchen might've had extra keys in the car, and when we got Ana inside, she'd drive off into the darkness just as quickly as she appeared. It was a possibility—one I very much feared.

We finally got Ana to the Eldorado and managed to work her into the backseat. Carolene pushed her legs as me and Gretchen, on the other side of the car, pulled her arms.

"Ok now, so where are the fucking keys?" Gretchen muttered to herself as she tore the car apart searching for them. "Ugh! This is just fucking great. Where the hell did that heifer put them?"

When she said that, my ears perked up. There was

something about hearing the word *heifer* that put the gears in my mind in overdrive. I closed my eyes to think for a moment, attempting to block out Gretchen's ranting.

And then it hit me.

Can't tell a heifer from a polecat without 'em.

I pulled Carolene close again, talking fast, anxiously, like I'd just figured out a Perry Mason case and was trying to connect all the details before Mr. Mason could coax the confession out of the criminal.

"He was right! Oh Care, it all makes sense now. My God. I don't know how but he was right. We gotta get out of here, and we gotta do it now."

"Jess, slow down," Carolene said. "What are you talkin' about? Who was right?"

"Frankie! Listen, I know it sounds crazy, but he was right about all of it. About Abraham—I know we were stuck on the *blind* part, but don't you remember? Abraham wore those thick, bottle cap glasses. So without them—"

"Oh God, Jess, you're right. Ok, let's get outta here. But how?"

I looked over at Gretchen who had a crazy look on her face. I already knew she was unpredictable, so whatever we did, we had to act subtly.

So with my back to her, I pulled out Gretchen's keys from my pocket, holding them tight so they wouldn't jingle, and whispered to Carolene, "We borrow their car."

30

"Well if they're not in here," I offered, "then they must be back at the campfire, just somewhere on the ground."

Gretchen looked up at me so fast she hit her head. But she didn't act like it hurt. Maybe the anger and adrenaline were keeping her from feeling the pain.

"Well why don't you run your ass back over there and look for them," she fired back, a patronizing tone to her voice. "But I always leave the keys under the seat."

Gretchen frantically rummaged through all the trash piled up in the car, throwing it over her head. I stared at Carolene and tried to communicate telepathically in order to make a plan, but it wasn't successful. So I started making motions with my head, which still didn't offer much success.

"Yeah, but ya remember, Ana had 'em last," I reminded her. "When she went to lock up the gun."

Right when I said that, I wished I could've lassoed those words back into my mouth. I knew I wasn't supposed to have heard that, even though Ana couldn't whisper to save her life. I didn't think it was a big deal, though. I was just glad they had it. But for some reason, this sent Gretchen over the edge.

"How the hell do you know so much about us?" she probed. "You been keeping tabs on us?"

"What? Of course not. I just, uh—"

"Yeah," she shook her head and pointed at me, getting closer and closer. "That's what you been doing all along. You're trying to put the slip on us. You want our car and so you were gonna use the gun as some sort of leverage, right? But now you're gonna use Ana, aren't you, you sick, twisted bitch."

"What? No, nothin' like that, I swear," I tried to reason with her, but Gretchen started following me around the car. "There was no leverage. Nobody was gonna use nobody. Just lemme explain."

When she tripped over a rock, I managed to get out of reach from her. But now me and Gretchen were on opposite sides of the car, studying each other, daring the other to slip up and lose focus. I felt like I was ten years old and she had my hair bow.

"Stop, Gretchen, we can work this out to where we both get what we want. I wanna get Ana some help just as much as you do. But I gotta think about me and my sister, too. You don't know what kinda mess we're in. So just stop playin' around."

"You think I'm playing, you twit? Listen, I liked you. I liked your sister. But I *love* Ana. She's my life. And no one is gonna take my life away from me!"

Carolene stood off to the side now, watching me and Gretchen dance and argue, looking back and forth between us like a tennis match, until finally interjecting.

"Gretchen, stop!" she pleaded. "Of course we're gonna help you. We owe you our lives. How could we forget how ya distracted Dave so Ana could get the best a Dale?"

Gretchen broke her gaze on me and flew over to where Dale and Dave's truck had been and began searching the ground. It took me a second to figure out, but I knew exactly what she was looking for, what Carolene had reminded her of.

Now drop the gun, loverboy...

I ran to our truck and grabbed the bag of money, then jumped in on the passenger side of the Eldorado and crawled over to the driver's seat. Gretchen still combed the ground, crying and cursing.

"Come on, Care, hop in, let's go!"

Carolene barely made it in before that V8 engine roared and we went flying, leaving a cloud of dust in the air. I was afraid to look behind us, but Carolene did and said she could scarcely make out a figure running after us, waving her arms madly in the air. But the figure grew smaller and fainter until it was long out of sight.

☙

I know that I referred to Ana as *Psycho* before I found out her name, but that was just referring to the movie. Seems Gretchen was the one I should've been calling psycho all along.

But as we sped down that dark road, Ana and Gretchen were already starting to become old news. Carolene and I were on our way to Detroit, and there was no way we were going to stop until we got there.

"Hey, Jess," Carolene spoke softly. "What do ya think'll happen to Gretchen?"

I drew in a deep breath and exhaled. Then I slowly shook my head from side to side.

"I really don't know. And I'm gonna be honest...I know it sounds harsh, heartless even, but I really don't care either."

And then we were quiet. I listened to the growling of the engine and the rumbling of the asphalt, but I knew Carolene had something else on her mind. And a few minutes later she spoke up.

"Hey, Jess?" she asked, even softer than before. "You think it'd be safe to pull over for a bit, just to get a little rest?"

I was just about to ask her why and tell her that we'd be crazy to stop now, but then the moonlight shined down and I caught a glimpse of Carolene's face. Her eyelids drooped and she wore the most troubling expression, as if it actually hurt her to be that tired. I couldn't say no to such a pitiful face.

So I didn't say anything, just smiled. But I swore to myself, after we caught a few hours of shuteye *then* we'd be on a nonstop drive to Detroit. I couldn't help it—when it came to sleep, I was a pushover. I figured I'd just get a catnap and start back up driving while Carolene slept. We wouldn't lose much more time.

I saw a hotel up ahead and figured we were far enough

away that there'd be no way Gretchen could catch up to us. So I parked and we both immediately let the seat back a little. Carolene seemed to be doing a lot of squirming. But I knew she'd be out in seconds if she'd just be still and close her eyes.

"Jess?"

"Hmm?" I acknowledge her, my eyes shut as I had already found a comfortable position.

"Ya know there's a dead woman in the backseat, right?"

"I know. But we'll be just fine unless she sits up," I smirked. "We'll figure it out in the mornin'. Just get some sleep."

And then I was out like a light. And Carolene obviously nodded off eventually too because when I woke up a few hours later to an unfortunately familiar smell coming from the backseat, right as the sun was peeking over the hotel roof, she was sound asleep.

And she must've been sleeping good because she was snoring. And Carolene's snoring could've stripped paint off the walls or pulled curtains off the windows, so I had to turn on the radio to try and block it out. I turned the dial a few clicks until I found a clear station.

I tuned in right as some man was talking about two women who were wanted for robbery and murder. And then he started talking to a sheriff who called the two women felons and said the police were hunting them down.

The host of the show paused his conversation with the

sheriff for a moment to announce his upcoming guest.

"Just a little later on the show, I'll be speaking with Mr. Dale Roberts, a witness who claims to have actually come in contact with these women, and who claims the women assaulted both him and his brother. Get your call-in questions ready."

And that's when my heart dove into my stomach.

31

As the police officer was going on about the robbery of Cheap Al's Quick Stop and the shooting of Ted, I took the map and jotted down a few notes, directions. I couldn't think about what had already happened. We were going to make it to Detroit, and it was going to be as quick as possible with no timely incidents.

I folded up the map and sat there until the sheriff's interview ended. I had no desire to listen to Dale's lies.

As Carolene slept peacefully, I debated on whether or not I was going to tell her what I'd heard, whether or not that would upset her too much. I knew she wanted adventure and all, but becoming wanted criminals is well beyond adventure.

But come to find out, I didn't have to tell her after all. I looked over at her again and she was still lying there just like before, but this time both her eyes and mouth were wide open and she wore the same face she did that time when we were kids and we snuck into that "haunted" house on the outskirts of Merilu. One loud noise and she took off like a scared cat.

I knew I had to step up and be the strong one here.

"It's all a big misunderstandin'," I told her as I rubbed

my eyes, still trying to get all the sleep out of them. "Don't fret too much over it. We'll get it all straightened out when we get back to Alabama. You'll see."

☯

"Help me put her in the trunk?" I motioned with my head towards the backseat, knowing we couldn't just leave Ana there and ride around in the daylight.

Carolene groaned and jerked open the door. It went pretty smooth this time—Carolene was on the same side as me and as I slid Ana out by the legs, she grabbed Ana's shoulders. Then, as gently as possible, we tossed her into the trunk. I said a little prayer and slammed it shut.

I was finally getting used to driving Gretchen's car and was pretty impressed. If I was back in my teens, and of course if it were under different circumstances, I would've been excited to show it off to Pete and go riding around town.

I strapped my seatbelt on and backed up, then out of the parking lot. Carolene was silent but sat up in her seat.

"We got about 200 or so miles 'til we're there," I told her. "So ya can lay back down if ya wanna, 'til we get there."

She watched out the window for a little while before finally giving in and lying back down. Occasionally I heard a whimper and knew that Carolene was probably mulling over the same thing I was—the consequences of being a felon, especially one on the run. I was just waiting for her to grab the steering wheel and force me off the road, demanding we turn ourselves in. But she never did.

※

As we made our way through the rest of Ohio, an uneasy feeling took over my stomach. But I didn't mention it. I knew it was just the silence causing me to worry and dwell on things. But I couldn't lose sight of what we had to do and what was at stake.

Then we passed the turn towards Bowling Green, and I thought it was kind of neat seeing signs for places I'd heard about and learned about in school but never thought I'd see in person.

Next thing I knew we were passing a sign for Toledo and I found myself realizing just how far we were away from home. It scared me a little, but I had to keep in mind that I was having to be the strong one, and the strong one couldn't be scared too.

Then I thought how maybe that was how the phrase "holy Toledo" came about. Maybe seeing the Toledo welcome sign is that moment when you realize you're a long way from home. Maybe even too far away. This made me chuckle a bit to myself.

※

Time must've been racing by because every time I looked at the clock it was approaching the next hour. I'd usually be surprised and declare, "Where'd the time go?"—but this time it was a good thing because I was beyond ready to get there. And the quicker we got back on the road to Alabama the better.

I was glad it was a beautiful day too. The sun was at its peak in the sky and I could feel the Lord's presence watching over us. Maybe even Mama was looking in on us.

And then I saw it, yanking me away from the daze I was in, snapping me back to reality. I perked up in my seat and patted Carolene on the leg to get her attention.

"Hey, Care, look—there it is!"

She sat up, a little dazed, looked at me, then followed my finger to see a big white sign. Breaking her four-hour stretch of silence, she read aloud the words. Her voice cracked a little yet had a faint hint of optimism to it.

"Welcome to Detroit."

Those three words made me smile, and I'll admit it made a few tears run down my cheeks. Carolene even seemed to be getting back to her old self.

But this meant a new chapter would begin. Now the traveling was over for a while and the search for Jolene was underway.

So I pulled over at the first gas station I saw, filled up, got a Coke, and asked the sweet, old lady behind the counter if she knew how to get to the Wayne County Jail. And thanks to her "good-for-nothing" son-in-law who was a regular there, she was able to give me some directions that were actually very easy to follow.

32

When we got parked at the jail, Carolene beat me out of the car. She stretched and held her arms to the sky as if she'd just been let out of prison herself. And I'll be honest, I did the same. I'm sure anyone would agree that stretching your legs in the sunshine after a long car ride is one of the best feelings in the world.

I grabbed the bag of money, took out just enough to pay the bail fee, and stuffed it into my purse. The brown bag I stuffed under my seat to stay out of sight. Then I clutched my purse tight and gave a comforting nod and smile to Carolene.

We followed the signs posted and they led us right to an officer standing behind a counter. His nametag read "Salters" and he looked like he'd had lumpy oatmeal with soured milk for breakfast.

"Um, we're here to pay bail money for my sister, Jolene Johansson."

I didn't know quite what to say. It was my first time in a jail. The officer just stared at me, so I, of course, continued rambling.

"She's in jail here, and we'd like to pay to get her out?" I found myself more so asking than telling him.

I shifted my weight from one foot to the other. Then, still staring at me and Carolene, Officer Salters finally called out to a much younger officer that had just walked up to the desk behind him with a stack of papers.

"Hey, Mackie, we gotta Jolene Johansson here? These two young ladies wanna post her bail."

The low rumble and crackle of Officer Salters' voice reminded me of the old looms at Fleabings when Mama took me on a tour of the factory once.

"Well, it looks like they're not gonna be able to do that," the young officer informed.

There was no way this was happening, I thought. I felt my blood begin to boil and rush through my veins like a river of lava down the side of a volcano.

"What?!" me and Carolene both exclaimed. "There must be a mistake, officers," I continued. "Check again. And look, we have the money."

I opened my purse and held it open for them to see. But the young officer started walking towards us holding out his hand in a stopping manner.

"Ladies, listen. Put your purse away. There's no need to get all worked up. The reason you can't bail her out is because her husband's dropped the charges. So she's free to go," he clarified with a smile.

I'm sure they could hear our sighs of relief back in Holy

Toledo. And as I instinctively glanced over at Carolene for her reaction, I saw her blushing a little at the smiling officer. Though this wasn't an appropriate time for all that, it was nice seeing her expressing an emotion besides worry or fear.

"You think that's a good idea?" Officer Salters scowled, still looking straight at me and Carolene.

The thought did cross my mind that he'd heard the radio report, Dale's interview. And I hadn't seen a TV since we'd been on the road, so we might've even been on there for all I knew.

Officer Mackie leaned down and lowered his voice, but I still heard him anyway.

"Well, her husband said he'd make sure she got some mental help."

Plus I'm sure it didn't hurt, as I later found out from Jolene, that Rodney's dad was fishing buddies with the sheriff.

So, me and Carolene sat in the waiting room while the officers did some paperwork for Jolene's release. I flipped through a Time magazine while Carolene looked disgustedly into a compact mirror I had in my purse. Every few seconds she'd make a sound like she'd just seen a runover armadillo.

When the doors opened and Jolene walked out, I barely recognized her. She was entirely too thin, her hair dyed, and her clothes were what I'd consider torn up rags. And that's coming from someone who made a lot of her own clothes. The Jolene I knew would've never set foot out the door dressed in rags.

But what really bothered me was the feeling I had after she ran up and hugged me. I mean, I could tell it was the same old Jolene I grew up with, but I also got the feeling that there was something wrong, something she was holding back. Still, we walked out with our arms knotted, laughing and crying with happiness.

☯

In the parking lot, Jolene saw the car I was leading her towards and asked, "Wow, where'd ya get the fancy wheels?"

"We borrowed it," I quickly answered, nonchalantly, then grabbed her hand and told her I wasn't getting in until she told me exactly what happened between her and Rodney, why she was in jail.

"Yeah," Carolene added. Something's not right. You seem kinda skittish, a bit nervous."

"I was just in jail!" she defended herself. "I mean, c'mon, how else *should* I feel?"

And with that Jolene pushed me away and lit up a cigarette. I groaned at the continued bad habit, but she assured me she had cut down tremendously over the past year. Said she just needed something to do instead of worry.

"You coulda called!" I shouted, immediately realizing the embarrassing hypocrisy. "But regardless of all that, there's somethin' else goin' on with ya, Jolene, I know it."

Birds chirping in the distance was the only sound during those moments as I stood face-to-face with my sister, my arms crossed, waiting for an answer. Carolene leaned against the car as if she could wait there all day.

"Ok," Jolene spoke up. "Ok, I admit, Rodney visited me earlier today when I was locked up in there, and, well...he kinda threatened to kill me if I left 'em again."

Mine and Carolene's eyes instantly connected and we silently argued over which one of us was going to ask about the *again* part. I gave Carolene a little jerking motion towards Jolene, trying to prompt her to ask, but she just did the same to me in return.

"I know what you're thinkin'," Jolene said, and I hoped she really did know what we were thinking. "You're wonderin' why I stayed with such a jerk, right?"

"No!" I blurted out. "Well, I mean, yeah I wanna know about that too but—"

"We wanna know about the *again* part," Carolene backed me up. "Ya said he threatened to kill ya if ya left 'em again. Now explain."

"Oh," Jolene replied timidly, almost embarrassed. "Yeah... Well, that was what got me in here. I told Rodney I was leavin' him. We got in this real big fight and he threatened me, said he wasn't gonna let me leave. We yelled some more then it sorta turned into this knock-down drag-out fight and I stabbed 'em. Just in the leg, though, 'cause I was down on the ground."

My eyebrows had now reached a height higher than ever before, and Carolene covered her mouth with both hands.

I knew I should say something comforting but it wasn't coming to me yet.

"I'm afraid he'll find me, no matter where I go. So there's really no point in tryin' to hide, right? So I just figured I'd go back to Alabama and see what happens."

"Jolene!" I yelped. "Ya can't do that. Ya can't just up and leave things unresolved like that, 'specially if you're gonna live in fear every day, always watchin' over your shoulder."

"Jess, it's my problem, not yours. Plus we ain't got much time, right? We gotta go. It'll be okay."

"No, Jolene," I stated firmly. "We ain't leavin' here 'til ya take care a this mess 'tween you and Rodney."

Jolene rolled her eyes as she bent down to put out her cigarette on the curb.

"Listen," I added, calmer, "we gotta little time to spare, so don't worry 'bout that. Ya gotta end this with 'em right now or else he's gonna always have a hold on ya."

"Yeah, Jess is right," Carolene agreed. "Ya gotta end it today. The fightin', the threats...it ain't healthy, Jolene. And the only reason he wants to keep ya 'round's 'cause he knows you'll put up with his nonsense."

As she spoke, Carolene had a distant look on her face, like she was reflecting on her own issues, her own mistakes.

"Jolene," she continued delicately, with melancholy in her voice, "he's just usin' you. It's like it's all one big mind game for 'em."

"Exactly," I agreed. "So do ya know where he could be now?"

"I just don't think confrontin' him's such a good idea," Jolene tried to change our minds. "'Specially not now. He's liable to get violent again, with *all* of us."

"Jolene..." I spoke in my most motherly *ya know better than that* tone. Carolene gave her the same judicious glare.

"Ugh," she groaned. "Well... His shift's done let out by now, so I'm sure he's at Doug's Pub—some stupid bar near his house he goes to nearly every day after work, instead of comin' home to see me."

Her mouth frowned with the thought of that. I sort of knew how she felt. Before asking me to leave, Pete started coming home later and later. Sometimes he said he volunteered to work over, and other times he just drove around for a while after work.

"Ok," Jolene agreed. "If we're gonna do this, let's do it."

"Good," I said and hopped in the car, followed by the others—Carolene in the front seat, Jolene in the back. "But on the way there, though, I need to tell ya a little story. We kinda ran into some bad luck on the way up here. We sorta got into some trouble..."

"Well I hope your story's gonna tell me why it stinks so bad in here," Jolene belted out, covering her mouth and nose. "Ugh, it's like somethin' crawled in here and died."

"Yeah..." I began. "I'll get to that. But first, see, we'd

stopped to eat at this diner and, well, we ended up getting robbed—by this...conman. And so we had to figure outta way to come up with some more money, right? Well, so then we had this crazy idea..."

33

"What?!" Jolene screeched, louder than I'd heard her yell since we were little kids and I'd stuck bubblegum in her hair. "There was a dead girl back here...right where I'm sittin'...an hour ago?"

"Well actually," Carolene corrected, "since we didn't hafta pay the bail it was more like *half* an hour ago."

"Gee thanks, Carolene! Now get me outta here!"

Jolene was freaking out, her body tight, her arms in the air, afraid to touch anything.

"I'm hurryin', Jolene, just hold on."

"Or don't," Carolene chuckled, noticing that Jolene had resorted to trying to hover above the seat.

❀

"It's just down one more block, I think," Jolene pointed. "Ugh, I don't know if I can do this. I don't know what he's gonna say, what he's gonna do."

"You'll be fine," Carolene offered her support.

"'Course she will," I said. "She's one a the strongest people I know. And that's what I've always admired about her," I added with a smile, glancing into the rearview mirror so she could see my eyes.

"Admired?" Jolene huffed. "That's crazy talk. I mean, you're the one that's got life all figured out," she sulked. "Always have. You and Carolene both. And then there's me, who's never even figured out where to start."

"Jolene, if you only knew," Carolene shook her head.

"Jolene, listen," I jumped in. "Ain't none of us had a perfect life. It's been far from it. So don't go thinkin' you're all alone and you're the only one with problems, 'cause trust me, we're all three in the same boat."

☯

It was strange to me that the parking lot of Doug's Pub was halfway full and it was still daylight. *A lot* of guys must not look forward to going home to their wives, I thought to myself.

From the outside the place was a dump and seemed pretty sketchy to me—from loose boards for steps to bars on the windows. But once we walked in, I saw where all the money went. The inside was much nicer, with pool tables, a jukebox, and a great big bar that was surrounded by men who looked like they either owned a motorcycle or were "saving up" for one.

"There he is," Jolene pointed out almost immediately.

Rodney didn't appear anything like I thought. He wasn't big or muscular, or even tall. He just looked like a regular, tattoo-covered idiot you'd never cosign a loan for.

"Yeah, I can't go through with this," Jolene backed away

towards the door.

I grabbed one arm and Carolene grabbed the other and together we pulled her back up beside us.

"Jolene, you can do it," I told her. "I have faith in ya."

"Me too," Carolene agreed.

"Now listen," I explained, giving Carolene a *be ready* look. "There's a time to be silent and a time to speak. So speak!"

And with that one last bit of advice, me and Carolene pushed her up to where Rodney stood facing the bar, talking to some other men. Jolene took a deep breath, fixed her hair a second, then shoved his shoulder. He turned quickly, his fist clinched, ready to fight whoever was there.

"Oh, it's just you," he recoiled his fist then started to turn back around.

But standing there with me and Carolene watching plus all of Rodney's buddies watching and laughing, all those bottled up emotions that had been building up inside her came rushing out. She grabbed Rodney's shoulder and snatched him back around so fast that two beer bottles fell off the table next to me. And while I was silently praying, Jolene began spitting fire.

"Listen, shithead," she snapped, her index finger digging into his chest with each word.

Yeah, I was pretty sure that wasn't what Solomon had in mind. But if that's what needed to be said to make that neanderthal understand, then maybe Solomon could just plug his ears for a bit.

"I'm done bein' your slave. I'm leavin' town and I ain't comin' back. Got it?"

Of course Rodney had to put on that stupid macho act in front of his buddies. So he jutted out his chest and stood as tall as he could.

"No, *you* listen, bitch. I don't know who the hell ya think you're talkin' to, but ya gotta lotta nerve comin' in here gettin' in my face. Besides, how ya gonna come up in here talkin' shit when I done dropped the charges on your crazy ass, huh? Your ass'd be locked up with the other nuts if it wasn't for me."

I assumed Rodney was excluding himself from the *nuts*, even though he'd seen the inside of a jail cell twice already.

"Listen, Rodney, I 'preciate ya droppin' the charges. See, you can be a sweet guy."

Rodney's buddies—all intently listening to the argument, of course—started aww'ing, which ended with some shoving back and forth between a few of them. You could feel the testosterone in the air, and those men had it oozing out of them as thick as chunky peanut butter.

"But I'm tellin' ya," Jolene continued. "I *am* leavin' here, *and* leavin' *you*. And if ya ever contact me again—I mean even as much as a phone call or even a postcard—I'm goin' straight to the cops and bringin' my arm full a bruises and medical charts with me."

"Uh huh, whatever," Rodney passed off her warning and turned back around.

Jolene looked over at me and Carolene and we encouraged her to push on, not to let him have the last word. We continued to cheer her on as softly as we could, trying not to grab the attention of any of Rodney's drunken buddies.

"Hey," Jolene yelled at Rodney, but he just continued talking to his buddies, drinking.

"Hey!" she yelled again, louder and with a shove this time, spilling his drink down his shirt as he went to take a swallow.

Slowly he turned, angrily, clenching his fist once again.

"Bitch I swear if you don't—"

"No!" Jolene cut him off. "You just listen to me, you ignorant, white trash, waste of my time, selfish son of a bitch. I meant what I said. And right now we may be runnin' from the law, but I'll be *damned* if I'm gonna keep runnin' from your sorry ass."

With a flip of her hair, Jolene stormed out of the bar with her head held high. We scurried after her like baby ducks after their mama. I'm sure she left Rodney a bit confused about the whole "runnin' from the law" thing, and it might not have been too smart to have mentioned that, but none of us were thinking about those types of details yet. We were still high on adrenaline, and once we got outside, we started up a hootin' 'n a hollerin'.

Me and Carolene, in homage to Ana and Gretchen, laughed as we recited lines like *dumbass men!* and *Annie Oakley never took shit from NO man!* Of course Jolene was in the dark about that and gave us strange looks, but I later explained it to her on the ride home.

I whipped out the Eldorado keys and went to open the door, but Jolene snatched them from me and flung them down the road.

"Ain't no way I'm gettin' back in that thang," Jolene stated, walking towards a truck parked nearby. "I ain't sittin' nowhere no dead woman's been. I mean, I know we had to move around Mama's body and all—and I know we gonna hafta do it again—but that's different. I didn't even *know* this girl. She mighta had some kinda disease or somethin' for all I know. Ya learn a lot about that kinda stuff when ya move to a big city. Besides, I gotta better idea."

Jolene unlocked a big, red—and turned out to be very loud—pickup truck and told us to climb in. I noticed the vanity plate on the front said *Hot Rod*, so I didn't even have to ask whose truck it was. I looked over at Carolene and shrugged my shoulders, then we both climbed on in.

And just like that, the engine roared and we were off.

"If ya gonna beat on your girlfriend," Jolene advised, beginning to smirk, "don't give her a spare key. 'Cause she just might get fed up and leave your ass stranded at the bar."

"Dumbass," Carolene snickered.

ಬ

Luck must've been on our side that evening because just

as we got a few blocks out of sight, the local cops came flying into the parking lot of Doug's Pub and swarmed the place. Of course the first person they started questioning was Rodney.

One officer told him they were tipped off by the Warren County PD in Ohio, who received a tip from two guys who came by the office down there. Said the women were on their way to Detroit. Said they'd already told their story on the radio but wanted to make sure we caught them.

Dale and Dave had struck again...

"A little bit of investigating," the officer began telling Rodney, "and we found out that you've recently been in a serious relationship with the third sister..."

Not sure why Rodney did what he did—maybe it was an act of decency or maybe he was just looking after his own hide, but come to find out that when the cops asked Rodney about where we were headed, he actually lied and said he didn't know.

"But I hope you catch 'em before they leave town," he barked. "Crazy ass bitch."

Rodney might not have been so obliging towards us if he'd known at the time that his truck was gone. Although he did get a very sporty hardtop Eldorado in return. Even though the keys were somewhere on Brush Street...and there was a dead hippie in the trunk.

As the officers were interviewing other patrons to see if they had any information, one of the officers turned around to see who was politely tapping him on the shoulder and was greeted by a man dressed in a purple suit, his eyes accented with mascara, and, yes, this time he was wearing a cape...

34

"Ahh, good eve, dear gents, dear keepers of the peace. I know these ladies well, these felons that you seek. I could tell you where their travels will soon come to a rest. A place they call home, but it will cost to disclose that quest."

"Uh, yeah, fella" the officer appeared confused but understood enough of what Frankie was getting at. "I guess we could setup some type of reward. That is, if the information you have is credible, if it helps us track these women down."

"My word is always credible. I've spoken with them face to face. I could pen you out directions to this very place."

I knew he knew we were from a small town in Alabama, but neither me or Carolene ever told him the name of it. But it was probably already all over the radio or on TV. Plus I knew he traveled around so much I'm sure he *could* have drawn a map. Probably to our front doorstep for all I knew. And that's probably the only reason the officer paid him any attention.

"Ok," the officer agreed. "You jot us down some directions to where they live and we'll look into getting you some type of reward. Just come on down to the station later on and you can pick it up."

"Oh no, my not-so-shiny badge sporting friend. I have information you want, so this chase you can win. These women are smart, so you'd better hurry, seize the day. But it's always payment before product, as my father used to say."

It was really no surprise that he'd sell us out when money was involved. And from the sound of it, looking for ways to make some fast, easy money was a family affair.

"Yeah, I can't help ya, buddy," the officer replied, licking his thumb and rubbing it on his badge. "Rules are rules. If you want the reward, you'll have to come down to the station just like everybody else."

Frankie crossed his arms and stared at the officer. Though the officer thought the mysterious stranger was a kook, he knew the kook was right about not having much time.

"Ok, fine," the officer broke, then lowered his voice, looking around. "Now here you go, you Shakespeare-wannabe looking freak."

The officer slid a folded bill into Frankie's jacket pocket, to which Frankie immediately took it out to check the amount, scowled, and put it back.

"There. There's your reward. Now write out the damn directions and we'll all be on our merry way."

Frankie did as the officer ordered—took out a pen from inside his coat, grabbed a napkin off the counter, and wrote out directions to our hometown. Even labeled things like "red barn on corner" and other helpful markers.

"Impressive," the officer admired Frankie's artwork and patted him on the back. "You just helped put dangerous felons behind bars, young man. You should be proud."

Frankie tipped his hat and turned to leave. But before he could take a step, the officer grabbed him by the arm.

"Hey, fella, it says here," he read from his notepad, "the women we're after aren't from around here but from the South, perhaps Alabama. Your little map doesn't look like it goes down to Alabama. So what gives?"

"Believe me or not, it is up to you. What you feel in your gut is what you are going to do. But I swear to you, officer, my word is pure like wine. Just watch out for the twists and turns and look out for the sign."

The officer waved the directions Frankie had given him in the air as he walked towards a group of officers, a couple of them sipping coffee.

"I'm getting nothing from these people," one officer said, others agreeing.

"Yeah, this is a waste," another stated. "You guys ready to pack it up?"

"Hey guys, check this out," the officer with the map gloated. "The Count over there says he knows exactly where our women are headed. Even drew out a little map. Looks fairly straight forward. He just rambled something about watching out for the signs or something. Not too sure—could barely understand what the freak was saying."

Having no other leads, the other officers asked if he could be trusted. One rookie even asked if he could be *counted* on. Which received no solicited laughs, only disapproving looks.

"Well," the officer with the map responded, thinking his under-the-table payoff assured accurate information, "he's a little offbeat, sure, but I think we can *count* on him," he said with a chuckle.

The other officers joined in for a hearty laugh. All except the rookie, who merely cut each of them a dirty look and walked off.

Frankie caught the eye of the rookie, and as he stood along the back wall, the officer watched as Frankie applied more mascara to his eye lashes. Chuckling to himself, the rookie just shook his head and walked out to his patrol car.

But a sneaky smile was smeared across Frankie's face as he left. And with everyone so wrapped up in the case and trying to find out what was going on, no one noticed as he took a handful of bills from the cash register before disappearing out the back door.

And even though he was the butt of the joke, Frankie was actually the one that should have been laughing. Because that was the day the Detroit Police Department unwittingly put all their trust into the word of the greatest illusionist of all time.

35

I must say, it was nice not having to drive. Jolene could've stayed behind the wheel all the way back to Alabama and I wouldn't have put up one word of a fight. I didn't even argue when she insisted on smoking while she drove. But I knew we'd end up trading places at some point. Probably when we stopped to get some rest.

Getting to sit there and not focus on the road gave me a chance to really zone out and reflect on the day, on our trip, and on what was in store for us when we got back to Merilu.

I guess it was because we passed a diner, but Abraham crossed my mind. I wondered what his story was. Everything seemed to happen so fast. I wished that one day I could meet him again, under different circumstances.

My eyes now shut, I could hear Ana humming along to Gretchen on her guitar. It was peaceful. And I realized that me and Carolene were the last people to ever hear them together. I would've loved to have seen them perform up on the big stage, opening up for Johnny and June.

My heart went out to Gretchen for her loss, and I hoped one day she'd forgive us. But I knew she and Ana would one day reunite and play music together again. But until then I couldn't help but wonder how Gretchen would get along without her partner. I knew she claimed not to have anyone who loved her or cared for her, but there had to be someone she could go to, confide in. Someone out there had to miss her.

☏

The sky was a beautiful rose color, and the sun hung low, peeking through the fluffy white clouds that seemed to stretch out and pull apart like cotton candy. I stared up at them, waiting for my eyes to pick up on a shape or face like I used to do as a kid. I finally did see somewhat of a face, but I couldn't make out whose it was.

I watched the clouds until the sun retired for the night. And I wished I was doing the same—in *my* bed. I kept telling myself it'd happen soon. But as for that night, if I looked half as bad as I felt, then I felt sorry for anyone that would have to see me wherever we stopped.

Though it had been a pretty successful day for the three of us—with Jolene standing up to her bullying boyfriend and me and Carolene having made it to Detroit in one piece, all of us now on the way back home—we still looked defeated, like we'd put in a long, hard double shift at Fleabings.

My mind continued to race in the silence and I wanted the thoughts to end, but I couldn't bring myself to carry on a conversation. But I obviously wasn't the only one tired of the silence. Carolene huffed and flipped on the radio. Since we were in Rodney's truck, I had no idea what to expect. I assumed some crazy rock 'n roll would come blaring through the speakers at a deafening volume.

But I was pleasantly surprised when the beautiful voice of Ms. Loretta Lynn filled the car with my favorite version of Ms. Sinatra's hit, and the three of us immediately perked up and started singing along:

> *These boots are made for walking,*
> *And that's just what they'll do.*
> *One a these days these boots are gonna walk*
> *all over you!*

Of course we all pointed as we shouted *you* in unison, pointing our fingers at each other. But we each had someone different in mind as we pointed, our own special person we wanted to tell off. That person we wanted to look in the eyes and exclaim, "I don't need you anymore! I know I messed up. But it's okay 'cause everyone messes up. But you weren't there when I needed you most. So to hell with you!"

The music revived us, gave us our second wind. And we laughed and sang so hard until tears were rolling down our faces.

"Ooh, turn it up," Jolene told Carolene as the next song began playing. "I listened to this song on my first day livin' in Detroit. Rodney left for work and I was alone and feelin' pretty blue, worryin' whether I'd made the right decision or not. So I crawled out of bed over to the record player, flipped through his records, and put on this album. I listened to this song over and over until I felt strong enough to get dressed and go see the doctor. Because that was also the first day Rodney struck me. Just one right hook to the eye, leavin' behind a black eye that took about three weeks to fade."

We were quiet after that, just listening to the words and enjoying the melody. And then Jolene began singing along softly, growing louder until the song reached the chorus. She patted us both on the leg, encouraging us to join in. So, me and Carolene came in right on cue, bellowing at the top of our lungs:

Just call me angel, of the mor-ning, an-gel!
Just touch my cheek before you leave me, ba-by!

And I about lost it when Carolene snuck in a different lyric on us, trying to sing over me and Jolene, causing us both to choke on the laughter—Jolene coughing uncontrollable, my face turning as red as a ripe tomato as I struggled for air.

Just brush your teeth before you leeeave, ba-by!

Singing made the time fly by, and once we saw signs to turn to go towards Dayton, we pulled over for gas. Since we didn't have to pay for Jolene's bail, I still had plenty of money in my purse for us to load up on some well-deserved treats—Twinkies, chips, and sodas. Jolene got some fried pork skins, which I've never seen her eat before, and a chocolate bar. Seemed to be a strange combination, but I guess that's just what she was craving.

As I figured, Jolene said she was tired of driving, holding her back as if she'd been sitting on a church pew for fourteen hours. So I climbed behind the wheel, with Carolene in the middle, and Jolene next to the window.

"Oh, God, I've been wanting to do this all day," Jolene wailed, leaning her head out the opened window, her hair blowing in the wind.

Me and Carolene just laughed at her. The breeze did feel nice, so I rolled my window down all the way too. In fact, we kept them like that even as we got some sleep that night.

Yep, another hotel. Parking lot, that is. But I was used to it. I knew we had the money for a hotel room—and that's what Carolene wanted, but I said it was too nice of a night to sleep indoors.

"Ya know what?" Jolene spoke up as we laid there, our heads resting on each other. "I really, truly hate Rodney. Is that wrong?"

The question had so many levels to it and I wasn't sure where to begin. So I just quoted the book that seemed to always have the best advice.

"Well, Jolene, there's a time to love and a time to hate. I know it ain't easy to forgive and show love for somebody when they're mean and disrespectful—and 'specially when that same person's abusive. But I just think life is too short to spend it hatin' people. It just takes up too much time and energy."

"Damn, Jess," Jolene replied with a half-smile, shaking her head in amazement. "Ya always know just what to say. Must be nice to have life all figured out."

I rolled my eyes. I wanted to explain to her how the praise made me feel proud, sick, and angry all at the same time. Proud that I was able to help out my sister and that she found comfort in my advice but sick to my stomach that she had no idea how false her statement was. And I was angry at myself for not living up to my expectations.

But I didn't feel like going into all that right then. So instead, I just dismissed the praise with one of the greatest words in the English language.

"Whatever."

36

The sun woke me up and it didn't take long before I was out of the truck, stretching as wide as I could. It took some coaxing but the other two eventually did the same. And while they were just getting out, I'd already hopped back in, ready to hit the road again.

"Hurry up," I yelled at them. "We're wastin' daylight. And if I'm gonna drive, I'm ready to go."

Because when the driver's ready, everybody else better be ready or they're going to get left behind.

And in no time we were off, back on the road. We didn't know what to expect from this leg of the journey, but we knew we had to hurry and that we couldn't afford to have any more major bumps in the road. So fingers were crossed, prayers were sent up, and our eyes were wide open.

Though we didn't take the time to site-see as we traveled, we did do a lot of looking out the window, seeing everything again for the first time, with somewhat familiar eyes.

Jolene was most amazed, not having paid any attention to the sites on her trip up to Detroit with Rodney.

"Most of what I remember is all a haze, a big blur. Mainly 'cause I was staring through tear-stained eyes."

After that we were quiet, just enjoying the peacefulness. I guess if we'd known that the cops were hot on our trail we'd have probably been a little more concerned, a lot more afraid.

And just like always, the quiet didn't last long. But what would you expect from three women crammed in a truck?

"Ugh, my stomach's just a gnawin' at my backbone!" Jolene complained, squirming and showing her disgust for the uncomfortable ride.

My stomach was growling too, so I didn't object when she insisted on stopping at a diner not too far outside of Bowling Green. But I did get an eerie feeling, because we were near where we'd met up with Ana & Gretchen. An accidental meeting that will stay with me forever, haunting me to my grave.

I also knew there was a chance that somebody might recognize us by our description, as told on the radio station and maybe even on the TV. So before we entered the diner, I advised my sisters to keep a low profile.

"Keep your heads down, don't look at anyone, and sit in the back. Try to look like nobody in particular."

We did our best, but I'm sure we made ourselves look even more conspicuous by trying so hard not to be. Either way, nobody recognized us and we ordered as though we'd been there a hundred times.

"Be right back," I announced, heading for the bathroom.

Carolene followed behind me, leaving Jolene alone at the table. But at least her face wasn't tied to any murders, so I was sure she'd be okay. After all, I was confident that all the bad stuff was over with. I mean, it had to be, right?

∞

Her face looked to be painted up with war paint, her eyes limp with exhaustion yet noticeably burning with rage. Her blond hair now brown from dust and dirt, her body skinned up and scratched so much that crimson stains were smeared all down her limbs.

Everyone's eyes followed her as she went from table to table, begging for help as if she'd been in an accident or maybe fleeing the scene of a crime with the lawbreakers right behind her.

But even from the back of the restaurant Jolene could hear that she wasn't asking for help for herself, rather she was asking for help in finding someone.

"Where is she?" she demanded of the frightened diner patrons. "Have you seen her? Oh please, just tell me you've seen her. Or even her sister."

The panicked woman grabbed the shirt of one of the male customers, pulling him close to her face, begging a response from him. This brought out the manager, screaming at her to leave and stop harassing his customers. He even had a big metal pot in his hand, which didn't strike a chord with

Jolene, though, since she'd never met Abraham and didn't get to experience his manic episode.

"Ok, man, I'll calm down," the woman backed away from the grasp of the manager. "You don't know what all I've been through. So just let me stay, ok? I'll go over here and sit down. Just please bring me a burger or something, man. I'm fucking starving."

The manager turned and walked back to the counter, told the waitress to bring her something and get her out of there quick.

She seemed to hobble as she walked, more than likely from a twisted ankle by the way she moved. With all the booths full now, she decided the least confrontational place for her was in the back booth where a woman who appeared to be harmless sat by herself.

"Mind if I sit?" she asked.

Jolene stumbled around for an answer, knowing that her sisters would be back at any moment. But even before she finished answering her, the woman had already taken a seat, smiling innocently as if the big scene she'd caused never happened.

"Sorry about all that. You'd never believe what I've been through the past couple of days."

"I can't even imagine," Jolene responded, trying not to say too much, hoping this woman would get the hint that she didn't want to talk and go to another booth, go bother someone else.

But she didn't take the hint, even asked Jolene for a cigarette. Jolene thought about telling her that she was out but the idea sounded nice, so she pulled out two and gave the woman one.

They both took long drags, filling their lungs with divine pollution. The mysterious women, who Jolene thought could have been beautiful under her layers of dirt-makeup, even gave a half-smile.

"Thanks, I needed that," she said, extending her hand. "My name's Gretchen."

Gretchen...Jolene thought, searching her mind's files to see why that name, while unique to her, actually seemed strangely familiar.

"So you from out of town?" Gretchen tried to make small talk.

Though Gretchen was now quite calm, Jolene was still freaked out and really just wanted the woman to leave her alone. Plus she was still racking her brain over the name.

"Yeah, we're on a kinda road trip," Jolene told her.

"We're?" Gretchen asked, looking around curiously. "Who all's with you?"

"Oh it's just me and my sisters."

As she spoke, she recalled the words Gretchen had said moments ago in her rant:

Have you seen her? ...Or even her sister.

And then she realized exactly who the sisters Gretchen was looking for were. Jolene cut her eyes over to the bathroom door, fearful they would be strolling out at any second.

37

And we did.

Carolene was the one to open the door, but luckily she stopped to tell me something, the door only partially open. As she turned back around, her eyes instinctively jumped to our table. Carolene flinched at the sight of a woman sitting across from Jolene, then squinted for a better view.

"Oh. My. God," she declared, quickly backtracking into the bathroom, easing the door shut so as not to make any noise.

I kept at her, asking her to tell me what was the matter, but Carolene's face was white like she'd just seen a ghost, and it took me grabbing her shoulders and shaking her to get her to snap out of the trance and tell me.

When she said her name, a cold chill ran down my spine. We blocked the door, just in case Gretchen decided to go to the bathroom. Even if she didn't, knowing our luck, she'd probably never leave, waiting us out.

I just shook my head, amazed by the irony of it all. I mean, what were the odds Gretchen would stumble into the same diner we were in *and* pick Jolene to sit with out of all the other patrons?

Carolene let go of the door and went over to the sink to splash some cold water on her face. I stood my ground but shut my eyes, praying that Jolene wouldn't say anything that would give us away.

☙

"Your sisters, huh? How many?"

In my eyes, Jolene didn't look much at all like me and Carolene, but still, you could probably tell a family resemblance. That's what I worried most about.

"Three," she lied.

"Oh wow—big family. So where are they?" Gretchen inquired, feeding the ashtray, Jolene following suit.

My clever sister was just about to lie again, tell her that we had to run some errands, wouldn't be back for a while. But her eyes uncontrollably flickered in the direction of the bathroom, which made Gretchen turn to look.

"They all in the bathroom? Why'd they leave you out here by yourself?"

Jolene told her she didn't have to go and tried to quickly change the subject to the weather. But Gretchen wasn't interested in talking about the weather. She wanted to know more about her sisters and why they were taking so long to come back.

"Don't know, but they need to hurry up. Maybe I need to go in there and check on 'em," Jolene said, beginning to push her way off the seat.

But Gretchen reached out and grabbed her arm before she stood, insisting to go in Jolene's place.

"Besides, I look a mess. I really need to freshen up. If I see them I'll tell them you're ready to go."

Jolene began to panic, but she tried not to show it for fear Gretchen would figure them out, if she hadn't already. Ideas ran through Jolene's head, like running and tackling her while Jess and Carolene made a getaway, or announcing dramatically that the woman who everyone already assumed was crazy had stolen her purse, even though Gretchen wasn't holding a purse.

But nothing good came to mind as the dirty, bloody woman with a crazy look on her face sped towards the bathroom.

༄

"Ok, here's what we're gonna do," Jess explained to Carolene. "On the count of three, you're gonna take off, push the door open as hard as you can so it don't slow you down, then you'll run wide open straight towards Gretchen, tackle her, and hold her down. Got it?"

"Why do *I* hafta do all that? What are *you* gonna be doin'?"

"While you have her pinned down, I'm gonna run over to the kitchen and grab a pot or pan or stack of plates—just whatever I find first. Then I'll race back to you and hit her over the head with it, hopefully knockin' her out or at least givin' us some time to flee 'fore she gets all her wits back. How does that sound?"

"Fine I guess. 'Cept for one thing."

It sounded like a pretty solid plan to me—the best I could come up with on such short notice with limited supplies and in a public place full of people.

"What if she's gotta gun? Or a knife? What if she stabs me while you're off decidin' what kinda dishes to get?"

"Come on, Care, this is our only shot at overtakin' her, to strike first. And, yeah, I'm sure she's prob'ly gotta weapon, since the last time we saw her she was searchin' the ground for a gun as we made off with everything important to her."

I knew that didn't make Carolene feel any better about the situation, so I offered to do the tackling while she went to the kitchen. Without hesitation she took me up on it.

"Ok then. Ya ready? Remember, grab somethin' quick 'cause she's gonna be like holdin' down a giant hornet."

I drew in a few deep breaths, pumping myself up for the attack, then backed up several feet for extra force.

"Ok. One...two...three!"

I darted towards the door, giving it a shove like I'd never shoved before. The heavy door swung open, the rage behind my push sending it farther out than I could've ever normally pushed it.

But it stopped abruptly.

I remember from one of my science courses, we learned

about this brilliant scientist who had this theory about objects staying in motion until being stopped by something else. This was a great example of that theory, because that door sure was in motion, and when it met that other object, it sure did come to a halt. Even swung back and knocked Carolene, who had taken off a second or two behind me, right on her butt.

My first thought was that I'd knocked out some little old lady. Probably took her a good minute to ease over to the bathroom door, relying on her cane, holding her aching back with every step. And now thanks to me, she was sprawled out on the hard floor, unconscious, if she was alive at all.

After helping Carolene off the floor, I slowly pushed open the door, easing my head out to see the damage. Then I heard Jolene calling out to me.

"Jess! Oh my God, Jess, come look."

Yep, I knew it. Judging by the alarm in her voice, I just knew I would look down to see that old woman, bleeding, a broken arm or leg no doubt. I didn't want to look, but my eyes were drawn to the floor like magnets.

And then I saw her.

Not the little old lady with a cane and broken limbs, but a filthy, blood-covered woman who you could barely tell was a blonde.

Patrons of the diner began to gather around. Then the waitresses and manager rushed over to see what the commotion was.

"It...it was an accident," I said, easing out of the bathroom, followed by my sister, a little dazed herself from her spill.

"Evelyn, run and call an ambulance—and the police," ordered the manager to one of the waitresses. "Tell them to hurry."

Then he pointed at me, waiving his finger from one Johansson sister to the next to make sure we knew he was talking to all three of us.

"You stay right here. You'll have some explaining to do when the cops get here."

He was very trusting to have walked away to help the customers back to their seats, assuring them everything was okay now. But he didn't know us, didn't know the predicament we were in. All apologies to him, but there was no way we were going to stick around until the cops came.

So we slid back further and further from where Gretchen lay, closer to the exit and eventually we were able to slip out the door without being seen. Unseen or not, we still took off running like three bats out of hades.

Once we were in the truck, I realized we hadn't left completely unseen, because Evelyn the waitress was running towards us, waving her arms, shouting, "I'm not supposed to let you leave. You have to come back in for questioning."

Her words grew faint, though, because we were speeding away as if we were nearing the finish line on a dragstrip. Like I said, they didn't know our predicament, and there was no way we were going to wait around for the cops.

We were down the road a good mile before I was able to take a breath.

"How 'bout no more diners," Carolene said, pulling her hair back into a ponytail. "They're nothin' but trouble."

38

The hours ticked away, and it must've been the eagerness to get back home that gave me the will power to keep pushing on, but long stretches of road between breaks were wearing on me. Watching that endless white line made my eyes cross and my head spin. I knew how truck drivers felt, or so I thought. I at least felt really bad for them now.

As we left the blue grass state for the rocky top, I started getting really homesick. I missed the friendliness of Merilu's townsfolk and the warmth of the gulf air. And longed to once again hear the ringing of the Mantioch Methodist church bells and even run through the lilies that grew around the creek behind the Old House, just like I was a kid again. Those things always brought a smile to my face, a sense of peace.

I knew we'd be home soon enough, but I couldn't let my guard down just yet though. The road is a dangerous beast that demands respect, even fear. But I couldn't help but to feel a little calmer, at ease, since it seemed like the road was actually being good to us this time. So far.

With all the madness that happened on the way up to Detroit, we were all really surprised that nothing crazy had happened yet, especially me and Carolene. Heck, we had even made wagers about what kind of bad luck we were going to run into before we made it back home.

Carolene bet two donuts we'd get robbed, again, and Jolene raised her with three donuts on us getting lost. But I knew that wasn't going to happen because me and Carolene had map-reading down pat now. And for the fun of it, I threw my hat into the ring with one donut bet on us having some type of car trouble. Or truck trouble, as Gretchen had insisted.

But luckily enough no one won. And once we saw it, we knew there'd be no more hitches, no more snags.

It was beautiful, comforting. If I had a camera with me I would've taken a picture of it and framed it. It was a warm welcome, a sigh of relief, even more so than when we entered into Detroit.

To me it said: *Welcome back, ya'll!* But I'm sure to most people it simply read: Welcome to Alabama.

∞

Making it back to the Alabama line with only one real mishap was by far the greatest magic trick ever. But as for the only magician I knew, Frankie VanTastic, whose face stayed with me like heartburn, I wished I had known then what he had done for us. Because at the time I still hated him.

Though he was a con artist and was really the one who started us on the downward spiral we were stuck on, I must give Frankie VanTastic some credit. I figured he'd sold us out to the cops just to make some money, but Frankie actually ended up helping us out by pulling off his greatest illusion yet—making our entire hometown completely disappear...

❦

The officers, of course, didn't find the women they were after, but instead found nothing but an empty field near Winamac, Indiana. They just stood there, dumbfounded looks smeared across their faces, their car lights still flashing and sirens blaring.

"So should I start knocking on doors?" the rookie asked the officer with the map, his lips curling into a smirk.

Writing out a map to an empty field was pretty clever, but how Frankie beat them there to put up that sign, that was genius. Maybe there really was some kind of magic to him. Or maybe he just had friends all over the country. But one thing I will admit—he was definitely a man of mystery.

❦

As it turned out, Frankie slipped town after his act of good citizenship and the cops were hot on our trail. They phoned in other officers from nearby and led a brigade to catch us, following Frankie's directions to a tee.

The directions were spot-on, which made the officer with the map feel a little better about himself. Like a checklist, the brigade passed everything on the map, even the red barn.

Nearing the end of the directions, though, buildings started becoming scarce, then houses became few and far between. The road turned into a dirt road and all you could see in any direction was field.

The sheriff was madder than a wet cat. There was one little sign off in the distance that he made the rookie go inspect. The sign merely read *WELCOME* in big, white letters and even had a note stapled to it. The rookie snatched the note off and read it aloud.

"I'm so sorry, officers, but don't blame your luck. Surely Shakespeare would have done the same for a measly five bucks."

39

After a while, the cheering let up and the excitement of being so close to home faded. We were back to silence. Jolene was zoned out, her head on her arm against the window. I'm sure she had a lot on her mind. But Carolene had obviously been using her time to think, too, and now she wanted to talk about it.

So I figured it was as good a time as any to take a little break from driving. I pulled the truck off the road and we all got out stretching. Then Carolene came up and stood next to me as I had my eyes closed, taking deep breaths of Alabama air.

"Jess?" she asked coyly.

I looked over at her. She was staring down the road, which curved and went up a huge hill and out of sight. Jolene was leaning on the truck, looking as if the smoke she was having was warming her bones like hot cocoa.

"Ya ever think life is just too hard?" she asked. "I mean, ya ever sometimes wish it was like when we was kids?"

"Well sure I do, Care." I could tell she was struggling with something by the way she wouldn't look at me directly, by the way she bit her bottom lip. "I'm sure everybody gets that thought from time to time. Growin' up is hard. And every year it seems to getta little harder."

"Yeah. I just been thinkin' 'bout that a lot," Carolene admitted. "'Bout how I wish I could go back, ya know, to right before things fell apart for me and start all over. Would *you* wanna go back and start over if ya could?"

I didn't answer. Instead, I just pulled her even closer. Jolene came and put her arm around Carolene, holding her cigarette away from both of us as best she could.

"I know exactly whatcha mean, sis," Jolene added. "A redo sounds nice. Sometimes I actually wish I was just someone altogether different, with a whole 'nother life."

Then Jolene flicked her cigarette butt and put her other arm around me, smiling, and told us she'd still want us as sisters, though. We both smiled in return.

But I was really disturbed over my sisters' jaded view of life and didn't say anything back. My face must've said everything I was thinking because Carolene and Jolene both started frantically apologizing.

"No, no, it's okay," I told them. "Really. I mean, it ain't like the same things hadn't crossed my mind too."

We loosened our holds and gave each other some space.

"Carolene," I came back. "You asked me if I'd wanna start all over if I could..."

Both of my sisters turned to look at me—Carolene with her arms crossed, her hair blowing in the wind, and Jolene with her hands on her hips, twisting the toe of her shoe around and around as if she was digging into the sand on the beach with old Abraham.

"Well, answer is," I confessed, "Prob'ly not. I mean, like the Good Book says: There's a time to mourn and a time to dance. And that's true. 'Cause life ain't always gonna be singin' and dancin'. It can't be good *all* the time."

"See," Carolene responded. "You're so strong. You can read one verse and be at peace. I wish I could be that way."

After a few moments of silence passed, I went to the truck to sit down. The gun lying causally in the seat reminded me of the sheriff on the radio calling us felons. Then I began wondering if the cops were still after us, because if they were, wouldn't they have caught up to us by now? Or even called the local cops to come track us down? Had we actually gotten away scot-free? After all we had been through, it only seemed fair, right? That eased my mind a little.

But no matter the case, family issues always came first, and the fact that my sisters were hurting troubled me so bad my stomach ached. They looked so defeated—and so did I—but I knew it was up to me to remedy the situation.

And then it hit me.

"Hey," I called out, my eyes now widened and my back straight. "I got an idea. And I think it may really help, if we all agree to do it."

"Sure, what is it?" both Carolene and Jolene questioned,

intrigued at my noticeable satisfaction.

As I explained the idea to them, it started to really make sense and I knew this was exactly what we needed. All of us.

In agreement we got back on the road. And along the way, Carolene and me each wrote a list of a few things we wished most for out of life while Jolene drove—said she needed some time to collect her thoughts. Once I finished, though, I took over driving again so Jolene could make out her list before she forgot everything she'd thought of.

"So, ya never said what we're gonna do with these..." Jolene urged me to explain.

"Yeah. And why'd ya want us to write 'em down instead a just sayin' 'em out loud?" Carolene added.

I told them just to hold on, that it'd all make sense soon enough. For now, I took the lists and put them in my pocket.

The activity must have drained us emotionally because no one spoke a word until I pulled off onto the side of the road right before the Sipsey River Bridge.

40

We all three leaned over the side of the bridge, staring in awe of the beautiful Sipsey River. Being a windy day, there was a rapid flow to the water and it looked like it would just whisk you away if you fell in.

It must've been a funny sight—all three of us' hair flying around as if the wind was going to snatch it right off like a wig if we didn't hold it down. But we didn't let that stop us from completing our mission.

I took out the lists from my pocket and gave them back to the respective writers. Carolene asked if we were going to read them, so I told her that sounded like a good idea, even though that's what I had in mind anyway. Jolene agreed and even volunteered to go first.

I wasn't sure if she was really cold or really nervous, but she spoke carefully and took her time with each sentence.

"I wasn't sure how deep we was s'posed to get, so I started out small and then dug deeper. So here goes... I wish life was easier, like when we was kids. I know I kinda stole that one from what Carolene said earlier, but I liked it and agreed with it, so... Also, I wish I had more money."

When we first talked about making the list, I told them to make it personal, not generic. I surely couldn't disagree with her about wanting more money, though, and I'm sure no one else would either. But there's no point in stating obvious desires that every single person has. I was hoping the rest of her list actually did dig deeper like she said.

But Jolene never stopped surprising me, and dig deeper she did.

"I wish a man would never strike a woman. It's degrading, offensive, and just morally wrong. But at the same time, I wish women were stronger so we could fight back, equally—ya know, be a fair fight."

What all had she been through? Jolene was so prideful she would probably never fully open up about it. From knowing a little about the guys she was with before Rodney, and from knowing their families, I was pretty sure they weren't abusive. Not physically, at least. So all fingers were pointed at Rodney when it came to physical abuse.

So what all had he done to this poor woman? Broke her down and brainwashed her? I wanted to drive right back up to Detroit and give that bastard a piece of my mind. Well, not really right now, but maybe I'd sneak away some day without my sisters knowing it. And stop at that gun shop on the way. If we couldn't have a fair fight like Jolene said, then I would need an advantage.

"And I know a lot of people have this wish too," Jolene

continued, "but I wish I was more attractive." With a half smirk she added, "Ya'll two got all the good looks and didn't leave any for me. That was pretty selfish, don't ya think?"

And then she smiled for real. But her eyes, despite the dryness from the wind, were becoming hazy. Neither me or Carolene said anything, just let her read.

"But seriously, I wish I was the kinda girl men fell for."

Her voice struggled to squeeze out of her tight throat. I put my arm on her back just to show her we were listening and that she could take her time.

"'Cause I'm just the girl men seem to go after once they've had their heart broke. And then after they get whatever it is out of their system, they leave. That's why I stayed with Rodney so long. No matter how bad a temper he had, at least he looked at me like I was much more than the ugly ducklin', much more than just a piece a ass. He made me feel desirable. Even if it was only for a short time."

Carolene sniffed and wiped her eyes and whimpered a sympathetic *Oh Jolene*. I just shut my eyes and waited for more.

"And—well, this was the last thing I wrote down—I wish I had more confidence. When I look in the mirror I see an old nag, beaten and broken down. Nothin' but a burden."

Jolene lowered her paper and stood there in silent tears.

"You ain't a burden, Jolene," I assured her. "In fact, you've always inspired me to have big dreams, 'cause I'd listen to ya go on 'bout yours."

This at least brought a smile to her face and she squeaked out a *thanks*. I looked over at Carolene and she, fighting back tears herself, said she wanted to go next.

"I didn't write as much as Jolene, but here goes. Like I said earlier and like Jolene said, I wish I was a kid again. Bein' innocent and carefree again just sounds really nice right now."

Again I couldn't argue with that. Life kills innocence.

"Also, I wish I had more self-respect. I think that's been a big problem with me lately, but I ain't sure how to go about gettin' more of it."

I really wasn't sure either. You can tell someone all day long what they need to do to better their life, but when it comes down to giving insightful suggestions on how to actually do it, people go blank. It may be because if they really started thinking of suggestions, they'd realize they also needed to be following them. And most people don't like to admit they need help.

"I wish I was a better person," Carolene continued. "I know that's pretty broad, but I mean like livin' a better life. I've been called a tramp, a slut, and I ain't gonna lie, I prob'ly deserved it. But I never been called words like loyal or faithful or honest. And I really wanna live the kinda life where someone actually calls me those things one day."

Carolene stopped as if she'd choked on the words. I didn't realize the activity was going to be so emotional, but I was really glad it was turning out to be enlightening.

"I just don't know if that's ever gonna happen."

Her words plowed into me as hard as Dr. Ellis' truck rammed into that deer years ago.

Jolene responded before me, "Of course it will, Care. The first step to gettin' to that point is realizin' your mistakes—which you've already done. Now ya just gotta work on fixin' 'em."

"Exactly," I added. "Couldn't've said it better myself. And we'll both be right there beside ya as ya try to figure it out. Just remember: there's a time to tear down and a time to rebuild—a time to keep and a time to throw away. Basically, Care, just keep on movin' forward and don't look back."

Carolene rushed over and threw her arms around me. We hadn't embraced like that in a while. Even when she came over to the house to talk about Scott she didn't let her guard down 100% like that.

Jolene reminded me it was my turn now, but Carolene, attempting to regain her composure, told me to wait because she had one more.

"Ok, now don't laugh," Carolene warned, "and don't think I'm bein' conceited—and no disrespect to you, Jo, after what you said,"—which of course grabbed Jolene's attention—"but I often wish I wasn't so pretty. I'd even settle for bein' kinda plain."

Jolene cut her eyes towards me and we didn't know whether to laugh or be angry. Both emotions felt right. Jolene asked her for clarification.

"So what are ya tryin' to say? You'd rather be like...me?" she sounded confused more than surprised. "One a the plain ones? Why the hell would ya want *that*?"

"A month ago," Carolene began telling her story, "I got pulled over by a police officer, and I'd clearly been drinkin' and was speedin'. I'd had a fight with Scott, and I'm not proud of myself, but it is what it is. But I had to practically beg him to give me a ticket. I didn't wanna be one a those pretty girls who uses her *powers* to beat the system like that."

Jolene gave a snort of laughter and asked if the cop ended up writing her out a ticket or not, to which Carolene pitifully shook her head no—"just a warning."

"Ha! I've had three tickets so far and I don't even drive that often!" Jolene declared. "Just when I used Rodney's truck to run errands and go grocery shoppin' while he was at work. If I had magic powers that'd get me off the hook, I'd sure as hell use 'em."

In a sudden change of emotions, Carolene's voice grew louder as she became more adamant in her point. Seeing her unravel before me like that made me realize that she had put a lot of thought into this particular wish, and into her list in general. I had to respect that.

"Ya don't understand, Jolene. I'd clearly broke the law," her voice struggled to stay steady, her eyes hazy, her arms animated as she spoke. "And I just wanted to be treated like every other law breaker. I know this all prob'ly sounds crazy to ya—or even stupid—but I was fall-down drunk, Jolene. I was sobbin' and speedin' and swervin' all over the road. And I just wanted to be given a goddamn ticket!"

Carolene burst into tears. The wind continued to throw our hair around as me and Jolene stood there, silent, listening to Carolene sob like she'd just repented her sins in front of the entire church congregation. Maybe it was because she felt bad, but Jolene was the first to speak.

"Care, listen, I'm sorry I didn't take ya seriously at first. I didn't realize it meant so much to ya, and I didn't understand the pains of bein', well, too pretty. I promise I'll never look at ya the same again, Carolene. And I mean that in the best possible way."

Carolene smiled, "I know what ya mean—thanks. That means a lot to me."

Wiping her eyes and trying to laugh off the sadness, Carolene said she was eager to hear my list. Jolene agreed. So, I took a deep breath and let it out. Like a rolling stone, I started off slow at first, then gained speed.

"I wish I could be satisfied," I began. "I never think anything's good enough. And I never think I've done enough, like I've let down everyone close to me, even let down myself."

I didn't stop for comments, just kept pushing through the list. I knew if I stopped I'd break down and wouldn't be able to finish.

"I wish I didn't give up so easily. I wish I wasn't so hard on myself. And I wish I could have kids."

I did have to stop for a breath after that but didn't look up from the paper.

"So put all that together and ya see why my life's gone nowhere—why my marriage failed and why I'm such a huge letdown to everyone."

"Jess," Carolene tried to interrupt but I wouldn't let her. I was talking uncontrollably fast now.

"And even though it might appear that I got everything all figured out—'cause that's what people always say: 'Oh, Jess, I wish I had everything figured out like you and know just what to say like you.' But that's the farthest from the truth. To be honest with ya, my life's in shambles. I ain't got *nothin'* figured out. And so with that said, the final wish I wrote down is: I often wish I was dead."

I stopped again to take a deep breath but quickly started back up before anyone else could speak.

"And before ya even ask, the answer's yes—but only one time. Pete was angry, told me I needed help. Then we got in a big fight and he said I wasn't the same person I used to be. So he told me to leave. That's why I moved back into the Old House. 'Cause I'm a failure."

I felt exhausted, drained. But I was sort of relieved that everything was out in the open now. I was glad they knew the truth. I just couldn't keep letting them look up to me when I was so far down. I hated to disappoint my sisters, though, but I hoped now we could all help each other out.

"Um, Jess?" Carolene spoke softly, like she was walking across a frozen lake, unsure if it would crack or not.

"I hope I ain't pryin' too deep here, but what happened that one time?"

I hated recalling those memories, but I knew I'd opened a can of worms that couldn't be resealed. So, embarrassed and ashamed, I described the details of that night...

41

"I took a knife from the kitchen—one a the big choppin' knives, and took it to the bedroom and laid it on the bed. I paced back 'n forth in front of it for a good hour, darin' myself to pick it up. I mean literally tauntin' myself to do it, sayin' aloud: *I betcha can't, I betcha won't.*"

"So...did you? Do it?" Carolene asked.

"Of course she didn't," Jolene fired back, I guess trying to defend me or something. "How could she've done it when she's standin' right here?"

"She could've done it and then the doctor rushed in and—"

"Wait, ain't nobody said nothin' 'bout a doctor," Jolene interrupted. "Plus, if the doctor did come then I'm sure ya woulda heard about it. Merilu's a small town, ya know. News like that'd travel fast."

"Wait a second!" I demanded, feeling the need to stop and clear things up, since I was the only one who actually knew how the story went. "Just lemme finish, ok? Now, to answer Carolene's question, yes and no. Yes, I used the knife, but there was no doctor."

"Told ya there wasn't no doctor," Jolene muttered to Carolene, which led to a light side-by-side shoving match that quickly ended when Jolene used her elbow.

I just shook my head at their childishness and continued talking right over them.

"Pete came home and found me layin' there sprawled out on the bed, bleeding from my side, all over the quilt his mother'd made us for a weddin' gift."

"So did Pete take ya to see the doctor then?" Jolene asked, stunned, noticeably ashamed of her juvenile behavior.

"Nope, I refused to go. Told Pete to just let me lay there and bleed to death, but he wouldn't let me. So he stitched me up himself with a needle and thread and put some salve on it and a bandage."

I pulled up my shirt for them to see the wound, which was beginning to scab nicely. But I knew it would leave a scar, and I was glad it would. It'd be my constant reminder that I'm not as strong as I often pretended to be, that I'm just as vulnerable and fragile as anybody else.

Carolene reached out to place her hand on the wound, and Jolene cocked her head to examine it. Both looked like they were about to bust out into tears.

"Now don't go cryin' on me. Ya know I'm not askin' for sympathy or nothin'. I just wanted to try to explain what I was feelin', what I been goin' through. I felt empty and overcome with emotion at the same time. That's why I felt like the knife was my only option. 'Cause no matter how hard I tried, nothin' I did would make it stop. And that's all I wanted, for it all just to stop."

"What exactly did ya wanna stop?" Carolene asked with innocence in her voice.

"Well, the sorrow over Mama that still tore me up inside, plus the guilt of not bein' the wife Pete deserved because of that. I just wanted all the pain to go away. Everything was so bottled up inside a me, it's like I couldn't function right."

As tears streamed down Carolene's cheek, Jolene took me by the hand. Not having talked to her in so long, I wasn't sure what she'd been through emotionally, but she must've been doing a lot of reflecting while she was off living in another state because she offered me some good advice.

"Listen, Jess. I been by myself a lot lately and had a lotta time to think. I came to understand that women have so much more emotion than men. We feel so much more. And men don't get it. They don't get women at all."

"Yeah, Pete didn't even try to understand. He just said I wasn't stable. Said he was afraid of me after my knife stunt. So afraid that he was even scared to sleep in the same bed with me—heck, be in the same house as me. That's why he said I should move out."

༒

We stood close to each other next to the side of the bridge and looked out over the water, taking a mental photograph, knowing we'd probably never come back there again. Then, like we'd discussed, we each took our lists and folded them into airplanes. A child could have done a better job than any one of us, but it wasn't a contest, so it didn't matter.

Just as I figured, everything we'd written about dealt with regrets, not our dreams. Dreams will give you something to live for, but regrets will keep you from living. Truth is, it's ridiculous to believe you can become anything you want to be. And you'll never accomplish anything in life until you learn to accept that.

"We can't keep dwellin' on these things," I told my sisters. "Everything we wrote on these pieces of paper has happened and we can't change that."

"'Cept gettin' a ticket!" Jolene interjected with a nudge to Carolene. "Some of us can't get one a those..."

We all laughed, even Carolene. Even though there was a deeper meaning behind it, she knew her wish sounded petty and most people would've loved to have been in her shoes. Because they were, in fact, really nice shoes.

"Yeah, well, or killin' yourself!" she replied, giving me a playful push on the shoulder. "That's one thing I'm *glad* you failed at."

I felt the anger behind her push, too, and it actually did hurt. But I had it coming, so I laughed it off.

"Well maybe not *all* our wishes need to come true then. I guess sometimes it's a good thing that they don't. Just like unanswered prayers. It's always for the best."

So with our arms drawn back, our planes ready to launch—the ones that contained our secrets, our fears, our shames—I gave a final dedication:

"Here's to unanswered prayers."

"And to ugly ducklings," Jolene tagged on.

"And here's to all the other pretty sluts out there," followed Carolene with a smirk.

Yeah, we all grinned at that.

Then we watched as our planes sailed through the air before gliding down towards the water. We stood there, our hands holding the railing as we leaned over, watching until all three had completely landed and the river had carried them out of sight.

Soon we were back in the truck and almost home.

42

"Hey, wake up!" I yelled.

Jolene and Carolene had decided to rest their eyes a bit before we got back. Carolene had her head on Jolene's shoulder and Jolene had leaned her head over onto Carolene's. They looked so sweet and peaceful, and I knew they were both tired, but after such an exhausting trip, the sight of the Old House made me so happy I couldn't contain myself.

"We're home! Oh thank you, Lord. Wake up, Care, we're back! Jolene!"

"Oh praise the Lord," Carolene perked up, working to get her head out from under her sound asleep sister's.

Jolene's head dropped and she sprung up, confused. But when she saw what was ahead, her face lit up.

And then the chattering began. The truck was filled with repeats of *Whatta we do now?* and *How'd we get back so fast?* and groans of *My back's killing me!* and *My butt hurts!*

Turning off onto the long driveway, we acted like we were pulling into Disney World, which I hadn't been to but heard was amazing.

Once we were out of the truck, I stood there in front of

the Old House and took it all in. I wanted to burn an image of it in my mind as best I could. The details, the colors—every rotten board and every loose shingle.

Click.

It was a photograph I hoped would never fade.

⚯

Jolene said she was eager to see inside, since she hadn't seen it in so long. But when she got to the door she stopped. Me and Carolene turned around, saw her hesitation, and asked what was the matter.

"Oh, nothin'," she said. "Just a little nervous, I guess. Not quite sure what I'm gonna feel once I step inside."

But as she slowly took a step in, joy crept onto her face. And the further she came in and the more she looked around, the bigger her smile grew, and her anxiety was gone in a matter of moments. Plus it seemed like walking through that door made her young again, picking at me and nagging me.

"Eww, Jess, this place is filthy," she groaned in disgust. "I thought you'd been stayin' here. Ya sure Pete didn't kick ya out 'cause ya forgot how to clean?"

I knew she was kidding, but I gave her a light shove anyway. And it's not like she wasn't speaking the truth—the place was pretty filthy. I just hadn't had the time or energy to do much tidying up. Isn't that what everyone says?

Me and Carolene followed Jolene as she toured the Old House, roaming around curiously, cautiously, reminiscing.

Jolene was surprised how much the place hadn't changed. I told her I had tried getting rid of stuff but just couldn't do it—not by myself. It just made me too sad.

Jolene stopped and stared at the attic steps, but I grabbed her arm and pulled her on passed.

"Later."

Then I escorted them back downstairs, and it didn't take long before we were piled up on the couch with a glass of sweet tea I'd made, telling old stories and laughing. Just relishing in the happiness of being back home, all together again.

∞

But sundown soon came, which reminded me we had a more pressing issue we needed to discuss. So I counted up how many days we had left until the construction crew would be showing up.

"So, today's Thursday—where did the time go?—and Mr. Poole said they'd start first thing this Monday morning. So, ladies, it looks like we got tomorrow, Saturday, and Sunday to get everything done."

I was upset we didn't have very long to work, but at the same time, after all that'd happened, I was grateful to have those three days. It could've been worse.

"Yeah I'm glad ya didn't count today," Carolene said. "I don't think I could do it. All I wanna do is sleep."

I told her not to worry about it, that I was physically and mentally exhausted too. All three of us needed a good night's rest. And I was so thankful to be sleeping flat again, in my own bed.

"Hey, Jess, is there any possible way to get some kinda extension from the man ya talked to?" Jolene complained. "I'm so tired I could *sit* here for three days. I mean just not move. Pee all over myself."

"Eww, Jolene!" I yelled at her.

She laughed, and so did Carolene. But I didn't find it too funny. Jolene knew that would gross me out, and I was far too tired and ill for all that. My nerves were shot and I just wanted to lay down, pull the sheets over my head, and close my eyes. I knew for a fact I'd be out in a matter of seconds.

"What?" Jolene played innocent, holding her arms out wide. "Don't worry, Jess, I ain't gonna do it. I'm just sayin' I could."

Then she turned back towards Carolene and continued planning out her idea.

"Yeah, then at the end of the day," she said, looking to make sure I was listening, "I'd just flip the couch cushion over to the dry side. No big deal."

Carolene laughed like a kid.

"Jolene!" I yelled out. "Stop it!"

43

The coffee pot was earning its keep the next morning. I didn't want to waste any time, so once I got dressed, I started going through the drawers of the buffet and the china cabinet, getting an idea of just how much junk had accumulated over the years.

Carolene joined me soon after, but Jolene took just as long to get ready as she used to. I even had to yell out *hurry up* several times to get her moving.

Once she was finally downstairs and had poured her some coffee, we all started sorting through the knick-knacks and dividing up the leftover furniture among us. Everything seemed to be going smoothly until Carolene had to go and be the voice of reason.

"So...what're any of us gonna do with this furniture? I mean, none of us really have a place of our own anymore. Me and Jess were kicked out and Jolene just got back. So what're we gonna do with it?"

She was right. As of Monday morning I was going to be homeless. We all were.

"This is a crazy idea, but what if we just stayed here?"

Jolene suggested. "All three of us."

"Kinda like old times, huh?" Carolene chuckled at the thought.

Then as we got quiet a moment and mulled over the idea, a smile spread wide across my face. My mind was buzzing with ideas, but I knew I couldn't get ahead of myself.

"Ok, how 'bout this," I began. "We clean up and clean out everything just like we'd planned—and take care of Mama, of course. Then come Monday mornin' I'll call Mr. Poole and tell 'em we decided we wanta stay and ask 'em—or *beg* 'em, actually—not to go through with tearin' the house down."

"What about the money?" Carolene asked. "He's already gave ya half of it, though, right?"

"Well don't ya 'member, silly?" I lightly bopped her on the head with my palm. "We robbed a gas station. We have more than enough to pay 'em back."

Carolene laughed and blamed her memory lapse on lack of good sleep.

"How could I forget? We gotta whole *bag* full a money!" she waved her arms in the air.

"Ok, here's...thirty dollars," I counted out all the money I had left in my purse. "I don't even 'member how much money's in the bag but it's definitely enough to pay back Mr. Poole. Plus we might even could buy some new furniture."

Carolene and Jolene jumped on that idea, already starting to plan out what we needed and arguing over what would look best where.

"Speakin' of the robbery," Jolene turned to me. "You're gonna hafta tell me that whole story. Ya just kinda skimmed over it before."

I agreed, and as I began telling the story of Ted and Cheap Al's Quick Stop, Carolene offered to go get the bag of money, saying she didn't want to hear it again because it made her sad. A minute later she returned empty-handed and asked me where I'd put it.

"Remember?" I began. "We were at the police station and I took out some a the money to put in my purse for the bail we *luckily* didn't have to pay. Then I put the bag under the driver's seat."

Solemnly, Carolene added, "Yeah, but that was in the Eldorado..."

"Oh good God, Jess!" Jolene shouted. "Tell me ya took the money outta the car before we left."

"Umm..."

My heart stopped while my mind raced. I racked my brain trying to remember what happened, backtracking my steps all the way back to:

Ain't no way I'm gettin' back in that thang.

"No, I 'member now—it was Jolene!" I recalled, pointing at her, her mouth open and eyebrows rigged, looking ready to go on the defense. "Ya threw the keys down the road! *That's* why I never got it out. 'Cause you was complainin' 'bout not wantin' to get back in the car just 'cause there'd been a dead woman back there."

"Hey now, don't go blamin' this all on me," Jolene snapped back, grabbing and attacking me like we were kids again, our fists full of each other's hair. "Sorry for tryin' to look out for your stupid health!"

We rolled around until Carolene jumped in and pulled us off of each other like a referee. We were all on edge, but I guess this incident pushed us right on over. Once the ref sent us to our own "corners" we stewed over our stupidity. Sitting there, I buried my face in my folded arms and was silent, my mind once again recounting the events of the past few days.

ಬ

Time passed. No one spoke, just worked. Me and Jolene had apologized to each other, but the notion that our wonderful idea had been stomped on by reality still stung like a wasp bite.

But it didn't stop us from trying to think of a new idea, though. The gears could almost be heard turning in our heads.

"What if..." Jolene started but trailed off.

"What if what?" me and Carolene both insisted, desperate for a good idea after having come up with so many bad ones between the two of us.

Silent, Jolene seemed to be working out the details, fine tuning her idea. When she thought she had it good enough to share, a big grin appeared and she sounded excited, rattling off the idea like it was an escape plan to break out of prison.

"Ok, so, I know we ain't got the money to give back for the house...but we *will* be gettin' the other half of the money the city owes us, right? And how much is that again?"

"Five thousand," I answered.

"So why don't we take all this old furniture and have a great big yard sale? Add that money to the five thousand we'll be gettin' and...then we buy a house. I know it ain't gonna be enough to buy a huge, nice house or anything, but I'm sure it'd be enough to put a roof over the heads of three homeless women."

It was a good idea. No, a *great* idea. And definitely the best we could've ever come up with given the circumstances. I really wish we could've figured out how to keep the Old House, though. But like Mama told me when I didn't win the costume contest we had at church one Halloween: "When life gives ya lemons, make a lemon pie out of 'em, then invite over all your friends for pie and fellowship!"

After some chattering and planning details of our new idea, we got back to work, loading some random stuff into some random boxes we'd gotten from behind Picket's Market and from the nice man at the nearby gas station. Then we stacked them into a big pile in the living room. The thought of where we were going to store everything until we had a house—or until we could have a yard sale—did cross our minds, but we were too busy to focus on that. We knew some kind of solution would present itself. Or at least that's what we prayed.

This routine continued for hours. I had stopped and made us some peanut butter and jelly sandwiches, just something to give us some energy. But we worked like machines, like machines on a mission.

Sundown came and the sky looked beautiful, but my muscles were screaming. Not like I did the heavy lifting by myself, but my body just wasn't used to being pushed that hard.

As I collapsed onto the couch, my arms were Jell-O, my stomach growled like a bear, and I had a really bad hankering for some lemon pie.

44

The next day was much like the last, but we'd moved on to the upstairs—the bedrooms. First up was Carolene's.

"Looks like it always did," I said. "Like a Barbie Doll lives in here."

Jolene laughed, picking up a pink tutu, slipping it on, and dancing around like a ballerina. But Carolene was defensive about it and told us to cut it out.

Digging through the pile of junk under the bed, though, Jolene uncovered a board game and we laughed at the sight of it, thinking about how much fun we had playing it as kids.

"Let's play!" Carolene yelled, and we wasted at least an hour coming up with crazy words, trying to outdo each other in Scrabble.

"Querzy?" I doubted. "Really, Jolene?"

Of course, I had to be the bad guy and start taking up the letters, reminding my sisters that we still had a lot of work left to be done. Carolene called me a bully and Jolene said I was being querzy. Whatever that meant.

I mean, I wished we could've played all day, too, but if we didn't do the work, who was going to do it? It stunk being the rational one.

We tackled one room at a time, putting stuff in boxes and carrying them downstairs. Then we'd go back upstairs for more, then back down. Up, down, repeat. It seemed like it would never end, and before it was even sundown, my legs were just about give out.

The pace slowed down every time one of us would see something memorable. *Aww* would be the beginning of a five-minute backstory on where the item came from and why it was so important.

"I said I'd never leave this behind," Carolene said about her favorite blanket. "Grandma made one for each of us, 'member?"

Me and Jolene looked at each other and smirked at the fact we were thinking the same thing: we had no idea where our Grandma-blankets were.

Then when Jolene entered our old bedroom, she instantly became just as sentimental.

"Oh wow—I been lookin' all over for this," Jolene said as she held up a ratty sweat shirt, which was at least three sizes too small now.

But I was just as guilty of acting that way as the others. As I sat there in the room I grew up in—Jolene on my bed, Carolene next to me on the floor—I actually cried over an old, headless doll. I'm not sure if I was more upset over the flood of memories she brought on or the fact that she was missing her head.

But as we sat there, taking advantage of our break, a thought hit me like a Rock 'Em Sock 'Em Robot.

"Hey, ya'll 'member what Mama always used to say 'bout how life's a backdrop?"

"Say, I ain't thought about that since I was a kid," Jolene said, smiling at the thought.

"Me neither," Carolene said. "Ya'll ever figure out what she meant?" she added timidly, hoping she wasn't the only one that didn't know.

"Well," I began. "I never put much thought into it. I always just nodded when Mama asked me if I understood. I figured if she was sayin' it then it must be good advice."

"Yeah, that's me too," my sisters agreed.

But it was like being there, all three of us together, sparked a sudden bolt of inspiration. And I started rambling off the top of my head, and was surprised it actually seemed to make sense.

"Maybe she just meant that all the things we regard as *life* are really just background for the real story, the story that's unfoldin' before our eyes. Ya know, like a picture or a movie'll have a backdrop. So I was thinkin', maybe she just meant not to get all wrapped up in unnecessary things, not to lose sight of what's important."

"Jess," Jolene said, her hands crossed over her heart. "You are my hero."

Then she slapped me in the face with a pillow from off the bed.

※

We worked until we got tired. And when we got tired, I would give pep talks like a football coach, telling them we had to keep pushing forward for Mama's sake. That would get us through another hour or two and then we'd hit another wall.

My body was ready to call it a day, but my mind was racing. Knowing we only had one more day left, I was starting to panic, wondering if we were going to get everything finished in time.

I knew the attic was going to take a while, and most importantly I wanted to be able to spend the bulk of our last day burying Mama and not be rushed. I wanted to give her the proper burial she deserved, what she had deserved to have a long time ago.

And though I wished we had at least another day so I could prepare a speech and jot down some Bible verses to say over her grave, we had to work with what we had and make the most of it.

With that in mind, I tightened the reigns and led my team to the finish line, at least for the day. And before I knew it we'd gotten the entire upstairs cleaned out, and everything had been brought to the downstairs pile, which was becoming a pretty massive beast of its own.

Looking around at the emptiness of the house, sadness

began to come over me, but still, I felt accomplished.

And I felt proud.

But most of all I felt exhausted.

45

Sunday morning and the sky was full of clouds. Jolene was in the back, with Carolene in front of her, as I took the first step up towards the attic. Taking my foot off the stairs and placing it onto the attic floor, I could feel the disturbing lies and taste the devious secrets lingering in the stale air. With each step the floor creaked as if it had something important to say, a secret it badly wanted to let out.

The door was heavier than I remembered and dust flew everywhere. I was worried about the insects and rodents and feces, but I should've been more worried about the smell, which slapped me in the face and tried to push me back down the stairs.

But once in, we all three stood there, our noses and mouths covered but our eyes wide, taking it all in.

"There's a lotta junk up here," Jolene stated the obvious.

So we decided to each take a corner and start separating things into four piles: one for each of us and a trash pile. This seemed to make the task a lot less daunting. And once we finally got our corners cleaned out, we all slowly walked towards the last one.

"Uh, how 'bout let's go through these boxes here first before...ya know," Carolene suggested.

So we did. First thing I pulled out was an old pie-baking ribbon—first prize. Then Carolene unwrapped a large solid grey t-shirt with a big rip down the back (I'm pretty sure it was mine, but I wouldn't swear by it) and uncovered a pair of glasses. None of us ever wore glasses so we assumed they must've been Mama's.

"But I don't 'member her ever wearin' glasses," Jolene said, trying to think back.

I said I figured they were probably just for reading and that she was probably embarrassed by them and never wore them.

"Prob'ly right," Jolene snorted, trying them on, looking uncomfortable and foolish. "I woulda been embarrassed too."

Under that was my diploma from Hopefield College. I snatched it up, wiped the dust off the glass, and read it aloud.

"Jessabelle Mavery Johansson. Associate of Science in History."

I gave a little huff and threw it in my pile.

Once we were through emptying out the boxes, my eyes got watery as I looked up at the blanket that covered my best friend, my mama. *How were we going to do this? Where was she going to go now?*

It was a whole lot easier in the beginning, when we first put her up there...

※

See, back when Dr. Ellis brought Mama home from the hospital, and after we'd exhausted all of our other options, I explained to my sisters that the attic would be the only logical place for the time being, until we could figure something better out. It took some debating, especially with Carolene who thought the idea was just too creepy at first, but we finally all agreed it was best.

I told Carolene to go up and prop open the attic door and start clearing some junk out of one of the corners. Once me and Jolene got Mama wrapped in the tissue, we wrapped a sheet around her and pinned it.

Honestly, Mama looked pretty ridiculous, if not scary, but we were young and thought we had done a good job. If I had to do it all over again, I would have definitely wrapped her better, maybe with some quilts. Just something thicker.

But the hardest part of the whole idea was carrying her. It took all the might of the three of us to carry Mama's body up those attic stairs. We moved carefully and as synchronized as an Olympic figure skating team. Didn't even drop her once.

When we were finished arranging her, we stood back and admired our work. Sitting in a rocking chair with blankets and newspapers covering her from head to toe, the pile of clutter that we called Mama was definitely a conspicuous sight to behold, if anyone was to ever behold it. But we made sure no one ever set foot up there, not even us.

Before we closed the door on the attic for good, we packed up a few boxes with some random things that we just wanted to get out of sight, mostly things of Mama's, like her apron and the handkerchief my father gave her when they were young and maybe even in love. Things we didn't want to throw away but didn't know what to do with. Things that would've been constant reminders and sad memories.

I guess along with all that stuff, my diploma found its way into one of those boxes. Funny how I never even missed it. All that work I put in—the reading, the studying, and trying to fit class time in with all my chores and other responsibilities—and I had nothing to show for it. Except that framed piece of paper, covered in a half-inch of dust.

☙

We all hovered around Mama, unsure of where to begin. It'd been so long since we put her up there that I was kind of afraid to touch her now. I mean, I'd been educated by enough *Hitchcock* and *Twilight Zone* episodes since then to know that flesh rots away, leaving nothing but bones. And though we couldn't—and didn't want to—see what her body had decomposed to, I had to assume that the wrapped up corpse was now a mere skeleton. And we'd have to be much gentler with her when we moved her.

So I leaned down to slide out the rocker from the corner. Just as the chair began to scrape against the wooden floor, Jolene grabbed my arm.

I jerked my head around towards her, yelling out, "What's the ma—"

But I slammed on the brakes and cut myself off when I saw her finger over her mouth, the universal symbol for *hush*.

Like a cartoon, I tried to swallow the words that had already slipped out, but to no avail, of course.

Carolene was frozen just like she was when Abraham was coming towards us talking out of his head, and just like when Ted had his gun drawn on us. At least she hadn't made a noise like I had.

Jolene glared at me, her eyes wide, the color fading from her face, just like she'd seen a ghost. And I actually wished that's what happened because I'm sure that would've been far less terrifying.

Carefully pronouncing each syllable so we could better read her lips, Jolene mouthed the words:

Some-bo-dy's com-ing.

46

Now there were three statues in the attic—me, bent over clutching a rocking chair with my mouth dropped to the floor, another statue with one hand on my arm and forever shushing us with the other, and one off to the side with her hands covering her mouth as if she was holding in a sound that couldn't be stopped, only contained.

"Jess? Carolene?" a voice called from downstairs. "You here? I saw a truck outside and figured it must've belonged to one of ya'll."

"Dr. Ellis!" Carolene exclaimed, a little too loudly.

The looks me and Jolene shot her instantly brought her hands back over her mouth.

"Carolene, that you? You upstairs?"

"Ya didn't lock the front door?" I whispered as angry as I could whisper. "You were the last one to go outside. Why didn't ya lock it when ya came back in?"

"Why would I lock it?" she asked sincerely, bless her heart.

Dramatically, I rolled my head around and Jolene wiped the sweat from her brow.

"Jesus, Carolene, you're a wonder."

As Dr. Ellis' footsteps grew louder, closer, I got a lump in the pit of my stomach the size of a cantaloupe. I couldn't think—I was dumbfounded. But Carolene, much to me and Jolene's surprise, came to our rescue and jumped up right as penny loafers clacked against the wooden attic steps.

"Dr. Ellis!" she exclaimed, rushing out the door towards him. "It's so good to see ya. How's things been goin'? And how's your father? I ain't heard one a his sermons in years. Betcha he figures I done skipped town or somethin'."

The string of small talk and open-ended questions she was able to rattle off was quite impressive. Yeah, maybe she laid it on a little too strong with a question overload, but she was able to fast-talk the doctor back downstairs into the parlor.

"Yeah, Dad's good. Listen, I'm sorry for barging in on you like this," Dr. Ellis told her. "It's just that I saw the truck, and the front door was unlocked, so I... I hope you don't mind."

"No, not at all, doctor. I'm glad ya stopped by. I'd offer ya a seat but there ain't none left. Done got 'em all packed up."

"That's quite alright, Carolene. So, is it just you here? Whose truck's that out there?" Dr. Ellis pointed out the door. "I'm sorry for all the questions."

"Oh it's fine. And yeah, just me. I was gettin' some stuff from upstairs and Scott lemme borrow his truck for a little while."

"Oh that was nice of him—is it new? And you mean

upstairs as in the attic, right? I heard you run down the wooden steps."

"Yeah, it *was* real nice of 'em," she sort of-not really answered.

After a brief silence, Dr. Ellis looked around at the mass of stuff and said, "Yeah, I heard you sold the house and they're going to put up a grocery store... So, what are you going to do with all this stuff—keep it or sell it?"

No answer, just another, longer moment of silence. Carolene stared at the door, thinking of her next move.

"So...what all's up there?" Dr. Ellis just pushed forward. "The attic, I mean. I've never been up there. Maybe you could show me around."

He looked in the direction of the attic and shifted as if he was going to begin walking that way. But Carolene sidestepped over in front of him and smiled in concealed discontent.

"That's right, a Food Giant," she quickly replied at last, now swinging her arms impatiently and noticeably cutting her eyes towards the door. "Yeah, we're all glad to see the house go."

She stopped, noticing her mistake, and gave a little chuckle.

"Sorry. I mean I'm really sad to see ya. You'll have to stop by 'n visit when ya got more time."

Dr. Ellis must have felt unwanted because he made a step towards the door and said, "Well, if you need anything, just let me know."

A loud *THUD* came from outside and both Carolene and Dr. Ellis jerked their heads around.

"What the heck was that?" he shouted, starting to run to the window before being blocked by Carolene like a point guard covering his opponent.

Though startled, she was trying really hard to remain calm.

"Umm, yeah I ain't too sure. But there's been a lotta dogs come 'round here lately. Ya know, lotta dogs live 'round here. So it was prob'ly just one a them. Pretty sure it was. Lots of 'em live 'round here, ya know."

If nothing else I had to give her credit for trying. Also, about that time, Jolene rushed downstairs, panting.

"Carolene, ya didn't tell me Dr. Ellis was still here—I mean, is here. I mean, it's great to see ya, doc. Been a long time."

"Well hey, Jolene... Yeah, it's been forever. I didn't think you were here..." he said in a leery tone, cutting his eyes over at Carolene, who looked like she'd just opened the door to a surprise party.

Between the puzzled look on Dr. Ellis' face and the thunderstruck expression on Carolene's, Jolene almost started laughing.

"Oh yeah? Well...I wasn't. I mean, I just got here," Jolene stammered out, still trying to catch her breath. "Came in the back."

About that time, I walked downstairs.

"Dr. Ellis! What a surprise."

"Jess!" Carolene exclaimed before Dr. Ellis could even react. "You're here too? Ya musta rode with Jolene, huh?"

You could tell Dr. Ellis was confused and somewhat suspicious. His mouth hung open and his eyebrows were all crinkled up.

"What's, uh...going on here, ladies? Nothing's really making too much sense right now."

"Carolene," I jumped in the conversation. "Why don't ya take Dr. Ellis on a little tour of the house, like a farewell tour."

"Ya know," Dr. Ellis replied, switching gears at the suggestion, "I'd really like to see the attic. I was just saying how I'd never seen it."

"Well there ya go," I said. "Carolene'll have to show ya the attic then, won't she?"

"But, uh," Carolene nervously searched for the right words. "Ain't the attic kinda nasty? Full a, ya know...dead things?"

"Nah, we took care of all those dead things," Jolene informed her, with a big ole fake smile spread across her face.

As Carolene cautiously showed Dr. Ellis around the house, Jolene and me quietly snuck out back where Mama lay on the ground with a rope tied around her waist. But I can't take credit for that. That was Jolene's brilliant idea.

∽

See, Jolene had tied one end of the rope around her waist while I tied the other end around Mama's. Then Jolene braced herself against the wall and grabbed ahold of one of the wooden poles that held up the roof while I, trying to be gentle about it, pushed Mama out the attic window.

Jolene had to hold on tight because when the rope slack ran out, it tried to pull her out with it. I stuck my head out the window to see how far down Mama was. I figured she was no more than ten feet from the ground so I told Jolene to let her go.

Jolene untied the rope from around her waist and it jumped out of her hands before she even knew it. I watched the wrapped up mass hit the ground with a loud *THUD*, hoping the bones stayed intact and that no one else heard it.

Jolene ran downstairs, assuming Dr. Ellis had already left. I followed shortly after. But first I just stood there a moment, staring down at the ground, wondering if we were doing the right thing.

But I didn't have time to think negatively. I may have had no idea what was going to happen next, but I did have an idea where we could bury Mama's remains, somewhere I was pretty sure she'd like after all.

47

Behind the house me and Jolene untied the rope around Mama and dragged her over behind a row of bushes, out of sight, and came back inside through the back door.

❧

"Dr. Ellis?" Jolene called out. "Dr. Ellis?"

He promptly came downstairs, shaking his head, declaring, "Dead rats, huh? I still don't think they'd smell *that* bad."

Poor Carolene looked plum frazzled.

"Dr. Ellis," Jolene interrupted. "I hate to say this, but we got lots a packin' to do before sundown, and—"

"Yeah, I was going to offer my help," he interrupted, rolling up his sleeves. "You got any big, heavy boxes you need a big, strong man like me to carry?" he asked with a laugh.

I responded immediately. The words slipped out without me even knowing it. And they were as dry and stiff as clothes on a clothesline.

"Listen, Doc. We came this far, just the three of us, so I think we can carry a couple a goddamn boxes ourselves."

Saying that brought me back to my days as a careless

youngster. And I didn't regret it. At that moment I thought my father—may he spend eternity in the fiery flames of hell—would have been proud of his daughter. Or maybe not.

Had I become that callous? That cynical? Was I now just a vulgar-talking, men-hating felon?

Dr. Ellis' jaw dropped and you could tell he didn't know exactly how to respond to that.

Taken aback and somewhat appalled, he told us, "I see you're all under a lot of stress, so I'll just let you finish your cleaning. I'll just check on ya'll later."

Then he walked out. Once he was outside, my sisters jumped all over me.

"Shh," I quieted them. "Listen."

Dr. Ellis' truck roared and the tires could be heard chewing up and spitting out chunks of gravel as it sped away. I took a deep breath.

"Ok, now, let's just finish this," I announced.

୧

Outside, we assumed our positions: Jolene held up Mama's shoulder area, Carolene underneath her back, and I grabbed her feet. She was actually a much lighter load than before, but all the wrapping still gave her some weight. While we walked—as fast as we could under the circumstances—Jolene filled Carolene in on how Mama got outside and in the bushes.

"Really?" she sounded somewhat impressed.

Then a couple of seconds later, the pieces started to come together for her.

"Oh! So *that* was the loud noise. But one more question..." she asked as we continued carrying Mama away from the house and towards the woods. "Where are we goin'? I mean, where are we takin' her?"

☙

The bushes and trees had really grown up since we were last out there. It'd been, oh, I don't even know how many years since I'd traveled through those woods. Where I used to fly through there with ease, jumping over stumps and pushing limbs out of my way, now it was a battle just to make it a few yards without having to stop and carefully step over the stumps and ease by those limbs. Of course I'd never been carrying a dead body through there either.

"Wait!" I began lowering Mama's legs and my sisters followed suit in easing her to the ground. "We need a shovel."

"Dammit!" Jolene yelled in frustration, slumped over with her hands resting on her knees, out of breath, sweat dripping off her brow and nose, her entire body covered in dust and dirt that we'd stirred up from our shuffled footsteps.

"I'll get it," Carolene graciously volunteered.

She took off towards the house but stopped and turned around.

"Hey, ya want me to getta wheelbarrow while I'm there?"

"Yes!" I exclaimed as if she'd asked if we wanted her to rub the magic lamp three times or not.

She was back before we knew it, and we carefully lifted Mama into the wheelbarrow. Then I held the shovel while Jolene pushed. Carolene helped me clear a path.

Finally out of the woods, we worked our way through a field of tall grass until we were finally there.

"My God..." I was beside myself.

"What happened?" Carolene asked, looking at me for an answer, but I was just as confused as she was.

"I don't know. It's not like I ever came out here. I ain't been here since ya'll have."

"The creek!" Carolene shrieked. "What happened?"

"Yeah how could a whole creek," Jolene added, "just... I mean, it's gone."

It had never occurred to us that those droughts we'd had over the years had played more of a toll on the land than just with the crops.

"So what was the plan anyway?" Carolene asked. "You never said."

I looked down at Mama's body, then at the stretch of dirt and rocks spread out before us, dead grass surrounding it.

"Everything's gone," I was still amazed.

I walked around with my arms stretched out and my fingers spread apart, imagining I was running my fingers through the lilies that once covered the now bare ground.

"Just didn't think it'd be like this," I said mostly to myself.

Looking around, I found what I thought was the spot where me and Pete had our first kiss and where I saw my first shooting star.

"But I guess it'll hafta do."

∽

We took turns digging, all the way up until sundown. Once we got a hole big enough and deep enough, we carefully picked Mama up, gently placed her inside—still covered from head to toe—and shoveled dirt on her until she was gone and the hole was flat. Jolene, Carolene, and me all held hands and prayed silently.

Tears poured from our eyes, mixing with the dirt on our faces, and fell to the ground. We cried so much that we could have filled that creek back up if we stood there long enough.

Jolene pushed the wheelbarrow back and I carried the shovel. Once we were back at the house, we just got in the truck and left, leaving behind all the boxes and furniture, having decided we didn't really need any of that backdrop stuff anymore.

Then for the last time, we slowly drove away from the house we'd shared so many memories in. Back to our own lives, back to our own personal issues.

I dropped Carolene off at Scott's, who luckily hadn't reported his truck stolen yet. But that didn't mean he wasn't beyond furious when he found out we'd taken it and left it on the side of the road somewhere that we'd probably never be able to find again. He tried to strike Carolene across the face like he'd nonchalantly done so many times in the past, but this time she stood up for herself. And her act of bravery landed her a trip to the hospital.

But there's a time to plant and a time to harvest.

Dr. Ellis took real good care of Carolene and—despite the fact that Carolene couldn't leave her bed—they became inseparable. Dr. Ellis would stay late by her bedside, share funny stories with her, and even leave flowers for when she woke each morning. The age difference didn't bother them, so it didn't bother me or Jolene none either.

It was nice seeing her happy again. I guess the feelings between them that had been planted long ago had finally grown to maturity. And now it was time to reap the joy of new love.

It didn't take Jolene long either before she took up with another man. Except this time I knew him, having grown up together in church. Dr. Ellis' nephew, Noah, was a few years her junior, but he and Jolene hit it off real well. At least I knew she wouldn't be dragged off across the country.

I joked with her about how living in Merilu now made it much easier for me and Carolene to keep an eye on her. Because we were done with traveling. Heck, we weren't even allowed back in parts of Kentucky. And I'm sure the rest of the country didn't want us coming to their cities either.

As for me, I went crawling back to my husband, begging for his forgiveness. I promised that I would do something about the depression if he'd stick by my side. I wasn't sure if he would be up for the challenge, but he surprised me by wrapping his arm around me, just like he did when we were kids and Mama was sick, and told me everything was going to be okay.

And although I couldn't stop the occasional bouts of depression or suicidal thoughts from popping into my head every once in a while, I knew my family would always be there to support me every step of the way. My life wasn't perfect, but I did have the endless love I'd fantasized about.

☙

Sometimes when I close my eyes at night, and there's no lights shining except a dash of moonlight sneaking in through the blinds, I picture the smile on Mama's face the day I graduated college. You would have thought she'd won a million dollars.

But then I start wondering if she'd be disappointed in me if she knew I was a housewife and—finally, after trying so many times—a full-time mother now. There's no shame in that kind of life, now don't get me wrong. And I'm sure Mama would be proud of me no matter what. But that was the whole reason I had begged her into letting me go to college. I mean, I figured me and Pete would one day get married, but back then I never wanted kids. Plus I'd planned on getting a job and making my own money and taking care of myself, Pete around or not.

Somewhere along the way, though, things got all messed up. Seems like that happens most of the time.

And every time I'd start to daydream about what I could have been, how I was going to make a name for myself, and how I thought I was going to be so different from all the other exhausted-looking mothers I knew, I pictured Mama kneeling down in front of me, pushing my hair out of my face, giving me her customary advice:

"No matter where ya go, and no matter how ya get there, life's a backdrop."

൞

That's how I *wished* our lives would have played out—like a real-life fairytale ending.

But just like Ana said, "There's no such thing as happily ever after."

And I guess that's true because I found out pretty quick that you can't drive across the country and cause as much mayhem and break as many laws as we did without suffering any repercussions, no matter the reason, no matter how good our intentions were. Our sins had finally caught up to us.

48

We had just gotten back from burying Mama, just starting to clean up, when there was a knock at the door. I was mid-leg into some clean pants, Carolene was splashing water on her face in the kitchen, and Jolene had already stripped down to her panties and was lying on the floor, sprawled out like a bearskin rug.

As Jolene covered up with a blanket, I opened the door ever so slightly.

"Dr. Ellis! What are you—"

And then another man stepped out from behind him and I jerked open the door.

"Pete!"

"Listen, Jess," Carolene's fairytale beau began, Pete just standing behind him, solemnly. "We know what's going on, what all ya'll have done. I mean, it's all over the news."

I was speechless, barely able to mumble out some sounds.

Carolene and Jolene were quiet, too. If I was Jolene, though, I wouldn't have worried too much. She really hadn't done anything wrong. But as for me and Carolene, I knew we had a lot of explaining and a lot of repenting to do.

"Pete, just listen. I know ya prob'ly think we're crazy, but it was all done for a reason. Ya gotta believe me."

"I ain't gotta believe a *damn* word ya say, Jess. I mean, I knew ya had some mental problems and all, but this...this is just... I mean, Jess, you're a criminal for God's sake!"

Seeing Pete so upset again made me feel wretched, disappointed. But very defensive, though I didn't have much of a case to argue.

"Well if you and Dr. Ellis and everybody else think we're a bunch a criminals, then why didn't he call us out on it before, huh?"

"I didn't mention it before 'cause I didn't know what ya'll were capable of," Dr. Ellis explained. "I had to be cautious. Plus, I was giving you the opportunity to open up to me. Instead, you threw me out."

Though his words were very sobering, I started to feel incredibly nauseous and woozy.

"But what about the attic?" I asked. "Why were ya wantin' to see it so bad?"

"Jess, I know what's up there. Pete does too. Heck, most everybody does. I'm surprised you even thought it was a secret. Merilu's a small town, you know."

"No," Carolene jumped in. "Ya wanted to go up there 'cause ya didn't know. Ya thought ya did but ya didn't. There's no way."

"Carolene, I just wanted to finally see for myself, but obviously you've moved her. You don't think I knew what that smell was when we went up there? Believe me when I say that everyone knows."

※

Faint sirens grew louder, followed by the slam of a car door.

"The cops!" I gasped as my heart leaped out of my chest and dove out the nearest window.

"Yeah, I know. I called 'em," Pete spoke frankly. "I was thinkin' 'bout gettin' ya some counselin' or somethin', but ya crossed the line, Jess. I gotta let 'em take ya."

As more sirens approached, all I knew to do was run to my sisters for comforting. I felt responsible—Jolene hadn't done anything and Carolene was so innocent, just going along with what I talked her into doing.

I knew what I had to do—turn myself in and say that I was the ringleader, that my sisters had unwittingly gotten themselves involved in my plans. Maybe that would keep them out of trouble.

And then the door was kicked in and two officers rushed inside, barking orders at us, just like in the movies.

"Freeze! Get your hands up. All of you," one of the officers pointed his gun in my, Pete, and Dr. Ellis' direction. "Now down on your knees."

We all did as he said, even Pete and Dr. Ellis. Though Dr.

Ellis continued trying to explain the situation and who he and Pete were.

The other officer's gun was aimed towards Carolene and Jolene. Carolene had done as the officer ordered, but Jolene stood there, her arms crossed in defiance, refusing to follow instructions.

"Nah, I ain't goin' back to jail," she announced, looking over at me and slowly shaking her head from side to side. "Ain't no way. They just gonna hafta shoot me I guess."

"Jolene, stop it!" I ordered. "Listen to me. Ya didn't do anything—ya ain't goin' to jail. So don't be stupid and just do as he says."

"Nah, Jess, we done got in way too much trouble," Jolene admitted. "They ain't gonna lemme go. I'm gonna be right back behind bars."

I wasn't sure what had gotten into her but I continued to plead with her to cut it out, to just calm down. The officer was getting noticeably nervous, shifting his weight to his other foot, sweat dripping from his forehead, his eyes and gun locked on Jolene.

"Ma'am I'm gonna ask you one more time to put your arms in the air and drop down to your knees."

But Jolene just continued ranting: "Right back in there with all those crazy women, always lookin' for a fight. And the guards treat ya like dog shit, orderin' ya 'round like ya was a slave. Stayin' up all night cryin', too scared to keep my eyes shut. Ain't no way I'm goin' back there."

As she spoke she flailed her arms around and, whether she unwittingly did it or not, continued to move closer to the officer.

"Stop right where you are, ma'am," he warned. "I'm serious."

"But, Jolene, just listen to me..."

"I'm sorry, Jess, but they just gonna hafta shoot me, 'cause ain't no way Barney Fife here's gonna lemme—"

BANG

My instinct was to get up and run to her, to grab her before she fell, press my hand on her chest to stop the blood. But I only made it a couple of steps before a loud, deep voice stopped me in my tracks.

"Stop! Stop right there. Don't take another step."

I knew he wasn't asking me but rather demanding me, so I froze. I watched as Jolene fell limp onto the floor. Her eyes closed as if she was saying a silent prayer.

In Ted-like fashion, blood gushed from her stomach and out of her mouth. Her body now elegantly posed, nothing on but her t-shirt and panties, just like she was in the opening scene of one of those crime shows.

I glanced over at Pete, but he and Dr. Ellis both had their heads down and turned away. Carolene collapsed, face planted in the carpet, her hands covering the rest of her face.

Tears fell from my eyes and I was soon kneeling in

puddles. Once again I felt faint come over me as time moved in slow motion. That is until a puff of blue smoke snapped me out of my daze.

And that's when Frankie VanTastic literally appeared out of the blue.

49

"Ladies and gents, hold your tongues and your fire. I am merely here to apologize for being a liar. Dear friends, I have felt guilty for my part in this whole mess. But to offer amends, I am here to valiantly confess."

One officer shouted at Frankie to put his arms up while the other officer yelled at Dr. Ellis to shut up, that he didn't care who he was.

"Great, Frankie, but you're a little late, aren't ya? Jolene's already..."

I couldn't even say it, just stared down at her.

"Whoever you are," the officer with his gun pointed at me ordered Frankie again, "if you don't put your arms in the air and get down on your knees this instant, I *will* be forced to bring you down myself."

To which Frankie just laughed, going on in his fancy rhetoric something about the officers being "boys playing cops for fun" and how they needed "a theme song like Peter Gunn."

With Frankie now drawing the attention of both officers, Carolene—confusing heroism with stupidity—took advantage of the opportunity and snuck up behind the officer closer to her. They tussled for a bit and Carolene was actually able to pry his gun away from him.

"Everyone freeze," she directed, waving the gun around the room at everyone but me, then held it on the officers. "Now get down, on your knees."

They did as she instructed.

"Now put your hands behind your head."

Seeing my sister take charge of the situation like that strangely made me proud. And for a moment, even though she was the one holding the gun, I felt invincible, god-like. And that gave me the courage to do what I knew I had to do. I knew it was foolish, but I told her I'd always have her back. I promised.

"Carolene, put the gun down!" Dr. Ellis called out just as I felt my muscles tighten. "Please."

My eyes were focused on the other officer's gun and I was ready to pounce like a cat on a chipmunk. And though it only took a second for Carolene to look over and tell the doctor to leave her alone, it was long enough for the other officer to pull his gun on her.

"Now, *you* freeze, bitch. Put the gun on the floor—nice and slow. Then back your ass up against the wall."

"Jess, what do I do?" she turned to me, pleading.

"Just do as he says," I advised. "Put the gun down."

"*Put the gun down*? That's all the advice I get?" she seemed disappointed. "Why not something more like: *There's a time to kill and time to heal—and this ain't the time for healin'.*

Whatcha think?"

"Care, this ain't the time for killin' neither. Sometimes ya just can't take those verses so seriously."

"Put the gun down *now*!" the officer ordered, his finger set on the trigger, his eyes now fully squinted.

Me, Pete, Dr. Ellis, and even Frankie (in so many words) chanted "no" and "don't do it" until it seemed we finally got across to her, and she lowered her weapon.

She knelt down, placed the gun on the floor, and carefully stood back up, her arms in the air.

"Looks to me," the officer began, "like this here felon got the jump on my partner, got his gun away from him. After doing so, I was forced to open fire. That the way your report's gonna read, Officer Morgan?"

"Wait!" I yelled. "What're ya'll sayin'? What's goin' on? She ain't got no gun."

I wasn't sure what kind of game these guys were playing, but I was confused and wanted answers. But they just ignored me and kept right on with their routine.

"Yep, that's exactly how my report's gonna read, Officer Smidt. I mean, you had to do what you had to do. I wouldn't be alive if you hadn't. And I thank you for that."

"It was my pleasure, Officer Morgan."

"Jess!" Carolene cried out, fear painted all over her face.

BANG

Sliding down the wall like a slug, my beautiful sister

clutched her stomach to keep as much blood from pouring out as she could.

Once again I was reminded of young Ted back at the gas station. The only thing missing was the shower of cigarettes.

This time I didn't care if the officers shot me or not, I darted over to be with my sister. I held her hand and looked down at her then over at Jolene. Both of my sisters lay there dying, and it was my fault.

"I take all the blame, God," I prayed aloud. "It was all me. Why did *they* hafta be punished for *my* sins?"

I could hear the officers shouting at me before turning their attention to a belligerent Dr. Ellis, still trying to explain who he was and begging them to put their guns away. But I closed my eyes and tried to block out everything around me until it finally vanished. And for a moment it was just me and Carolene.

"So," she looked up at me, the fear in her eyes slowly turning into peace. "Where do we go from here?"

"I, uh, don't know..."

And then a slight smile crept out of me as I realized where she was going with this.

"Australia?" I suggested.

Carolene smiled as best she could.

With every cough, blood sprayed from her mouth and airbrushed my face, but I didn't care. I didn't care about anything anymore.

"You stole my line," she reprimanded. "I thought *I* was Butch Cassidy."

"Oh yeah. Sorry, lot goin' on."

I brushed back the hair from her face and petted her comfortingly.

"Jess?"

"Yeah?"

"Me and Jolene'll tell Mama hey for you. Ok?"

That hit me like a grand piano falling from the fourteenth floor.

She looked so innocent, and I wanted to tell her to hold on, not to give up, to wait for the ambulance a few more minutes. But I knew there was no ambulance coming. There would be no hospital, no pacing in the waiting room. No doctor coming in, looking relieved and even proud, telling us, "Well, we finally got the bleeding to stop and got her stitched up. I think she's going to be just fine now."

I wanted to tell her that everything was going to be okay, but I couldn't do it. I couldn't lie to her. As I watched her eyes close—no doubt imagining herself soaking in a tub of hot, relaxing water—there were a thousand things I could've told her. A thousand things I *wanted* to tell her. But it took all I had to choke back the sobbing long enough to answer her with one short word.

"Ok."

50

I looked up just in time to see Frankie throw a series of knives at the officer who shot Carolene—two in the neck and one in the stomach. I thought Frankie had only thrown one until I looked at the officer. I swear I'd never seen anyone throw so many things so quickly before.

"In a position of such power, it's never right to tell a lie. But never forget, in my line of work, the hand is always quicker than the eye."

The other officer rushed to check on his partner. Pete joined him, along with Dr. Ellis, whose life-saving instincts kicked in and he began barking out orders.

"Pete, look for some towels. I'm gonna run and grab some stuff from the truck."

But when he hopped up, he was immediately grabbed by Frankie, who must have sensed what was about to happen because the officer grabbed his partner's gun and started firing at him. But instead of hitting Frankie, the bullets hit Dr. Ellis instead, who Frankie was using as a shield.

Out of bullets, the officer threw the gun down, and Frankie threw more knives. This time they all went into the officer's throat. He fell over onto his partner and Pete tried to help him as best as he could.

I walked over to Carolene's body, took the officer's gun from her hand, and pointed it at Frankie.

"I should shoot ya right here," I slowly moved towards him. "You're nothin' but a liar, a thief, and a murderer. You can just keep your damn apologies. They ain't gonna bring back Dr. Ellis, and they sure as hell ain't gonna bring back my sisters!"

At this point I was merely a few feet away from Frankie. And as he tried to talk his way out of it, telling me to act rational and be logical, he eased his hand inside his coat.

"Keep your hands where I can see 'em, Frankie," I called out.

But he continued reaching inside his coat, and just as he was sliding out what I assumed was going to be another knife, Pete dashed towards him and tackled him like a linebacker rushing the quarterback.

And as Frankie landed flat on his back, birds flew from his coat and a huge puff of confetti covered everything. But Pete had already grabbed his throat and wasn't letting go. Frankie fought back but Pete squeezed harder, and the magician's face turned a mixture of red and blue until he stopped fighting and went still.

Donning such a bright purple suit, it was almost fitting that Frankie would go out with a purple face.

☙

I was silent, my arms wrapped around my knees, until Pete sat beside me. I was waiting for him to tell me everything was going to be okay—and I was ready with a snappy comeback—but he didn't, just apologized.

"Jess, I'm tore up 'bout how all this turned out, what happened with your sisters and all. It's just horrible."

I told him thanks but didn't have much else to say. So he rubbed me on the back and stood.

"But ya know I'm gonna hafta turn you in, right Jess?"

I nodded as I went over to Jolene and took her by the hand.

"I'm so sorry," I whispered.

Then I lay my head down against hers and began singing softly:

Soon we'll reach the silver river.
Soon our pilgrimage will cease...

"So," Pete stopped just short of the phone. "Not to sound insensitive or anything, but is it really true? Is your mama really up in the attic?"

He didn't know! For whatever reason, Dr. Ellis hadn't told him. I knew I had to play it to my advantage...

"Yeah," I reluctantly admitted. "It's true. Go look for yourself if ya want."

So he did. I wasn't sure why he hadn't gone ahead and

phoned the police, but I didn't take the time to dwell on it right then. We all make stupid mistakes, and this was his.

I listened for his shoes to click-clack against the wooden steps towards the attic. And once I heard them, I shot out the door and towards Dr. Ellis' truck, praying that the keys were in there.

I jerked open the creaky door and climbed in. My eyes were closed, too scared to open them. But when I did, there they were.

"Thank you, doc!" I squealed. "So naïve and trusting."

Out of curiosity I stopped a second to look around for Frankie's car. I figured he had to have driven there but there wasn't another vehicle around. I just shook my head as I cranked the truck and mashed the gas pedal. The tires slung rocks and dust as I tore down the driveway.

And then I was gone.

EPILOGUE

After having finished reading the letter, Shane walks over to stand beside Mr. Bennet. A young reporter is asking him to describe the scene inside the house, to which Mr. Bennet declines to comment. But of course this opens up a series of further questioning.

Shane turns to the side, as if to appear nonchalant and to shield himself from the questions. Clearing his throat to grab his boss' attention, he tells him he's finished reading the letter and asks what he should do next. Talking through his fake camera-ready smile, Mr. Bennet gives Shane one final set of instructions.

"You carry a lighter don't you, Stevens?"

Shane, having quit smoking a few months ago, whispers, "No sir."

"Here, use mine then. And do exactly as I say."

Shane looks down, his attention caught by a shaking lighter behind Mr. Bennet's back. Shane awkwardly takes it, looking around as if he'd just participated in a drug deal.

"Good. Now take that lighter—"

Mr. Bennet pauses to decline any comments for another

reporter. Shane fidgets and prompts him to finish by clearing his throat again. Mr. Bennet waits until one of the officers begins speaking to the camera before giving Shane his last instruction.

"And burn the letter."

~

Shane is torn. He doesn't want to disobey his boss or get the company in any kind of trouble, but he also knows destroying evidence is a crime. But if he's the only one that has seen the letter, he thinks to himself, then no one would know it was missing. Regardless, he's hesitant to move and tightens his grip on the paper buried in his hand.

As the ambulance pulls down the driveway and a couple of officers run over to assist, Mr. Bennet now fields more questions from another reporter pleading for answers and Shane seizes his chance to slip away. He figures no one was really paying him any attention anyway, and he's right.

With the letter in one hand and the lighter in the other, Shane walks towards the house. But before anyone sees him, he shoves the letter and the lighter into his shirt pocket.

A few of the construction workers gather outside the house, talking, some of them smoking. One opens a thermos of water and takes a drink, wiping his mouth with his sleeve. He then turns to offer a drink to the man beside him, along with some information he'd overheard.

"Hey, I heard that paramedic in there say that one a

those dead chicks was pregnant."

"Really? Which one?"

"Uh, the one in the panties, I think."

Shane shakes his head in disgust as he thinks about that and about the gruesome scene in general. The whole thing baffles him more than he lets on, much more than it should.

He rubs his forehead, thinking through all the questions left to be answered, all the uncertainties. *I have to find out the truth. There's a reason I found this letter.*

"Hey, anybody got a lighter?" asks another construction worker as he searches his pockets, an unlit cigarette dangling from his mouth.

Before anyone else could react, Shane speaks up and hands him the lighter from his shirt pocket. The construction worker nods in appreciation. Once the cigarette is lit, he reaches out to return it.

But instead of taking it, Shane puts up his hand as he's turning to leave.

"Nah, you keep it. I won't be needing it."

Shane walks towards his truck, unfolding the bulky letter again. He shuffles through all the blank pages until he gets to the last. Running his hand through his hair, he stares at the two sentences once again, trying to figuring out their meaning and admiring the unique penmanship.

"Seek and ye shall find the answers you aspire to know. Hidden deep below the surface in a place where no lilies grow."

CPSIA information can be obtained
at www.ICGtesting.com
Printed in the USA
LVHW041344110623
749360LV00003B/116